A Friend of Kissinger

Also by David Milofsky

Playing from Memory
Eternal People
Color of Law

A Friend of Kissinger

A Novel

David Milofsky

THE UNIVERSITY OF WISCONSIN PRESS

The University of Wisconsin Press
1930 Monroe Street
Madison, Wisconsin 53711

www.wisc.edu/wisconsinpress/

3 Henrietta Street
London WC2E 8LU, England

1   3   5   4   2

Printed in the United States of America

Library of Congress Cataloging-in-Publication Data

Milofsky, David.
A friend of Kissinger : a novel / David Milofsky.
pp.   cm. — (Library of American fiction)
ISBN 0-299-18520-6 (hardcover : alk. paper)
1. Boys—Fiction.   2. Madison (Wis.)—Fiction.
3. Milwaukee (Wis.)—Fiction.   I. Title.   II. Series.
PS3563.I444 F75   2003
813'.54—dc21   2002152956

This novel is a work of the imagination and while it does draw on real places, any resemblance
between characters in the novel and people, either alive or dead, is purely coincidental.

Terrace Books, a division of the University of Wisconsin Press, takes its name
from the Memorial Union Terrace, located at the University of Wisconsin–Madison.
Since its inception in 1907, the Wisconsin Union has provided a venue for
students, faculty, staff, and alumni to debate art, music, politics, and the issues of the day.
It is a place where theater, music, drama, dance, outdoor activities,
and major speakers are made available to the campus and the community.
To learn more about the Union, visit www.union.wisc.edu.

To Jeanie, with love and gratitude
To John Kelly and Carole Oles
And also to the memory of Bella H. Selan

But often, in the world's most crowded streets,
But often, in the din of strife.
There rises an unspeakable desire
After the knowledge of our buried life;
A thirst to spend our fire and restless force
In tracking out our true, original course.
—Matthew Arnold, "The Buried Life"

Acknowledgments

I wish to thank the National Endowment for the Arts for a creative writing fellowship generously granted and the College of Liberal Arts of Colorado State University for several timely travel grants. Twice during the time I was writing this novel, I received fellowships from the MacDowell Colony, the best place in the world for a writer to work. I'm also grateful to my friends Clint McCown, Dan O'Brien, and George Cuomo for their advice and support. Amy Solar Mills was very helpful in sharing her extensive knowledge of the people and culture of Guatemala with me and David Hull, probably without knowing it, provided an insight into foreign experiences that I've made my own. Teresa Harbaugh and Stephanie G'Schwind were sources of shelter and cheerful enthusiasm at crucial times and Patti Thorn and Tom Walker created a literary context and invited me in. I'm grateful to Joyce Meskis, Margaret Maupin, and Cathy Langer of the Tattered Cover Bookstore for supporting my work in countless ways and to my children, Sam, Mimi, and Jennie for understanding things I often didn't understand about myself. As always, my greatest debt is expressed in the dedication.

A Friend of Kissinger

One

A New World

When I heard of my father's death and made the trip back, it had been almost thirty years since I left Milwaukee, time in which to grow and change, to eradicate what I thought of as the insidious effect of that somnolent city on my personal and psychological development. But after leaving Durango and changing planes first in Denver and then in Chicago until I finally arrived in Milwaukee just after five, I experienced the same physical feeling of falling as I walked through the terminal with my brother and his son, along with a familiar sense of dread, though what I might have dreaded was unclear. I had gotten away from all that. I lived in sun-drenched Colorado and took skiing vacations with my wife and children. I had made a modest success of my life. But Milwaukee was like a sponge drawing everything into it, and as we walked to the parking lot in the blue light of a winter afternoon, I realized that though I might have obscured the past, I would never lose it, whatever I might tell myself.

The impact of coming back now, even for such a specific and temporary purpose as a funeral, filled me with anxiety and it had little to do with mourning my father. His had been a miserable life that lasted too long, until he was left old and toothless in a nursing home with little to do and few visitors. We hadn't been close, and now I was glad he was gone, glad for him, though he would never have taken the out of suicide that many in his condition might have considered. But I didn't feel guilty about the failure of our relationship. My anxiety had only to do with my life in the city in which I had come to adolescence and then left as quickly as possible. I had always thought, somewhat melodramatically, of going away to college and then settling in the West as an escape, and now that I had returned I imagined behind me a gate had been erected and I would never be allowed to leave. Though I was well into middle age and had a family of my own, here I was and would always be small and ineffectual. A person of no power and little consequence, even to those I knew, even to those for whom I should have mattered. But that was all many years ago, I told myself. None of that should matter. I should feel different coming back as an adult in a Burberry raincoat and Italian shoes. And yet it was the same. For the experiences that shaped my life had happened here and so I had the same anxious reaction now I had all those years ago, when my parents made their unilateral decision to move to Milwaukee. For in my previous life I had neither known gangsters nor been aware of evil in the world. Riding into the city from the South Side with Lake Michigan on my right and my brother's family all around me, I felt it all come back with a vividness that was frightening.

～

Madison in the sixties was, if not exactly paradisal, close enough to excuse the impression. Built on an isthmus between two lakes, the city was home to both the University of Wisconsin and the state capitol. My parents had moved there ten years earlier from New York when my father was offered a position in the School of Music. His Town Hall debut had not been as brilliant as he had hoped and the solo career for which he had trained first at Peabody and later at Juilliard seemed less promising than before. Hurok had not called. For him, teaching was a compromise: he had no desire to be an academic,

4

but the steady paycheck was inviting after years of freelancing in Manhattan.

Our life revolved around trips to the beach and the Unitarian church, in those days a sort of ecclesiastical front for the Democratic Party, which met there clandestinely on Sunday mornings after services. In Madison, professors, like my father, were accorded the kind of deference that might have been reserved for a prince in a satrapy, and my teachers generously handed on this presumption of brilliance to me. My father's response to this adulation was ambivalent. Of course he thought he deserved the praise he was given, but since he and his colleagues regularly derided the unsophisticated Wisconsin audiences and the subsequently unimaginative programs they felt obliged to present at their concerts, as musicians they were frustrated as well. Still, it was hard not to enjoy the perquisites of a professorship.

Yet for all this, my childhood was absurdly normal, consisting largely of Little League, Boy Scouts, and summer camp. And the idea that this might be an insular existence never occurred to me; I assumed that the world outside was nothing more than an extension of life as I found it. For while we shopped at Sears, lived in a modest house, and drove an old Plymouth, in Madison society I was a prince, no less gifted nor privileged than a member of the royal family. If the terms of my entitlement were modest, I desired nothing more.

All of this changed abruptly for us in the fall of 1969. It is unusual to be able to date something so precisely, yet it was then, that fall, that things began to fall apart just as surely as the new Fords and Chevys sported fins. Our descent would not have seemed so dramatic had what came before not seemed so ideal. Of course it was not really that precipitous. I had been aware of certain changes. I had overheard without attending to my parents' urgent late-night conversations when they assumed my younger brother and I were asleep. I knew that my father had taken a leave from his job the year before and that my mother had accepted a position as an art teacher in a junior high school. We had moved from our comfortable bungalow on the West Side to a cramped duplex near the stadium, which allowed my father to avoid climbing stairs. Here, we lived in four rooms on one floor with my mother's ancestors looking down disapprovingly in dark oils from the crowded walls.

Things had been changing slowly and I was aware of these changes, but somehow they didn't penetrate. There had been visits to doctors, near and remote. We had all traveled by car to Indiana and Michigan, to Chicago, and Minnesota, and in the process I had spent more time sitting in hospital waiting rooms than most twelve-year-olds do. And my father, never the type to play baseball in the park or accompany me on camping trips, had become even less active and now spent most of his time sitting in his bathrobe reading or making cryptic notes for concerts he would never give. Though great care was taken to shield my brother and me from the reality of his condition, I had heard the word arthritis mentioned *sotto voce* in those small rooms at night, and I knew vaguely but definitely that something was wrong. What was confusing was the fact that despite all this my life remained very much the same, and thus I thought it would go on in this fashion—through junior high, and finally high school. Even without the ritual benefit of a bar mitzvah, I recognized intuitively the subtle strivings of manhood and the persistent ache of sex, and so was not as aware as I might have been of the crisis through which my parents were moving that summer and early fall.

Looking back, it seems impossible nevertheless that we were not prepared for what was about to occur. One imagines the small family huddled together in the tiny living room and my father saying, "Boys, we have some bad news." But at least in memory, no such announcement of my parents' intentions was ever made. And thus my first real knowledge of our family's move from the only home I had known occurred the morning of the August day we packed up our car and drove down Route 30 to Milwaukee, leaving Madison behind for good along with any childhood illusions I might have had.

Even now, I remember that day vividly; if I close my eyes I can hear the humming of the tires on the road, the wind rushing through the windows, my mother's low voice speaking in the front seat, the sense that if I didn't open my eyes things would be as they had been before. I remember stopping at a hamburger stand thirty miles from Milwaukee called Korky's Korners and my father joking in the way he had with the waitresses. It was as if we were only on a family outing, to Mount Horeb for Norwegian food or Devil's Lake to swim, and that after lunch we would get back in the car and go home.

Then suddenly we were in Milwaukee, driving down Wisconsin Avenue, which was the only way into town in those days, before they built the freeway. Skyscrapers and movie palaces crowded the streets; the Riverside and the Strand boasted large marquees layered with neon. I remember Boston Store and Gimbel's on the river, the cosmopolitan bustle of the city. The top was down on our Plymouth and wind ran through my hair as we crossed over from the West Side toward the lake. I heard foghorns and my father explained that Milwaukee was a port with large ocean liners from Europe arriving daily. And even then—is this possible—I remember feeling reassured because the ocean liners that came would surely be leaving, thus guaranteeing my escape. This would be a persistent fantasy, extending beyond my childhood into adulthood. I would never live in an apartment nor go to an office where I would not establish an escape route before settling in. I would never be comfortable anywhere again until I knew how I would leave.

My parents had rented an apartment in a triplex on Frederick Avenue, a nondescript street on the East Side, not far from the university extension where my mother had taken a position as an instructor. Though I was just thirteen, I remember the details. She would be paid $6,500. And there was small hope for tenure. Still, since her only prior experience was as a junior high school teacher, she was pleased to have the job and pleased for reasons I didn't yet understand to have left Madison. Our apartment, modest even by the standards of the neighborhood, was in a large dusty-rose building with a peaked roof and asphalt siding. There were three stone stoops flanked by rusty red railings leading to the units—two down, one up. A small bay window in my parents' bedroom faced the street but otherwise

7

the rooms were arranged like a railroad flat, with bedrooms opening off a narrow corridor at the end of which was a bathroom and the kitchen. There was linoleum in the kitchen and living room, but the bedrooms had pine floors, which had long since begun to deteriorate. Early on, my brother and I learned never to go barefoot, but splinters were hardly the worst of it as far as I was concerned.

I can still feel the sense of panic and shame that settled first in my stomach and then radiated throughout my body. I was desperately lonely yet I wouldn't have wanted any of my Madison friends to see us living in such a place. Frederick Avenue wasn't Calcutta, and our flat wasn't a tenement, but as far as I knew there were no such streets in Madison where simply living in an apartment would be a declaration of poverty or failure or both. Somehow our family had come down in the world and this wretched place with its sooty walls and greasy floors was the tacit expression of our fall. I experienced a feeling not only of despair but also of actual abandonment by those who were supposed to be looking out for me. How, I wondered, could my parents have let this happen? How could they have rented such an apartment, paid money for it? Now in adulthood, I rationalize and make excuses. I understand of course the gravity of my father's illness, a form of arthritis that afflicts only the young and is inevitably progressive just as I appreciate the anxiety my mother must have felt at having to adjust not only to a new job but really to a new life. I realize that the future of their marriage must also have been on their minds and that the very fact of their thinking this way must have made it all seem even more problematical. Which would have rendered them incapable of understanding—or even acknowledging— the effect these changes would have on me. Probably they were right. I wasn't the most important consideration, given the strains on my parents at that time. Yet, my feelings of isolation from my family and my past would not have been greater had they simply pushed me out of the car in Oconomowoc and driven away. In a way, I might have preferred that.

Everything around Frederick Avenue seemed gray and hopeless. The other houses on the block were not quite as forlorn as ours, but

for the most part they were duplexes or small single-family struc-
tures, all with an identical metal pipe extending from their front
door, serving as a handrail but reinforcing for me the sense that I had
wandered into some kind of residential factory. I rarely saw anyone
on the street and when people did emerge they tended to walk with
heads down, examining the sidewalk beneath their feet. This feeling
of bleakness was reinforced when I explored the new neighborhood
on my bicycle and found a small business district two blocks away
consisting of a bowling alley, two taverns, a drugstore, and a pawn-
shop, along with a second-run movie theater. On the corner was a
house that apparently doubled as a garage with a sign saying Sound
Horn mounted on its door, though I never saw a customer in the
five years we lived there. My first impressions were thus confirmed:
we were now truly poor since we lived downtown. I had no idea that
all of Milwaukee was made of small business strips like this or that
eventually I would come to value the propinquity of diversions like
the Oriental Theatre. For now, I was convinced that our move had
been globally transforming and that the grim working-class reality of
the new neighborhood would forevermore be mine.

At home, I settled into a routine that was as unappealing as the
milieu. Because of my father's incapacity, I had taken care of the yard
for several years, mowing the lawn in desultory fashion and shoveling the walk in winter. But now my duties increased. Our building
was heated by a coal furnace, which had to be tended several times a
day. As the oldest boy, the job of shoveling coal and cleaning out the
furnace fell to me without discussion, though I later came to understand that my mother had made a prior agreement with the landlord
who in exchange lowered the rent by a few dollars a month. Each
week, I lugged a metal pan of spent clinkers to the curb on collection
day and made sure adequate coal remained in our bin to heat the
house. Similarly, it was necessary to light a burner in the kitchen if
we wanted hot water for dishes or baths, something I had simply
never heard of before. I hadn't read Dickens at the time, but if he exaggerated the poverty of his childhood, there was good reason. What
difference did it make how many days or weeks he spent in the

blacking factory, how long his father was in debtors prison? What mattered was how it *felt*. And this regimen felt like forever to me. It was as if a huge gray cloak had been dropped over my world rendering everything dull and devoid of color. Yet in its own dreary way, my labors were a relief from the oppressive atmosphere in the apartment, where my father and brother ignored me and sat hunched over the chessboard studying grandmasters like Casablanca and Alekhin.

In self-defense, I took a kitchen chair down to the cellar and spent hours there reading adventure stories by the light of a simple bulb that descended from the ceiling of the furnace room. I wore a cap to protect my fair hair and skin from the coal dust and in time my parents began calling me the super and referred to the cellar as my office, which amused them and suited me. As August turned to September, the one thing I knew was that the farther away I could get from my family the better things would be.

~

Although my mother's position at the university was only a junior appointment, and temporary at that, it offered one important benefit in her view. The admissions committee of the Campus Laboratory School gave children of faculty members preferential treatment, and while my brother's grade was full, there was one place open in the eighth grade. Though we had applied late, I was admitted, and my mother was excited by the idea of small classes, experimental educational techniques, and the fact that my teachers would be professors and graduate students in the School of Education rather than run-of-the-mill public school teachers.

As is usually the case, things at Campus weren't quite as advertised, but the place had a reputation for being a good school for the gifted, something that was unusual in Milwaukee. As a result, many parents of children of ordinary intelligence applied to Campus, hoping that through some alchemy the brilliance of the other students would be transmitted to their children. My class had only eight boys, not even enough for a baseball team, but the boys at Campus didn't care much for sports. And while the laboratories, workshops, and library were impressive, if such things impressed one, there was only a small playground outside and no gymnasium. It was at Campus School that hot September day in 1969, my new shirt sticking to my back, that I first felt the almost crippling anxiety that was to become a constant in my life. If I were to characterize it—and do so badly—I would say that I felt as if I couldn't breathe, that the walls of the large classroom were about to close in upon me, and, worst of all, that there was no possibility of escape. At least part of my discomfort was due to the fact that this feeling was new and completely unexpected; I had never felt this way before and now felt sure I would never regain my composure again. It was all I could do to hold back tears, but miraculously, my classmates seemed unaware of my discomfort—indeed they hardly noticed me. And the teacher, a gaunt, apparently disfigured woman with a large head and grotesque features, slouched against her desk, hip thrust out provocatively as she swung her long leg rhythmically in time to some unheard music.

Her name, I would learn, was Irene Harmon and I was fascinated both by her ugliness and by her elegant clothes and legs. Though I couldn't put a name to it then, it was Miss Harmon in her perfumed blouses, open at the neck, with a scarf obscuring her décolletage, who first awakened sexual desire in me. In fact, it was the ugliness that drew me to her because it seemed interesting and mysterious and she was oblivious to it. Yet that day even Miss Harmon could not blunt the force of my anxiety and after a tortured morning, I skipped lunch in the cafeteria and ran two blocks to the college gym where my mother was working registration. In retrospect it seems too easy that I could have found her in the crush of students. Perhaps she had given me instructions; perhaps we had arranged to meet beforehand. In any case, I found her and immediately burst into tears.

"Mom," I said. "I hate that school. The kids are all either brains or queers."

An unfair judgment, yet it proved to be uncannily accurate. Even after I had adjusted to Campus, I would not have veered far from this characterization of my classmates. For the children at Campus had been culled from schools all over the city for their intelligence rather than their social skills or athletic ability and at least half of them were certified geniuses. Accurate or not, though, my reaction could not have pleased my mother, who as a new instructor with a sick husband and two young boys to support, had troubles of her own. Still, she left whatever she was doing and took me to the drug-store across the street where she bought me a milkshake and listened sympathetically to my tale of woe.

Even then, I did not expect her to do anything, in part because my despair was so great that I had given up hoping for positive change. I didn't ask her if I could transfer to the public school my brother was attending or, better yet, return alone to Madison. Just having someone listen to me was enough. After a half hour she returned to registration and I went back to school, oddly relieved.

—⁓—

With only eight boys my age at Campus, my options were limited regarding friendship, especially since many of them lived in other parts of town and were delivered to school and called for by drivers in black coats or by dutiful parents. This struck me as both exotic and a little ludicrous, but given our newfound poverty, my immediate reaction was to become pugnacious and combative. So much so, that I remember standing in a stairwell throwing lefts and rights at a phantom sparring partner, prompting one of my classmates to ask innocently if I had been a boxer in my former life.

As strange as this new world was to me, I must have seemed equally strange to my classmates, stuck in my conventional ideas of pre-adolescent masculinity as it was expressed in my world. The norms of Madison in which boys rode bikes to school, punched each other in the halls between classes, and competed in sports year-round were clearly not normal here and it would do me no good to pretend that they were. In Madison homogeneity reigned, even if it was born of membership in an equally exclusive society, the university. Given that, however, there was a remarkable degree of parity throughout the school. While there were smart kids and some people had more money than others, there were neither geniuses nor millionaires, or at least none I knew about. No attention was paid to one's social standing; indeed, as far as I knew, there was no such thing as social position in Madison at all, unless one counted rank at the university, and that applied only to our fathers. Yet here I sat among scions of great fortunes or the possessors of towering IQs, and occasionally both. Possessing neither, I had no idea how I would fit anywhere and apparently my teacher agreed. After a few weeks, my mother received a request for a conference from Miss Harmon and came to school for a meeting.

"I'm afraid Daniel isn't making a very good impression," Miss Harmon began.

"I don't care what kind of impression he's making," my mother snapped. "And you shouldn't either. All you have to do is teach him."

Miss Harmon was a professor in the School of Education and wasn't used to being talked to this way by parents. I remember feeling enormous pride in my mother, who had never forgotten her ties to the Southern aristocracy. Though she was only a temporary instructor, she was not about to be lectured to by a social-climbing schoolteacher, even if, improbably, Miss Harmon meant well.

"My father lost more money twice than most of these people ever saw in their lives, if money is supposed to matter," my mother said as we walked home. "Don't you let them make you feel bad, Danny."

Yet the conference achieved at least part of its purpose. Miss Harmon's treatment of me improved markedly as, apparently, did my adjustment to the school. Perhaps she just decided to make the best of things, as I was doing, but in time we became quite close and I even visited her in the run-down residential hotel where she lived before accompanying her to the Milwaukee Symphony. But that was much later.

⟿

Sometime early in the year, I was walking home by myself and became aware that I was being followed. Turning quickly, I recognized one of the boys in my class trying valiantly to control an English bike too large for him. "Are you following me?" I asked.

"Not really," the boy said. Then he appeared to stop and think about my question. "I mean, I'm behind you, so I guess I am, but I didn't really mean to. I think we both live in the same direction, actually. I'm just going home."

I immediately liked his willingness to accept my terms. Technically, he was following me, but it was an unusual way to answer the question. Now I looked at him closely. He was small, like me, but had more delicate features, brown curly hair, and large blue eyes. His nostrils were prominent and flared, bringing his nose to a tip as if it had been bobbed, which gave him an odd, fishlike appearance. I couldn't think of anything to say to his reasonable response, so I shrugged and moved to the side of the walk. "We can share the sidewalk, I guess." And the boy smiled and dismounted his bike with obvious relief.

My new friend's name was Joey Goodstein and I was to learn as much about him from others as he ever told me himself, because he came from a family that was well known in Milwaukee, though perhaps infamous would be more accurate. His father was Abraham Goodstein, a prominent lawyer who had appeared before the Kefauver Committee and subsequently ran afoul of Bobby Kennedy. On national television, Abe had bragged that he had personally placed more than $3 million in bets annually, though Senator Kefauver was more interested in his connection to organized crime. The conventional wisdom, faithfully reported in the *Milwaukee Journal,* which ran full-page pictures of both Abe and his wife on the front page, was that Abe set the national betting line for the mafia, which made him a central figure in the investigation, but he knew enough not to talk about that. As much as anything, however, what made Abe contemptible in the eyes of many was his absolute lack of remorse. It was his Jewish cockiness that got him in trouble more than anything he had done, though in the end they got him for tax evasion. But for Abe this was never the issue. He was proud of what he did.

Wearing a sharp blue pinstripe and a white-on-white shirt, he bragged, "I'm at the top of my profession. I'm very good at what I do. Why should I feel bad about that just because I happen to live in a hypocritical society?"

The result of Abe's appearance on television was that he was sentenced to five years in Terre Haute and the family had to sell its home in Whitefish Bay and move to the East Side, which is why Joey and I were walking home together. Despite his family's having apparently come down in the world, as far as I could tell the Goodsteins lacked for nothing. Their apartment was much larger than ours and filled with large overstuffed chairs, thick carpets, and mahogany tables with dishes of candy and nuts displayed upon them. Joey's mother, whom we called Mrs. G., was working as a real estate salesperson, but spent most mornings in bed reading through a lorgnette or talking on the telephone with friends.

Joey's older brother was a student at the University of Michigan, but Abe's temporary incapacity had not left the household without a masculine influence. At regular intervals, two large men named Al and Pete appeared with armfuls of groceries or toys asking Mrs. G. if she needed anything. "We got a car outside," Al would say. "You want me to take Joey somewhere?"

More important to me was the fact that I now had a friend. Joey and I quickly became inseparable despite my mother's concern that through him I had made contact with the underworld. I liked eating roast beef at Mrs. G.'s table and I liked Al and Pete who would do things with us that my father couldn't, simple things like taking the car out for a ride on Saturday afternoon or getting takeout food at the Pig 'n Whistle on Capitol Drive. And even my growing sense of Joey's being ostracized at school by our classmates, who were less enamored of his family's colorful past than I was, did little to dampen my enthusiasm for him. We were both boys with crippled fathers; that was our bond and it would endure. As the cold weather set in, Milwaukee began to seem more hospitable to me.

Two

Anna

The apartments in our building were called floor-throughs because each occupied one half of a floor. We never saw the families above us, or at least if we did I have no memory of it, and for the first few weeks I heard nothing from the people who shared our floor, though occasionally someone would pound on the shared wall if my brother and I were making too much noise. Still, even if I hadn't met our neighbors, I knew they must have been very different from us. Though there was no discrete boundary between the apartments on the landing outside, the neighbors' side of the vestibule couldn't have been more dissimilar. While ours was cluttered with stacks of newspapers, milk bottles, overshoes, and the occasional sack of garbage, in contrast, our neighbor's floor was waxed and the golden wood shone; there was a clean doormat, a spray of dried flowers mounted on the door, and a plaque offering welcome to visitors in German. On my trips to and from the basement, I would often pause, wondering about the neat, thrifty people responsible for all this before entering the chaos of our apartment. On one such occasion, the door opened and a short, squat woman in a burgundy velour caftan looked out at me.

It would be generous to say she was five feet, and with no exaggeration she was as wide as she was tall. She wore what I at first thought was a cap but later discovered to be a wig of matted brown hair, but what was most amazing to me was her nose which looked as if it had been professionally flattened and then tilted toward the east. I had never seen anyone like her, but if she was self-conscious about her appearance she didn't show it. Instead, she smiled broadly showing a faintly yellow denture and when she spoke her accent was so heavy that I thought she said, "Who are you, I'm tight."

"Tight?" I repeated, not understanding.

"That's right," she said, rhyming and smiling. "I won't bite. I'm Anna."

She said this with the kind of assurance that led me to think she must be famous, too, but she was completely unlike the Goodsteins. "Come in," she said, and stepped aside to make room. My mother had not been mindful enough of urban dangers to warn me about strangers, but I hesitated anyway, unsure of what I wanted to do. "Come," Anna said insistently, and smiled again. Finding her irresistible, I let her pull me inside.

The bright kitchen I entered was spotless and the table was set for three with green place mats, though no one else seemed to be at home. It was all so different from the depressing monotony of our apartment that I wondered vaguely how they could both exist in the same house. Perhaps for the first time, it occurred to me that what I had previously considered to be inevitable was actually a choice my parents had made, though a very eccentric one. I'm not sure I would have called what we had a lifestyle, but looking around Anna's small kitchen I could see that she had done things my mother would never have dreamed of with the same basic material. And though I immediately felt guilty, I knew instinctively that I preferred this neat bourgeois arrangement to the thrown-together collection of Salvation Army furniture that occupied the space across the hall.

Anna took stollen from a bakery box and put it on a plate and set the plate in front of me. "Just out of the oven," she joked. "Go ahead, don't be shy." I hadn't realized I was hungry until then, but I think now that what I was really hungry for wasn't just pastry but the kind of mothering Anna offered me then and in the future. While I ate, she told me that she and her husband were German refugees who had come to Milwaukee after landing first in New York and working there for two years. Both had been in concentration camps, and Anna's parents had been killed by the Nazis, though she was so matter-of-fact about it that it seemed as if she was telling me where she had gone to school. More remarkable to me was the fact that she had been born without a nose, something she had attempted to remedy with plastic surgery as soon as she arrived in America and started to make some money. Now, she looked at me slyly and said, "It's all right to be curious about it, Daniel. I'll bet you never met anyone without a nose before."

I admitted I hadn't and she invited me to touch it. "Touch your nose?" I asked. The idea filled me with dread, mixed with sick fascination.

She nodded. "Everyone wonders about it, but most people are too polite to ask. I don't give a shit about being polite."

The word *shit* stunned me, that someone my mother's age would use it, but Anna seemed nonplussed. "Go ahead," she said. So I reached over and gently palpated the twist of ligament the surgeons had attached to her face. It felt oddly like silly putty, but I was afraid to squeeze it too tightly for fear it would come off in my hand, something that seemed too catastrophic even to imagine.

Given the intimacy of the moment, it seemed silly to hold anything back. "Can you smell?" I asked.

"Not very well, but how well do you need to? We're not dogs, are we? But the nose is a complicated organ; it protects against disease, for example. Mine is useless for that." Anna shrugged as if this, like everything else, was only to be taken in stride. "I have false teeth, too," she added irrelevantly. "My teeth were lousy and then we couldn't take care of them in the camps, so they all had to come out."

Under the circumstances, I thought she was a triumph over physiology but she wasn't through. "And you've noticed I'm too fat.

That's because I like to eat. I used to try to lose weight, but then I realized that I really enjoyed eating so why not have that in my life? Who cares anyway, I'm not a *Playboy* bunny."

The idea of Anna as a centerfold made me smile and then we laughed together, enjoying our new friendship in her warm kitchen. "That's about all," she said. "But if you think of anything you want to ask me, just go ahead. I really don't care."

And she didn't. It wasn't that Anna was particularly open; she was actually quite private about family matters. But the things most people considered to be intimate didn't matter to her and she never stood on ceremony. The main thing was she didn't want imagined sensitivities about her bizarre appearance to come in the way of friendship. Anna and her husband Paul shared their apartment with a professor whom Anna had met when she started taking classes at the university. He lived in Chicago, but spent three days a week in Milwaukee as a visiting lecturer. Though she had little formal education, Anna told me she didn't want to be an interior decorator all her life. In my naïveté, I couldn't imagine one *having* a life after being in the camps, but to Anna what I would later know as the Holocaust seemed only and always part of a past in which she had little interest. She never spoke German or read classic literature and she had an obsession with everything modern, whether furniture or fine art. Anna was moving forward and Alfred, the professor, was helping her. I asked her what she wanted to do, having little idea what adults did do, apart from my parents and teachers. Everyone couldn't be a professor or an artist.

"I want to be a therapist," Anna said. "I've been listening to my friends complain for twenty years; I might as well get paid for doing it."

I nodded, but leaving aside the practical difficulty of her plan, it seemed incredible to me that this *Hausfrau* actually wanted to change her life in such a dramatic way. I didn't know what interior decorators did exactly, but her neat kitchen testified to her skill. I had the idea that being a therapist was more complicated than choosing a bedspread, but I didn't want to argue. After all, she might be right.

"That's enough about me," Anna said decisively. "What about you?" Then she surprised me by already knowing most of what I would have told her. There had been a short article in the *Journal* about my father when we arrived in town, but most of what Anna knew seemed to grow out of her native intelligence. She knew, for example, that my mother taught at the extension, that I went to Campus School, even that "the Goodstein boy" was my friend. "I'd love to meet your parents," she concluded. This seemed odd to me since we lived next door. Yet it was only then that I dimly understood that despite our shabby housekeeping and my father's illness, other people were in awe of my mother and father, simply because they had been distinguished in another life. I had no idea of course whether my father would deign to notice this odd-looking woman, but it was the first real hint that anything had traveled with us from Madison to Milwaukee and so I offered to make the introductions.

"I'd like that," Anna said now, and despite her girth and the nose I was carefully avoiding despite having held it in my hand, there was real delight in her eyes, and I was glad I had made her happy. As it happened, there were other things I wanted to ask her, not just about herself but about Milwaukee, which at the time was still a German city with German newspapers, restaurants, and even a Kino. But Hitler was just a name to me and while there were no doubt survivors in Madison, I had not known them. It was an odd thing to grow up in Wisconsin, separated not only from family, but also from great events and even that part of history that cousins, aunts, and grandparents represent. I wondered if my parents had thought of that when they decided to move away from their past. Probably they hadn't considered it as important as establishing a new life and furthering my father's career—and who's to say they were wrong? Yet here I was talking of nothing with Anna, an embodiment of everything unknown and avoided by the people who had brought me into the world.

"I guess I'd better go," I said, exhausted by the weight of what had happened and satiated for the moment.

Anna rose, shorter than I was by inches, and held me to her. Then she smiled again. "You're a good boy, Daniel. I can tell even though I just met you. You'll be a good man someday, and we'll be friends for a long time. You remember that."

I told her I would, thanked her for the pastry, and left.

Three

Chocolate Nut Sundae

As soon as we moved, my father got worse. While in Madison, he had felt it incumbent upon himself to keep up appearances and would generally dress in a shirt and tie and often made the three-block walk to Macaws for lunch or a cup of coffee. Now, however, alone and a stranger in a strange city where he knew no one, there seemed to be no reason for such efforts and days went by without his leaving the apartment. Often I would return from school and find him still in his bathrobe puzzling over a chess problem at the kitchen table. I can't say this had no effect on me, but I didn't know what to say that would not sound like criticism—and I didn't want to criticize my father, though I often felt angry at him for his indolence. As a nod to the idea of rehabilitation, a physical therapist had come and installed some parallel bars and occasionally the therapist would visit and my father would venture upon them, his long slender arms trembling under the weight of his body as he dragged his skinny legs along after him. But my father soon lost whatever enthusiasm he might have had for this and settled into inactivity, though he still avoided the wheelchair whenever possible.

At this time, we had no television, not even a radio or functioning record player, and the quiet in the apartment was eerie, especially considering two teenaged boys lived there. Often I took long walks to escape the silence, heading south down Farwell Avenue and then up North Avenue to the lake where I sat on the bluffs overlooking Bradford Beach listening to the foghorns and imagining I was going somewhere. Inevitably, however, the only place for me to go was back home, to my room with the red splintered floor and my Chip Hilton books. I don't remember my father or mother complaining about the path their life together had taken, but there was an ineffable sadness about that apartment, that time, which I have never forgotten and never altogether shaken. It was the sadness of faded brilliance, of rescinded gifts, and thus early in my life I was introduced to the idea that all things are only given to us temporarily and may be reclaimed at any time by fate, capriciously, and for no reason.

Our major diversion and, incidentally, the only way in which Milwaukee exceeded Madison, was going to the movies. In those days there were probably fifty or sixty movie theaters in Milwaukee. There was one a block away and another a mile east. Though we seldom ventured downtown to the first-run movie palaces with their velvet-roped entrances and costumed ushers, we often drove to other parts of the city where the theaters specialized in different sorts of films. We would go to the South Side or even to the Kino in Germantown when there was something my father wanted to see, like a Marlene Dietrich film or one directed by Fritz Lang. Always I went with him eagerly because in my mind there was a romance associated with the movies that television could never hope to imitate. In a darkened theater with images of handsome men and beautiful women before me, the reality of a crippled father and a dingy apartment simply seemed impossible—and for those hours nothing that I hated or feared was allowed to exist.

There was also a practical reason for me to accompany my parents as my father needed help either walking the few steps from car to the door or with the wheelchair that we brought out for longer journeys. On this evening, there was a Garbo festival at a theater on Twenty-seventh Street and I had been pressed into service, though I knew nothing about Garbo. Still, it was worth going if only because it had been months since I had seen my father so excited. My brother was doing something at school so my mother and I helped my father into the car, loaded the wheelchair into the trunk, and drove off to the West Side. My father disliked the wheelchair and seldom used it in our neighborhood, preferring crutches or Canadian canes, though he had suffered some embarrassing falls of late. It was snowing and the streets were slick, but the car seemed warm and safe and it was nice to see my parents happy.

Driving from the East Side, where we lived, to the West was like traveling to another country in those days. Working people referred scornfully to the neighborhoods near the lake as the Gold Coast, even if our small apartment bore little resemblance to the mansions of Newberry Boulevard and Lake Drive. I could see the city change as we drove down State Street past the *Journal* and the Safety Building and the courthouse, past the small bungalows and the breweries, the corner taverns advertising Pabst and Schlitz and Braumeister and Gettelman's, knowing of the brooding ghetto that lay just to the north and the Poles, Serbs, and Greeks to the south. And all of them living together not in anything that could be called harmony but rather in a precarious balance that could be disturbed at any time by almost anything.

In those days, a bandleader named Louie Bashell was holding forth at a small nightclub on Twentieth Street that advertised dancing and cheap drinks. When I saw Louie's picture in the entertainment section of the paper, next to the movies, I sometimes imagined our stopping one cold evening and going into that bar where my father would be greeted like long-lost kin and asked to sit in by the band. But not on this night. My mother drove past Louie's bar without comment and then turned south on Twenty-seventh, toward the theater.

My parents were children of the Depression when movies had been virtually their only diversion. My father often talked nostalgically of going with *his* father, of whom I knew almost nothing, to triple features for which they paid a dime. It was about the only thing he ever mentioned doing with my grandfather and in this respect little had changed, as our one constant family activity was going to the movies together once a week.

The streets were clogged with snow and since the concept of handicapped parking did not yet exist, we had to park a block away, though the long neon sign of the Tower and its marquee were easily visible from the car. I got the wheelchair out of the trunk and lined it up as best I could next to the passenger door.

"Bring it closer," my father snapped. "I'm not an Olympic gymnast, for Christ's sake. Why are you so damned far away?"

I inched the chair closer, but I had my reasons for keeping some distance between us. Now he unscrewed a plug from the rubber tube that ran down his leg and hot urine spurted into the street. My mother and I discreetly looked away, as if we had no idea what was going on, and when the bag had emptied, my father refastened the plug and wiped his hands on his pants. Then he looked up at me. "Give me a hand, kid."

I need to say that this was hard for both of us, hard for him to ask for help from his teenaged son, hard for me to acknowledge his weakness. But I didn't know this then; I only felt a kind of dull anger, directed at no one in particular. I loved my father but I wanted to be away from him, from this; I wanted to live in a normal house where the father left in the morning with a briefcase and returned eight hours later carrying the evening paper. I wanted our dinner table conversation to revolve around family activities, for my parents to ask us about school, and to be tolerant of our prattle. But in our family there were no shared activities, no church or synagogue, and few friends. We had neither dog nor cat, never took vacations, and had left the Boy Scouts behind when we left Madison.

Now I climbed halfway into the car and reached around my father, wedging my hands into his armpits, aware of his closeness, of the subtly mingled smell of sweat, piss, and aftershave. I lifted as hard as I could and was greatly relieved, as always, when I was able to heave him into the waiting chair. Then I strapped his shoes to the footrests, careful always lest a muscle spasm cause one to shake loose, and draped a tweed overcoat around his shoulders for the trip down the block to the theater. Neither of us spoke during these preparations and my mother walked a few steps ahead, as if she was unaware of what was going on behind her.

The time I'm speaking of was far removed from that of the elegant movie palaces that had drawn people in the thirties, but multiplexes had yet to be invented and theaters in the late sixties still felt obliged to make a nod in the direction of distinctive decor. The one we went to that night seemed to have tried to accommodate everyone as the designers had settled on an odd melange of things, with black panthers ready to spring in the lobby, minarets with peaceful Buddhas in the auditorium, and everything topped off by a starry cerulean sky. Before the show started, different colors washed the screen in sequence and kids on dates tried to guess which color would come next.

There were no special accommodations for wheelchairs inside the auditorium, so I left my father sitting in the aisle while I went back to the lobby for refreshments. His requirements in this area, as in most things, were precise: he wanted a large tub of buttered popcorn, orangeade, and a box of Jordan Almonds. Fortunately everything was available and I was able to get back inside just as the lights went down.

The newsreel was ending when I heard my father mutter "Shit," and when I looked over he was bathed in popcorn. "Goddamned hands don't work," he said.

My mother and I brushed him off and retrieved what we could of the nuts. I heard Garbo speaking and was about to take my seat when my father said, "Get me some more popcorn, Daniel."

His voice was soft, even plaintive, as if this was the most reasonable request in the world, despite the fact that the aisle was full of popcorn already. I looked at my mother for help, but she just shrugged. This was between my father and me, so I climbed over them and went back to the lobby.

This was to be a pattern in our lives: my mother would resolutely refuse to ratify truths I saw as obvious, apparently because she thought they would destroy my father. There is no way now to say whether this was so, but her silence had the effect of pitting my father and me against each other in a unique way. That is, I wanted him to *be* a father, someone I could push against and, if necessary, turn to in times of crisis. I didn't want him to be sick and dependent and pathetic and angry at me for all of it. Painful as it was to witness my father's deterioration, it would have been better for me if my mother had simply acknowledged the vision I had; if she had been able, in effect, to say, yes, awful as it is, you're right. This is the way our life is and is going to be. Instead, she practiced a kind of stoic denial of the obvious in which we were all forced to pretend that my father's condition and his behavior were in some sense normal, which led to a kind of organized psychosis in our household.

I got the popcorn and by the time I returned to my seat Garbo was in the middle of it. She was a spy and I had never seen anyone, spy or not, as beautiful. She was different not only from people I knew or might have known, but also from every other movie star. Women like Elizabeth Taylor or Kim Novak seemed ordinary, even cheap, compared to her. As I watched the film, I had the thought that this woman would now be sixty, but this had no effect. For the first time in my life the idea of timeless beauty assumed meaning for me. She was like the lovers on Keats's clay pot; she was something.

My mother nudged me and when I looked over I saw that my father was once again covered in popcorn. This time he said nothing and I didn't ask. The humiliation was too great. I simply got up and returned to the refreshment counter where the usher gave me an odd look and fired up the cash register. This time, in addition to the popcorn I got a refill on the candy since I figured that might have gone on the floor too. Fortunately, this held him through the rest of the feature, which ended tragically for Garbo.

I don't remember Ramon Navarro, except for those wild, staring eyes and slicked-back hair, but the plot and acting meant little to me. I was just watching Garbo, her slim hips, her smallest gesture. The slight steeple of her ruby lips, her eyes, her nose, and the fact that I would never meet her or even anyone like her made it all better. This was an illusion that you could hang on to, something that hurt no one, which gave only pleasure and fulfillment and no pain.

I was so entranced by the movie that I hardly noticed my father, but apparently he made it the rest of the way unscathed and by eleven we were out on Twenty-seventh Street again rolling the chair toward our car. There was a moment of panic when we were transferring my father into the car, but somehow my mother and I got him inside and we drove home feeling the quiet satisfaction one gets from accomplishing something unreasonable. It was a feeling I would come to associate with my father: he didn't seem to understand that there were certain things a cripple simply couldn't do. He did whatever he wanted and dragged his world along behind him. I wouldn't have said his disability was worth it because of the greater rewards he received in this way, and it wasn't particularly pleasant to be with him much of the time. But he was the only father I had and it seldom occurred to me that I could change him. My problem was rather that I had trouble accepting things as they were, while at the same time I knew that I had no choice but to do so.

At home we negotiated the concrete steps with difficulty and everyone got inside. Then my mother and I sat in the kitchen silently drinking tea. The warmth of the room lulled me and I was about to excuse myself and go to bed when my father called out from his room. "Daniel, come in here, will you?"

I walked the length of the apartment and found him sitting in his undershorts at his desk. A book was open in front of him. Now he looked up and said, "I'm hungry. Go down to Marc's and get me a chocolate nut sundae." This was not a request but a demand.

Kernels of popcorn lay on the floor, apparently transported home from the movie, but I wasn't so much annoyed as amazed that he was still hungry. "I'm kind of tired, Pop," I said, which was an understatement.

"Okay," he said briskly. "To hell with it. But you know, Daniel, the trouble with you is that you'll never do anything for me."

In memory, this scene has the quality of a tableau: the world-famous concert artist sitting in a small room in his shorts surrounded by the detritus of invalidism. And now I began to tremble with anger. It wasn't just that we had driven to the other side of town in the snow to indulge him, or that his wheelchair and demands made it more a chore than a pleasure, because that wasn't true. I had enjoyed the movie. Garbo had been worth whatever my father had put me through. And had it not been for my father, I would have been sitting home alone. None of that was to the point. He was difficult and demanding, but I accepted that, or mostly accepted it even if I didn't like it.

The important thing was what he had said: that I never did anything for him. For what he meant was that I didn't do *everything* for him and never would. It struck me as an incredible thing to ask, to expect of anyone else. And in that moment, I realized that finally no one will get you the chocolate nut sundae, that no one can. If it is there to be gotten, you have to find a way to do it yourself. And if this wasn't quite what my father meant—if, that is, he was just being childish—it was still the meaning I took from it. And it made me angry to have to understand this. Angry with him, angry at the world. "Sorry," I said. "I'm going to bed."

Four

A Life of Crime

Fall turned to winter. Things gradually worked out at school. Miss Harmon began to see some incipient talent in my writing, in part because it was necessary for me to be good at something. And I made a few friends, though none as close as Joey Goodstein. We spent all of our free time together and though my parents found Joe's manner annoying and his family objectionable, it was at least preferable to my moping around the house and having no friends at all.

My brother wasn't doing as well. Unable to find space for him at Campus, my mother had enrolled Charlie at Maryland Avenue School, two blocks away, where he was a freak among the children of pipe fitters and brewery workers. Unable to fit in, Charles spent more and more of his time alone in his room working on chess problems until one night at dinner he announced that the previous evening a spaceship had come in his window.

My brother had always been imaginative, the genius in the family. At three he had constructed towering block buildings so impressive the *Capital Times* had sent out a reporter and photographer to memorialize the event. And the strength of his convictions was great enough to persuade others to follow him in unlikely directions. At five, for example, he had convinced some friends to begin construction on a battleship in our basement, which only ceased when they realized there was no way to get the ship out of the house and down to Lake Wingra; at seven he had defeated the state chess champion, a mathematics professor at the university; at ten he beat my father blindfolded and began playing postal chess with people of his own ability. School had never been much of a challenge and my mother was used to eccentricity in her younger son. "You were just dreaming," she said now.

"At least he has some friends," I put in.

"Shut up, Daniel," my father said. "What do you mean a space-ship, Charles. What kind of spaceship was it?" His question was typical of our family. Everyone liked to talk, whether what he had to say made sense or not. Rather than acknowledging the obvious, that spaceships weren't common in our neighborhood and my brother was delusional, my father's inquiry attempted to normalize the abnormal. It was as if Charles was simply passing on something that had happened at school.

He thought for a moment, his handsome young face serious. "It was blue," he said at last. "And there were these little guys inside. Actually, they stayed for quite a while."

"Oh," I said. "The *blue* spaceship; I've only seen the yellow one. You should have brought the pilot out and introduced him to every-one." But my parents ignored my sarcasm. They were making eye-signals to one another.

"They were shy," my brother, said, oblivious to the rest of us. "The guys inside, but maybe next time I will." The spaceship's visit followed an earlier episode of sleepwalking and the combination so alarmed my mother that she immediately arranged for my broth-er to see a psychiatrist. This didn't stop my father from asking for progress reports on our visitors from outer space, however, which resulted in my spending more and more time in my basement hideaway.

It was on a long Saturday afternoon in December that I first met our neighbors' boarder, though of course I knew something about him already. I was rereading a John R. Tunis novel when I became aware of someone standing in my light. When I looked up, I saw a short, meticulous man with thinning blond hair and a sweater thrown around his neck standing in the doorway. For some reason I remember noticing his feet, which were tiny and encased in highly polished oxblood loafers. His features were too large to be called handsome, but there was something attractive about him. There was an awkward silence between us because there was no reason for this man to be here. Then he extended his hand. "I thought we should meet," he said. "Anna speaks highly of you and said I might find you here. I'm Alfred Leach."

To my knowledge no one had ever spoken highly of me before and I had no idea why Alfred Leach thought we should meet. Shaking hands was also foreign to me, something I might have done twice in my life prior to this. I saw no reason to be unfriendly, so I took his hand, or rather his fingers since it would be more accurate to say he squeezed my hand rather than shook it. I wondered if he was from some other country as he was so small and precise in his speech, yet his accent was no different than mine. It was something in his manner, the way he held his head, and the way he looked at me.

"Nice place you've got here," Alfred said.

This was ridiculous since we were standing in what used to be a coal bin, but his voice was so quiet and sincere that I wondered if perhaps I had missed something. The coal was actually stored next door now, and I had scrubbed the floor and whitewashed the walls besides adding a small desk, a bookcase, and an easy chair I had found on the street on garbage day. Still, I would not have expected anyone to notice these improvements or to think they were attractive. "Come on in," I said, uncertain what to say.

Alfred walked into the room and examined the rack of sports books as if they had been the complete works of Spinoza. "What do you like to do?" he asked.

I was not accustomed to adults showing interest in me, and Alfred's sudden questions made me uncomfortable. My father had called him a fruit after having dinner with Anna, but beyond assuming this must have something to do with Alfred's masculinity, I had little idea what the term meant. "Baseball," I said. "Basketball in the winter."

Alfred nodded. "Reading, too?" He gestured at the bookshelves.

I shrugged. I didn't think of myself as liking to read; it was just something I had always done obsessively and without discrimination, first comic books, then sports and adventure novels. I liked biographies, liked to imagine myself living somewhere else, being someone else. "Sometimes, when it's too cold to go outside," I said carefully.

Alfred smiled. "Sometimes I get tickets for the Packer games. Maybe we could go?"

"Really?" The man's deferential manner put me off, but I wasn't afraid of him and my father had never taken me to a professional game of any kind.

"Sure," Alfred said. "It's a date then?"

I thought of my father's remark, but I was beginning to like Alfred. "I'd like that," I said. "I'm usually around."

Alfred looked down at his feet, then smiled again, his teeth white and even. "Good meeting you, Daniel." He pressed my hand again with his fingers and then he was gone, though the room did not seem empty, as if his aura had stayed behind.

~

Often on weekends, Joey and I would go with Al and Pete on what they called their rounds, though I never knew the exact purpose of these trips. When I asked, Al said something about collections, but what he was collecting was a mystery to me. Once he sent me into a barbershop whereupon the barber announced loudly, "Jesus, they're using kids now. Abe must be up to his ass with the Feds," before handing me a white business envelope. I smiled stupidly, thinking I had inadvertently stumbled into a partnership with J. Edgar Hoover. But ordinarily Al went into the taverns alone and came out whistling, with Pete in his wake. The fact is I was grateful to Al and Pete for rescuing me from the dreary sameness of our apartment where

34

my father sat attenuated over a chessboard facing my brother and his extraterrestrial companions.

Al and Pete presented quite a contrast. Big cheerful men with thick necks sticking out of loud sport shirts, they wore Canoe and bragged about their sexual exploits as we toured the East Side in Al's Buick. They spoke of a world that was tough and straightforward and, perhaps most attractive, they included me, which made me feel more at ease with myself than anything my parents could have said. And if I didn't know precisely what my new companions were doing, I suspected it was illegal, and thus I knew instinctively it was just as well not to know. Still, I was curious and Joey who was normally garrulous and, if anything, a know-it-all, was surprisingly close-mouthed in connection with his father's business associates. All the same, I thought that if he really didn't want me to know what was going on he wouldn't have included me.

"What are they doing in there?" I asked once when we had been waiting outside a bar called the Cummerbund for a half hour.

"Why don't you ask them when they come out?"

"I don't want to ask them. I'm asking you."

Joey shrugged. "Business, I guess."

"What kind of business?"

"I don't know, Danny. They don't *discuss* it with me. My father's business. They work for him."

"I thought he was in prison. How can anyone be working for him when he's there and they're here?"

"Why not? You've heard of the phone, haven't you?"

He sighed and looked out the window. "Look, people think my father and his friends are some kind of joke, like the gangsters in *Guys and Dolls,* but it's not really like that. At least I don't think it is."

"What do you think it's like?" I really wanted to know, though I had never read Damon Runyon. My only experience, if you could call it that, grew out of watching *The Untouchables* on television, but there was nothing lovable about Al Capone and Eliot Ness always won. Although Al and Pete were big, they weren't menacing, or at least they didn't seem so to me. They were always laughing, joking around, always in a good mood, in contrast to my father. I liked being with them.

"My father's in Terre Haute," Joey said simply. "That's not very funny is it?"

I had to admit Joey was right about that, and yet there was nothing sinister about those afternoons and the two men could not have been kinder to me. It was Al, after all, who came to watch the Saturday morning basketball games we inevitably lost, not my father. After one particularly humiliating loss, when half our team walked off the floor before time had expired, it was Al who put his arm around my slender shoulders and said, "You'll get them next time, champ." And, improbably, it was Pete who showed up to hear me solo in the Christmas pageant at school, my father being too refined in his musical tastes to stoop to such things. Al and Pete were tough and manly and interested in us. And their interest extended to rough displays of affection and impromptu basketball games on public courts when they slid around wildly in their Italian loafers and waved their hands in our faces as we moved swiftly around them toward the hoop. Most of all, they seemed willing to do almost anything we wanted and they'd pay for it too. While I knew, or thought I did, what they were up to, I didn't judge them for it. Having allowed us our freedom, it seemed only fair to allow them theirs.

After an hour or so of collections, we would usually go to a bar where Al and Pete were known and eat hamburgers and watch football or basketball on television. At one point Al said, "I wish Abe was here. We could make some money on the games."

"Can it," Pete said, indicating Joey, but if my friend heard he didn't say anything. I didn't know whether or not Al was joking, but other than that I never heard either of the men refer directly to the activities that had put Abe in prison.

Not that it mattered, for Abe Goodstein was everywhere. Whenever I visited Joey's apartment, Abe's presence was palpable. And while I hadn't met the great man, I was growing increasingly curious about him. I had never known anyone, least of all a man, who had his own dressing room. Yet just off the bedroom Abe shared with Mrs. G. (they slept in twin beds), was a kind of anteroom with double racks of suits, all hung neatly one inch apart. The rods would rotate so that Abe could select from summer suits, heavier fabrics, or resort wear, depending on his plans. Once Joey pulled open Abe's dresser to reveal piles of silk shirts, braces, and gold cuff links. The top of the dresser was littered with perhaps a dozen bottles of cologne and to the right twenty or thirty pairs of shoes were displayed on a standing shoe rack. All of this represented unimaginable luxury to me. I thought of my father in his drip-dry shirts from Sears and his battered brown shoes and wondered what kind of man Joey's father could be because it presented itself to me in just this way: that he must be of some different species than any of the men I knew or had known, men for whom clothes would never be anything more than an afterthought, if that. But as with Al and Pete, whatever loyalties I might have developed toward my father and his way of life vanished before the absent Abe Goodstein.

I knew that my parents would consider the Goodsteins to be showy and cheap and that my father would be infuriated to know how much time I was spending with Al and Pete, but I didn't care. For whatever Abe Goodstein had was what I now decided I wanted for myself. And whatever value my parents might place on art, politics, and intellectual concerns did not matter to me. I wanted an apartment with thick rugs, cut glass, and soft leather sofas; I wanted many television sets, phones in the bathrooms, and more shirts and shoes than I could ever wear before tiring of them and buying more. I had seen enough of the misery life could bring and as far as I could tell art did nothing to relieve that pain. Simply being a good person could neither guarantee happiness nor provide succor when life dealt out its blows, and I thought, mistakenly or not, that having some of the things I saw in the Goodstein's home might cushion the inevitable fall. I hated to go back home at the end of the day.

Occasionally, Al would consent to take us downtown rather than touring the bars, and on one such day, having admonished us to be standing in the same spot in two hours, they dropped us off on

Wisconsin Avenue, in front of Gimbel's. Before he drove off, Al rolled down his window and called me over. "Take good care of him, Danny," he said. Then he winked at me.

I knew what he meant. Joey had a tendency toward wildness. He would taunt gangs of boys wearing jackets from other schools and then take pleasure in being chased for blocks. Or he would throw snowballs at police cars or try to sneak rides on buses. It was part of his charm that heedfulness had no part in his nature, especially since I was never able to do the simplest thing without first calculating the risks or consequences. Yet today he seemed quiet, almost distracted, and it wasn't until we stopped for ice cream at Heinemann's that he let on about what was bothering him.

"My Dad's coming home," he said simply.

Joey never referred to his father as the old man, as other boys did, or seemed disrespectful in any way. Abe's absence was palpable but not something we talked about very much. It was as if he was away on a business trip. "That's good," I said. "When?"

Joey nodded. "I guess it is," he said slowly. "I was only ten when we went away and I didn't see him that much. I suppose it'll be okay. There'll be a big party. You can come."

"A party?" I imagined gun molls in sequined gowns and men in double-breasted suits with heavy pockets.

"We can get drunk," Joey said. "No one will notice."

Despite the fact that he was talking about a party, a homecoming, there was no joy in his tone, no hint of anticipation, and it made me wonder if life with his father would be hard. I knew about difficult fathers, but of course, his would be difficult in a different way. We walked through Boston Store and then down to Gimbel's where we found ourselves on the fifth floor surrounded by sporting goods. We weren't shopping in any real sense, as there was nothing we needed and we had already spent our money on ice cream. I inspected the baseball gloves, trying on a model endorsed by Nellie Fox as I worked my way up to a Wilson with Mickey Mantle's name scrawled across the thumb. Joey was on the other side of the section looking at golf bags, a rich guy's sport in which I had little interest. When I joined him, he flashed a pack of Titleists in his open palm.

"What are those for?" I asked stupidly, not understanding.

Joey put the golf balls in his pocket. "Come on," he said. "We've got to go meet the boys."

In some instinctive way, I knew I should distance myself from this, but in the munificence of Gimbel's, one pack of golf balls didn't seem to matter very much. Now, in retrospect, I wonder if Joey was trying to impress me with his daring, if having asked him about his father and organized crime, I had in a sense forced him to play this role. But there was no way to know then, so I followed Joey down the escalator and we were approaching the Wisconsin Avenue door when two large men blocked our path.

I started to excuse myself. "We have to meet someone," I said. But the men weren't moving and Joey now seemed to have become even smaller.

"You boys better come with us," one of the men said. He was carrying a walkie-talkie and seemed to be in charge.

"What's this about?" I asked.

"Ask your friend," the man said and spun me around by the shoulders.

They took us to a small office on the mezzanine with light green walls and two metal desks pushed together in the center. In no time, they had searched us and the golf balls were on the desk, dimpled accusers but still innocuous enough, or so it seemed to me.

"What's your name?" The man seemed bored and I couldn't blame him. Busting kids for stealing golf balls wasn't going to get him on *Crimestoppers*. Yet when Joey told him his name, the man looked at him with a mixture of curiosity and sympathy. "Abe Goodstein your old man?"

I wanted to answer for my friend, to say that while Abe was his father this had nothing to do with Joey's family. But I said nothing and Joey just nodded.

Now the other man spoke for the first time. "The apple don't fall far from the tree, aina?"

Even at fourteen, I realized that this was outrageously unfair. It was as if Joey had learned the art of shoplifting at his father's knee. Yet there was no point in arguing, and *something* had made Joey take those golf balls just as something drove him to pick fights he couldn't win. Wherever it came from and whatever you called it, it was real. That's why we were in this office while Al and Pete waited for us down on the Avenue.

"So what do we do with you?" the first man asked rhetorically. "Run you in?" He smiled as he said this, as if he knew it was pointless to try to scare the son of a famous gangster, but Joey didn't respond and I now understood that it was because he was acutely embarrassed. There was nothing smart to say in this situation, no act of daring with which he could impress me. In its own way, considering who he was, it was a piker's crime, not worth getting caught for, and therefore not worth committing in the first place. That's what Al would have said had he been there, but it was just the two of us and Joey had taken the golf balls and I had seen it all and said nothing to discourage him. Stupid or not, we were in it together. As if the store detective understood this and sympathized on some level, he rose and put his arm around Joey's shoulder.

"Don't let me see you in here again," he said gruffly. "Get the hell out of my store."

Joey and I descended the elevator again and went out on the street. Al and Pete were waiting and wanted to know what had kept us, but I made up an excuse and we got in the car and drove home. It seemed somehow that something should have come out of this, some greater understanding between us, but Joey and I never discussed that afternoon at Gimbel's, though I always thought he was grateful to me for not saying anything about it to anyone else.

Five

Homecoming

Abe Goodstein was released later that month, a fact duly noted in our newspaper of record which ran a scare headline reading "GOOD-STEIN RELEASED." Accompanying the article were pictures of Abe and Mrs. G. along with a sidebar detailing the history of the case for those readers who were not familiar with it. My parents noticed the article and I could tell by the small tight worry lines around my mother's mouth that in her mind this just made matters worse. Although she wasn't crazy about Joey, she was sympathetic toward his mother and didn't like to make judgments on others based on the newspapers. Too many of her friends from New York had suffered similar fates during the McCarthy era. At the same time, she worried about these new influences on me in the moments when she wasn't taken up with her concern for my father, her new job, or talking to my brother's psychiatrist.

I think she was fascinated in her demure way by Abe Goodstein for many of the same reasons I was, though she had made none of the choices he had and nothing in her experience would have prepared her for Al and Pete. For her, Abe was a larger-than-life character who wore a pinkie ring, was surrounded by Runyonesque characters, and dispensed extravagant tips to hatcheck girls, if there were any hatcheck girls in Milwaukee. In reality, Al and Pete were the only family retainers I ever saw, though like my mother I assumed there was a large dangerous organization behind them. In any case, it was only with some difficulty that I was given permission to attend Abe's welcome-home party and then only over my father's strident objections.

The party itself was a somewhat lackluster affair though someone had gone to the trouble of ordering a blue banner with "Welcome Home, Abe" printed on it and Mrs. G. was playing "Happy Days Are Here Again" on the piano when I walked in. Since I had seen pictures, I already knew what Abe looked like, but while he was paunchy and seemed tired, there was an undeniable vitality behind his small, blue eyes. He wore a cashmere cardigan and an ascot and his gray hair was combed back in wings over his temples. He might have been a corporate executive relaxing at home after a hard week on the Street. He had the quality of making everyone seem important, so that when he took my hand and said in a gravelly voice, "Nice to meet you, Danny, I've heard a lot about you," I thought he meant it and that somehow news of my escapades had reached him in the slammer in Indiana.

Other than that, however, the evening was uneventful. Mr. and Mrs. Goodstein played bridge with another middle-aged couple while Al and Pete watched a football game on television.

Joey and I tended bar and no one noticed that with each drink we made for someone else, we added a finger for ourselves. My exposure to alcohol had previously been limited to the occasional glass of table wine my mother would share with me and by the end of the evening the borders of the room had begun to seem indistinct and the ceiling had receded into the distance, where it circled sedately in a rhythm foreign to me. Eventually, someone put me to bed in a back bedroom but sleep came only fitfully.

—✐—

Sometime later, I became aware that Joey was there and had taken me in his mouth. At first, I was uncertain whether or not I was dreaming but as I felt myself getting hard I became excited and pulled him to me. I was too tired to even consider whether this was something I wanted, but now I think that I did; I think that I always had. For this wasn't sex in the way adults think of it; rather, it was comfort, something I needed badly, chronically. Comfort for leaving my home in Madison and moving to a strange place; comfort for the awful gravity of my father's illness; comfort for my mother's distraction, taking from me a love I had always assumed was permanent. Comfort.

And for Joey? I don't know. As with the shoplifting, we never discussed what happened that night, but I would guess he had similar feelings and needed to be comforted as badly as I did. Certainly, things had happened to him for which he bore no responsibility but had to suffer the consequences anyway. It is a truism of childhood that kids are the innocent bystanders to their parents' misfortunes, powerless to assert themselves but able to suffer nevertheless. What we had that night in bed was some kind of recompense for all that, a way for each of us to forgive the other and in the process forgive ourselves for allowing our parents to fail.

What we shared was certainly sex, though the result was more labored than passionate, and far from expert. I suspect Joey had more experience than I did, but then, anyone would have had more experience than I since I did not even know how to give myself pleasure. Except for the odd nocturnal emission that left me embarrassed and confused, I had never had an orgasm. And while it may seem contradictory, I'm sure neither of us would have considered ourselves to be homosexual or even thought of this as a homosexual interlude. We would still make fun of the men who cruised Juneau Park, would still tell faggot jokes, for in our culture homosexuality was a shameful thing. It never occurred to either of us that we might prefer boys to girls. We desired each other that night, but our desire existed outside the theater of sexual preference. We loved each other as friends and there were no artificial boundaries to our love and no need to restrict its expression. Still, if either of us had had the opportunity to be in that bed with a girl, Dana Bowman, say, or Carol Maxwell, the choice would have been easy and there would have been no hard feelings. We were prisoners, as Abe had been, but in our case the prisons were the families into which we had been born, the lives that they had imposed upon us.

As it was, we comforted each other with our hands and our mouths and then we slept. Yet when I awoke, Joey was gone, bright sunlight was streaming in, and Mrs. G. was standing in the doorway. "Your mother just called," she said. "She wants you to come home."

~

Like my mother, Alfred Leach taught at the university; unlike her, he had achieved some distinction in his field at a relatively early age. His specialty was the history of science, which was news to me because I had not known that science had a history. I had always assumed that history was only and always history and that science would be the same, but Alfred confused things further by telling me that he was really a philosopher interested not so much in either discipline as in the way people had thought about them throughout time. It was this area in which he had made his reputation and this was what had brought him to the university as a distinguished visiting lecturer. While he claimed to think Milwaukee was chauvinistic and boring, he had for some reason remained for five years and now seemed to have become a fixture, though he was only in town for a day or two each week. During these periods, Anna was his slave, maintaining his room in pristine order, doing his laundry and cooking special dishes whenever he wished, which wasn't often since Alfred was always on a diet.

Paul's opinion of Alfred was muted. Though I suspected he must have resented having another man in his house, especially one his wife idolized even if he was homosexual, he welcomed the extra money and Alfred was really very little trouble to anyone. Now, however, things began to change in subtle ways. Alfred was an agitator and Anna was his cause. Why should a woman with Anna's intelligence stay home and clean house? Just because Hitler hadn't allowed

44

Jews to be educated was no reason to compound the problem now. Alfred encouraged Anna to go beyond the continuing education courses she had been taking at night and enroll in something called the University without Walls, where she could receive a combined high school and college degree in two years. He would be both her instructor and advisor. Much of the time required to receive a conventional degree was wasted on social life in Alfred's opinion, and the new program gave Anna credit for her life experience. Although Paul was a cultivated man, he wasn't prepared for this, with the result that he and Anna grew steadily apart.

Sometimes on weekends, Anna would accompany Alfred to Chicago where they stayed in Alfred's North Side apartment with his lover, Joe, who taught art in one of the high schools. I knew of this from my mother, who had become Anna's intimate. I would hear them talking in hushed whispers after Anna's Chicago visits and sometimes, to my surprise, I actually heard my mother giggle in delight at something Anna had said. The two women seemed very different to me, but their friendship thrived nevertheless and I suspect it had to do in part with my mother's need for companionship. She had even taken to discussing things with me, as if I were an adult friend. Still, Anna's behavior was in its own way shocking to my mother since initially she had seemed like a typical *Hausfrau,* content to limit her world to home and family, and dramatic change is foreign and disturbing to most of us. Even at that age, I could see that there was something attractive and forbidden about Anna's new life to my mother, trapped as she was by an invalid husband and two young boys. Yet I did not learn that Anna had a new friend in Chicago from my mother, who must have known, but rather from Alfred during one of our basement conversations.

"Haisuss?" I said. "You mean, like Jesus?"

Alfred smiled patiently. "I was using the Spanish pronunciation," he said, waving his hand in the air. Alfred looked a little Spanish this afternoon with his orange serape and huaraches, so I supposed that he knew what he was talking about. Still, in my world, married women did not have male friends in other cities with whom they spent stolen weekends. And I still didn't know why Alfred bothered to tell me anything.

"Where did she meet this guy?" I was also having trouble imagining Anna as a sexual being. I didn't know how she would move her bulk around without crushing the other person. I had previously assumed this explained the fact that she and Paul had no children, but now Jesús had been added to the equation.

"The grocery store," Alfred said. "I think it was the produce aisle. He was working there and introduced himself." He shrugged. "I don't know exactly."

Meeting over the carrots and celery didn't strike me as being very romantic, but I supposed that if you were built like Anna it wouldn't do to be choosy. I took a moment to be sure I understood what I was being told. Anna was involved, that much was clear, and involved with a Central American man whom she had met in the grocery store. Alfred sensed my bewilderment. "What's the matter?" he asked.

I didn't know how to put it, especially given Alfred's own sexuality. My night with Joey had increased my curiosity about him and his lover. It still seemed odd to be talking about sex in a dusty cellar with an older man. But I was interested and wanted to know more. "I just never thought of Anna that way." Thinking of anyone in a sexual way was new and exciting to me, but I didn't say this. I felt foolish enough as it was.

Alfred seemed to understand and was kind enough not to draw attention to my awkwardness. "Some men like big women," he said. "I'm told men in Guatemala think American women are too thin. Of course they have a much broader view of sex than we do."

I decided not to probe further in that direction. I liked Alfred and didn't want to have any reason not to like him. "She's big all right," I said. "But does this guy, Jesús, speak English or what?"

Alfred shook his head. "They speak the language of love, Danny," he said. "Anna's studying Spanish, but it's not an intellectual relationship. It's passionate." He raised his eyebrows as he said this, but I had already figured it out.

46

I tried again to imagine Anna in bed but couldn't. Oddly enough, however, I found myself accepting whatever she had done or would do. It made no difference to me and I don't know why since if I had been asked I would certainly have said that adultery was wrong. This wasn't for some reason; I knew that immediately, even if I didn't know why I felt this way. "What about Paul?"

Suddenly, Alfred looked very serious. "You can't say anything to him about this. Remember, his heart." Alfred patted his chest, though I thought this was somewhat insincere since I knew he didn't care at all about Paul's health. "Paul can be a very violent person," he added.

I doubted this since he had always been kind to me, but now I thought about loyalty. If this could happen to Anna, then why not to my mother, who was smaller and prettier? I thought of it in exactly this way: of her being the passive recipient of Jesús' passion. After all, my mother was a young woman and my father was growing steadily weaker. Shouldn't my mother be as entitled as Anna to have a man in her life? But even if I could justify this hypothetical affair, such thoughts were upsetting to me. What would my responsibilities be then, to my mother or my father? Would I even blame her? Without ever thinking about it before, I knew I wouldn't. Though I had never really experienced either and had no reason for feeling as I did, I decided then that there was a difference between sex and love. "I won't tell anyone," I said. "I promise."

"Good boy," Alfred said approvingly. "Let's go to the movies."

In winter, Milwaukee seemed to draw in upon itself and the limited world of the city was even more limited, or so it seemed to me. The sun was gone from November until May and if a scrim of snow appeared in early fall it remained until summer, simply growing grayer and meaner over time. The wind was cold but also wet and with a penetrating quality I have felt nowhere else. While school was seldom cancelled and everyone went to work no matter what the weather, the streets in winter were mostly empty and there was a dismal quality to the air. Yet for me there was no school now and so to escape the linoleum sameness of our apartment, I roamed the neighborhood looking for surcease from my depression. My mother was often at the university or working in her studio and my father and brother were at work on a perpetual chess game I was not invited to join.

The part of the East Side in which we lived bore little resemblance to the sumptuous neighborhoods with stately mansions that overlooked Lake Park, which had been designed by Frederick Law Olmstead. East of Downer Avenue, the streets grew progressively wealthier, culminating in Lake Drive; to the west, however, the houses were smaller and less prepossessing until they ran finally into the Milwaukee River beyond which lay the working-class ghettos of the poor whites who were defending a few miles of double-deckers from the spreading area called, appropriately, the Inner Core, where the Negroes lived piled on top of one another like so many pieces of coal.

Our neighborhood represented a kind of border society made up of lower-middle-class families trying to escape from whatever was beneath them on the social scale. Men who had grown up on the North Side, or on Brady Street in the small Italian section, had worked all their lives for the meager purchase of a run-down duplex on the wrong side of Downer but still on the East Side. It was for them a kind of triumph but our family was, to say the least, unusual in this mix; I never met another child from a professional family in the five years we lived on Frederick Avenue and finally such distinctions came to lose their meaning for me. Mainly, I was struck by the sameness of everything, the lack of distinction or distinctiveness, the lack of color anywhere, and it made me feel desperate. Sometimes with Joey, or less often with my brother, I would take the number thirty bus downtown to Wisconsin Avenue for entertainment, but more often I frequented the Century Lanes, where one could bowl for thirty-five cents a line or go for hamburgers at the Oriental Drugstore.

Walking through that world, I found little diversion from the gray asbestos siding of the houses belted by black metal railings with cement porches on which sad collapsed gliders sat piled high with snow. The air was damp and smelled of cinders. Though no one I knew had a fireplace, everyone heated his house with coal, as we did. And then, just beyond Farwell Avenue, our district took on an institutional flavor as a Catholic orphanage, an old folks home and Saint Mary's Hospital spread east to the lake bluffs.

It would be inaccurate to say that there was nothing to do, and my parents demanded little of me beyond my chores. But what friends I had made at school were far away in the suburbs and Joey's family had gone to Florida for the holidays, an unimaginable extravagance in my mind. I would sometimes shoot baskets with a flattened ball at the Maryland Avenue playground and there were matinees at the Oriental. But I felt terribly alone and indeed I was. It seemed to me as if the holiday would never end.

Ironically my lethargy was not ended by anything I did or could have done, but by Anna knocking frantically on our door in the middle of the night to say that she was taking Paul to the hospital. He had suffered another heart attack and now she said she was instructing the doctor not to go to extremes to keep him alive. The word she used was heroic, but it seemed odd to me to speak of heroism in this context. In any case, it seemed to all of us that she was being somewhat premature.

"Why doesn't she just put a pillow over the poor bastard's head," my father said.

But my mother, as usual, was understanding, even sympathetic. "I thought you liked Anna," she said.

"I do," my father said. "I just don't want her taking me to any hospitals."

My mother assured him that she would do the driving if that was ever the case and immediately began preparations for a siege. My mother had liked Paul instinctively from the beginning and he had always been courtly and attentive to her. But more important, in the South, where she had grown up, you did not desert family and friends to strangers in their hour of need. Now my mother took crackers, cheese, candy, oranges, and bananas and put them in an old shopping basket along with pillows, blankets, and an extra pair of socks. There was no question of my father going along and my brother was too young, so my mother and I got into our old Plymouth and made the short trip to Columbia Hospital to wait out Paul's crisis with him.

Without anyone having to tell me, I knew that Anna and Paul were unhappy, and it had little to do with Jesús or even with Alfred. Their unhappiness was structural and inevitable. He was older and had been a friend of her brother in their hometown of Fürth. Later, Paul had become the administrator of the Jewish hospital and had married before being sent along with his wife to Buchenwald. The difference in their ages was enough, along with Anna's lack of beauty, that Paul had never given her a thought when they were both in Germany and he probably would never have looked at her in this country had she not taken it upon herself to rescue him when he arrived alone and without language in New York in 1946, a reluctant survivor of the Holocaust. Paul, like many people, didn't know why he had lived, but more to the point he felt that he shouldn't have, that he didn't deserve to be here when his wife had been killed. It would have meant more to have died defending her, but that wasn't a possibility and so he had improbably lived to regret his new life. Furthermore, his experience and education meant nothing in America. Small and slight, he was offered only menial labor, washing dishes in a Jewish community center in Brooklyn, which he found not only inappropriate but insulting. It would have been better if this had made Paul angry, but whatever anger he had was turned inward with the result that he walked with a stoop and wore a habitual scowl on his face.

Anna had arrived six months before, having been saved from the camps by the children's crusade that sent Jewish children to England to live out the war. Often, they outlived their families as well and this had been the case for Anna. She had arrived in New York at eighteen with no education beyond grammar school and little experience, but she was able to find a job as a doctor's baby nurse and with her first three paychecks bought herself a new nose. She came across Paul by mistake at an *oneg Shabbat* in a temple where she had gone with the express purpose of meeting new people, though she was not religious and often derided Jews who were. Not expecting to know anyone at the *oneg*, Anna cried out in relief when she saw Paul and threw her arms around him. Despite his pallor and weary expression, he represented the older, more stable world she had lost. All the same, perhaps because of her luck in escaping to England, Anna had no interest in dwelling on the past, preferring instead to be as American as possible and leave Germany and its horrors behind.

Paul couldn't do this. His wife was dead and there was no suitable work for him. He believed that if he ever drove a car, a buried psychotic rage would impel him to run people over, so he was limited to public transportation, though driving would have made his life easier. For a time, he worked for a Jewish grocery as a runner, then at a newsstand; finally Anna and Paul moved to the Midwest, where he found work, improbably, as a salesman for a company that sold beauty products. Over time, what had begun as a friendship, evolved into mutual coexistence and finally resentment, since Anna felt Paul limited her opportunities while Paul believed she had unrealistic expectations. Having seen his life end once in the camps, Paul was now forced to live in humiliation as he watched Anna's infatuation with Alfred develop. Slowly, he retreated into himself, with his Dürer prints and Goethe, and said little to Anna, who wanted to go out and meet new people. Though they never discussed it, Paul's acquiescence to his heart problems represented escape for both of them.

At the hospital, Anna had set up headquarters in the hall outside Paul's room and when we arrived she offered fruit and drinks, as if we had stopped by for a social visit. "How is Paul?" my mother asked.

Anna rolled her eyes. "The nurses are terrified. He thinks he's back in the concentration camp. He yells out in German and won't let them near him because he thinks they're Nazis doing experiments on him."

Tears formed in my mother's eyes, but when we saw Paul he seemed completely lucid. He smiled shyly and said, "I'm sorry you had to come to this place."

"Oh, Paul," my mother said. "I'm sorry, too." Then she took his hands in hers and they both began to cry.

Though my father's illness should have inured me to doctors and hospitals, I had never been this close to death. One advantage of moving away from relatives is that death is always kept at a sanitized distance, and when one does occur it has the immediacy of something read in the newspaper. Now, however, while no one said anything, someone I knew, indeed someone who had lived in my house only steps from our kitchen, was going to cease to exist, and in all likelihood it would happen very shortly. This had a predictable effect: it made me think of my own mortality, for even if I was young, Paul's situation made my own end seem more inevitable than it had, and it also seemed closer.

At the same time, I was to learn from this experience that death had its mundane routine, just as life did: whenever we entered Paul's room, my mother would rearrange his pillows, which had just been fluffed by Anna or a nurse; then she would refill his water glass from the plastic pitcher on his table and retrieve whatever magazine or book had slipped beneath the bed. Finally, she would take orders for whatever Paul might desire from the gift shop in the lobby, mark the slow decline of his condition, and then leave promising to return. And we did faithfully each day, knowing that the next time we came we might find the room empty, the bed stripped, and the room tenanted by someone else. Anna seldom made an appearance while we were there, though I knew she was often in the hospital, talking to the nurses or sitting in the cafeteria. I imagined she was asking if they couldn't speed the process and help Paul die faster than he was managing to do on his own.

In the interstices of visits by the adults, my mother often left me in the room in the belief that it was bad enough to die without having to do so alone. At first this made me uncomfortable, but Paul quickly put me at ease. "You don't have to say anything, Daniel," he told me. "I'm not sad particularly."

"You mean you want to die?" This seemed incredible to me.

Paul wrinkled his forehead in thought. "I wouldn't say that, exactly. I didn't commit suicide, did I? But I don't object to it either. It seems logical under the circumstances."

I couldn't argue with that. He looked terrible, gray and drawn, but I had never thought of illness in these terms. There was nothing logical about my father's illness, for example. I hadn't thought logic really governed life, though some people liked to pretend that it did. But it was absent from my life. In my experience things just seemed to happen, usually for no reason. Oddly enough, however, Paul seemed more cheerful than usual and I wanted to keep him talking. "Aren't you going to miss everybody?" I asked.

He smiled. "I hadn't thought about that," he said. "Actually, I don't know if the ability to miss anything is present in death. I guess that's one of the things I will discover. But, no, not really." Then he corrected himself. "That's not quite true," he said. "I will miss your mother. She is a lovely person, and I would like to see you grow up."

I was pleased but not satisfied that this was the whole truth. "What about Anna?" I wanted to know if he resented her as she prepared for his death. I suppose I thought that he should. But Paul didn't seem angry.

"Anna?" he repeated, as if it was a question. "Oh, she will get along quite well without me, just as she has gotten along very well with me. I think that I will make no difference at all in her life, either here or there."

I waited but there was nothing more. I thought Paul had been quite generous but it seemed to have cost him nothing. He drank some water, then he said, "There's a chess set in that cabinet over there, Danny. We could play a game if you don't object to playing with someone who is not nearly as good as your little brother."

"That's okay," I said. "I'm no good either." I got the board down and set up the pieces. Even though I disliked chess, confining the world to a grid of black and white squares seemed comforting under the circumstances.

When, after four days, Paul finally died it was in midafternoon, as though he regretted the inconvenience he had caused before by getting everyone out of bed in the middle of the night. For the last day of his life he regressed entirely into German, which only my father understood, and then imperfectly. And while they weren't close friends, it happened that my father was with Paul at the end and he reported that he had sat erect in bed and fastened his gaze on the wall in front of him and said only one word: *Warum?* Why. Of course no one had anything to say to this. It was the great unanswerable question, whether addressed to Nazis or people like us.

Anna was untroubled by philosophy, however. Her response to Paul's death was businesslike and immediate. He was cremated the next day and there was no funeral, supposedly at his direction. If Anna mourned at all, she did so privately, but then all real mourning is private, whether one wishes it to be or not, and I could not judge Anna for this. She never said anything to me beyond asking if I wanted any of Paul's clothes. He was short, so they might have fit, but his wardrobe consisted almost entirely of gray suits and cardigan sweaters, which would have been an odd choice for a boy my age, even one who had few clothes and little money to buy more. It seemed a little morbid to be wearing a dead man's clothes, but I didn't want to hurt Anna's feelings. So in the end I took one of the sweaters, which I took to wearing in the drafty basement, and a copy of *Das Lied von der Erde,* though I neither spoke nor read German. Anna said it would be worth something someday if I held on to it.

I had liked Paul, liked his gentleness and acceptance of the violence in the world and within himself, and I resented Anna's alacrity in expunging every trace of his life from their apartment. Although I had never even had a girlfriend, I possessed a youthful certainty about the requirements of marriage, and in her hurry to be rid of her husband, Anna had confronted them, whether she meant to or not. What made it confusing was that I couldn't bring myself to dislike her. What did I know of death or grieving, after all? I only knew that things hadn't turned out well for Paul. Though in some way death is always a return, I wished an exception could have been made in Paul's case and that instead of returning to die in Germany, he had been allowed to journey to some new place, somewhere he might have found happiness.

Six

Complications

Joey's family returned from Florida just after New Year's and our friendship resumed as if nothing sexual had happened between us. I had felt both excited and somewhat ill-at-ease, unsure how I was to behave toward him and willing to take my lead from Joe. The fact that he said nothing allowed me to do the same and I think we were both relieved. The only real change lay in his father's constant presence, rather his dominance, over the scene. I don't know that I thought Abe should have seemed chastened by his time in prison, but I expected him to brood a bit, to spend time staring out the window into the winter twilight, wondering why fate had dealt him this cruel blow. Instead, he was upbeat, cocky as he walked around his apartment, like the lord of the manor, shaking peanuts in his hand and then throwing them into the air and catching them in his mouth. Previously, we had spent evenings with Mrs. G. playing Monopoly or dominoes, with Al and Pete making occasional appearances to run errands or take us places. In retrospect, it all seemed wonderfully simple, as if we had been campers sitting at the feet of a beneficent matriarch.

Abe, on the other hand, was hard and tough and seemed to want everyone to know it, especially Joey. Perhaps it was necessary for him, returning from prison, to reestablish himself as the head of the household by ordering everyone around, but I wasn't thinking about that. Short and broad, with long muscular arms, Abe projected a menacing masculinity that made me want to stay out of his way, though he was always polite to me. And, though he seemed glad to have his father home, Joey could seemingly do nothing that didn't irritate Abe. One night at dinner, Joey was showing off, playing spoons, when suddenly Abe's right arm snaked out and caught him across the face. I remember the sound being like a piece of wood breaking and then blood appeared on Joey's lips. For a moment everything stopped and I expected Mrs. G. to speak up, perhaps to confront her husband. But her only reaction was to hand Joey a napkin and say, "Go wash your face."

Joey left the room and Abe looked directly at me. "I'm sorry you had to see that, Danny," he said, ignoring the obvious. That is, I didn't have to see it because he didn't have to do it. But of course I said nothing. Then Joey returned and dinner resumed without comment.

Even now, after almost thirty years, I'm not sure what to think about Abe Goodstein. He was a little peacock of a man with his white-on-white shirts, Rolex watch, and Bally shoes. Though he had graduated from the university with honors and made law review, he had never been as interested in law as he was in gambling. He was defiant and I'm not sure he wasn't right to be. In fact, when I see betting lines routinely listed in the daily sports section today, it's hard to feel that Abe was doing anything wrong. Furthermore, he was full of contradictions. Though the government had surely not treated him well, Abe had nothing but contempt for war protesters or those who burned draft cards. He was a man out of time or at least in his own time, which had little to do with anyone else. But he had self-respect and that seemed to be the thing that propped him up and protected him from the negative opinions of others.

Far from allowing anyone to think he had learned his lesson in prison, or even that he had a lesson to learn, Abe now set up a new

office on Wells Street in sight of the courthouse and began petition-
ing the state bar to reinstate his license. I don't know if this was right
or wrong any more than I did then, but I wish my father had been as
angry at what had happened to him, even if it would have meant
that he hit me from time to time. Instead, he sank slowly into mel-
ancholy, no longer bothering to try to negotiate the parallel bars and
in time neglecting even to get dressed if he didn't have to leave the
house. Of course it's a flawed comparison. Abe wasn't ill, and he even
had the chance to rehabilitate himself if he chose. But what I admired in him was his tenacity, his unwillingness to see himself as
anything less than his peers. So I became ever more fascinated with
my friend's father, even as my own father complained that my best
friend was the son of a gangster and refused to accept the Goodsteins' invitations to the symphony or the opera.

"They think I'm a goddamned trophy," he told my mother.
"They want to put me on the mantle piece and show me to their
friends."

"I think Mrs. Goodstein is just trying to be sociable," my mother
said. "They've been very nice to Daniel and you never complained
when people invited us out in Madison."

"That was different," my father said, and I knew what he meant.
In Madison, any invitations they might have received had been in
recognition of who he was; now it was a question of what he used to
be and he didn't want to be reminded of that. Beyond this, my father
had never enjoyed concerts or what the world in general considered
culture anyway. He preferred the movies. But there was no way for
the Goodsteins to know this and in time the invitations ceased.

━╴

School resumed in its desultory way, but owing to the sort of school
Campus was, beginning and ending seemed even more arbitrary
than they had to be. The principal had earnestly informed us that
the task of a laboratory school was not so much to master a body of
knowledge as it was to study the ways in which people learn, and to

ask *why* we learn the things we do and not other things instead. Valuable as this quest for learning might have been, it didn't seem to mean as much to elementary school children as Dr. Patterson might have liked, which was something he needed to learn. The practical result of the school's philosophy was that we studied mainly what we wished to study and, not surprisingly, few children wished to study grammar or algebra. Dr. Patterson's response to this was, as he said publicly, "At Campus, we teach children to articulate, not punctuate." And so they did, with varying degrees of success, but this lack of structure made itself felt in other ways as well. There were, for example, no bells at Campus, announcing when school or classes began or ended. And there were no tardy slips. It was common for students to leave class with no explanation and wander the halls, and while it was generally acknowledged that school began around 8:30, children frequently arrived later than that and suffered no consequences. Once, Joey appeared at 10:00 and was sent by Miss Harmon to Dr. Patterson's office. Afterwards, I questioned him about it.

"He asked me why I wanted to be so late," Joey said.

"Wanted? He asked you why you *wanted* that?"

Joey nodded. "He said that if I had wanted to be there on time, he thought I would have made it a point to be there. Since I was late, he figured I must have wanted that too. He thought I was trying to make some kind of point, I guess."

"What did you tell him?" I had never heard of an adult asking a child questions like this. In my experience, adults seemed to have no concern about what children wanted, though they had lots of ideas regarding what they might need. Even my parents didn't seem to care what I wanted, if I wanted anything.

"I just told him I wanted to sleep late," Joe replied. "And he said, 'Today, you wanted to sleep late today, but another day you might want to come to school when the other kids do?' And I said it could happen that way, and that's all there was to it."

Such interviews were grist for the educational mill. We were constantly being asked what we were interested in, if we wanted to study this or that, and since we often had no idea, we would say whatever came to mind, as on the day I announced I'd like to learn something about astrophysics. This impressed my teachers to no end and in due time I was sent over to the physics department at the university where a retired professor and I tried valiantly to communicate for several weeks. Though I knew little more about physics than the word, the experiment was eventually declared a success and I was deemed a prodigy, something that raised my stock with Miss Harmon considerably, which made it a success as far as I was concerned.

Just as there was no morning bell at Campus, there was some confusion about exactly when school ended with the result that children stayed in the building until they felt like going home or until their parents came inside looking for them. Whatever strain this may have caused the teachers never entered our minds and was never alluded to by them. The wealthier kids, raised in privilege, must have assumed that they were roughly equivalent to servants, there for our pleasure, to do what we wanted, and the rest of us simply followed along. It was a wonderfully freeing feeling for me to be so important, or at least to be allowed to think of myself as being in control of my own destiny as it was expressed in school. The teachers often said that they were there to learn from us, and as questionable as this might sound, I think they were sincere for the most part.

This laissez-faire attitude on the part of the faculty had the effect of generating a cheerful chaos, in which students came and went as they pleased in the school, as well as a wonderful confidence among the children in their own abilities, ideas, and talents. If this delight in oneself was inevitably to be tarnished in later life, it was an incredible change for me to come to love school, and remarkably, to be appreciated and loved in return. And everyone was appreciated for something because, as Dr. Patterson remarked, "You are all exceptional."

This may have been true or an exaggeration, but what I remember as ordinary for Campus is in direct proportion to how unusual it truly was for an elementary school: Miss Harmon in high heels circling the class with one hand on her right hip or sitting on her desk and clasping her knees to reveal inches of nyloned thigh; Carol Maxwell reaching beneath our joined desks and massaging my leg, before pinching my penis hard; being called on to recite a Keats ode and later having an autobiographical essay read aloud to universal astonishment and praise; our boys basketball team—the worst team I ever observed at any school, on any level, in any sport—that lost every game by a minimum of thirty points.

Yet the high point of the school year occurred shortly after my adventure in physics when I was assigned two graduate students, who were apparently going to write seminar papers about me but instead became my friends. As older confidants and, unlike Alfred, heterosexual, they were helpful in procuring dirty magazines and were an endless source of hamburgers, milk shakes, and long talks on Saturday afternoons. If they ever did write anything about me, I never saw it, but as far as I was concerned, they were welcome to whatever they could learn. Certainly, I couldn't have been of much help. But Campus was sui generis, absolutely unique, and an odd place to land for a boy who understood none of the worlds in which he moved. Yet in that long, sad winter, it became my base, both physically and emotionally, the place I felt most free to be whoever I was and whatever it was I was to become. For all its peculiarities, I was grateful for that.

My father's condition continued to deteriorate. What had originally been described to me as a minor annoyance and then, later, incapacitating, was steadily tending toward decrepitude. Although my father retained his essential brilliance in conversation and manner, and had always related to me as a rather puzzling satellite in his universe, he now seemed to shrink physically before my eyes. Not that he was simply shorter or smaller, but that he actually began to contract, as if his disease was affecting mass and causing him to collapse upon himself.

Ironically, however, I saw more of him than I ever had when he had been out in the world and, in a peculiar way, we became closer. Often, when I came home from school he would be in the kitchen,

61

seated next to the stove, waiting for a saucepan of soup to boil. And though we would later have violent fights, I remember this period as an oddly tender interlude in what was otherwise a fractious relationship. I don't remember what we talked about on these afternoons, only that we did, and it was this that was valuable. There would be a book on his lap or open upon the table and I would sit with him while he ate his soup, ladling the liquid with trembling fingers only with difficulty into his mouth, then spilling it on his pants. An essential part of our relationship at this point was an unspoken agreement to ignore his growing infirmity. It was important to him to appear strong and impregnable, but it was at least as important to me to continue to think of him this way despite the obvious evidence to the contrary.

When he was done eating, I would help him get up and walk down the long corridor to his room where he would read or write until my mother's return at the end of the day from the university. This was a role reversal that my father bore with more patience than I might have expected considering he had been the center of attention since childhood when his parents maintained a funereal silence in the small apartment, shushing his brother and sister officiously so that the genius could practice in peace. Now, however, there was no such dispensation. It was he who ordered the groceries and oversaw what cooking or cleaning was done, and he who sat and waited for news of the outside world. Now, he was vestigial to the business of the family and yet he bore this with grace, uncomplainingly. What had happened to him was manifestly unfair, but I never heard him say that. Not that he was one to see silver linings, for he had a rather pessimistic view of the world. But he was not bitter. Indeed, when he spoke of his condition, it was with a detachment that was intellectual rather than passionate. In his view, the disease had simply happened; he had gotten sick, as had thousands of others, and there was no point in acting otherwise.

"Considering the number of illnesses they've identified, it's kind of remarkable we don't get more of them," he observed logically. He also disliked the romantic images of illness, or the military terms utilized by the popular press. He never thought of himself, for example, as "fighting" the disease, or of arthritis as invading his body. "I'm a conscientious objector," he said ironically. "I don't believe in fighting."

My father didn't believe in God either, nor in redemption nor even punishment, feeling this was more sentimental nonsense. To him, what had happened wasn't personal. "How can bacteria punish anything?" he asked. Instead, he was a true agnostic and embraced the randomness of the universe, even as it affected his once graceful, now useless, limbs. I thought even then it was a heroic way to behave. While I had been in awe of my father before, I had not admired him as I did now.

He was using a cane when he went outside, which he did less and less frequently, but inside he would careen along the hall when no one was there to help him and the dim light of the hall revealed his handprints, like the prehensile remnants of the past in a cave. I liked the feeling of his heavy hands on my shoulders as we walked; I liked thinking of myself as a weight-bearing instrument since I seemed to have no weight of my own.

At some point, however, without anyone ever discussing it in my hearing, the decision was made to hire a maid to care for my father when no one else was around. It is hard to imagine how my parents could have afforded this, even assuming that such a person would have cost little in those days. For there was very little to spare. The apartment had been furnished from the Salvation Army store; my mother wore secondhand clothes, as did my brother and I. We had a used Chevy station wagon that was on its last legs. We were broke, or close to it, most of the time and even at that age I was well aware of this. Nevertheless, I remember my mother interviewing a series of women sent by the state employment service, all of whom were black and sat immobile in their coats holding shopping bags while my father held himself proudly aloof in the next room, as if this process had nothing to do with him.

I remember thinking then that the progress of the disease was like a slow, sad slide down a mountain, which accelerated as one approached the bottom. Yet the fact that we were actually going to have a maid represented a kind of cachet for me, something that proved we were not quite as poor as I had thought. Since many of the kids at school came from wealthy families with big homes on the lake, the fact that we lived in a small apartment on the wrong side of Downer was something that I had borne silently until now. Except for Joey, I had invited no one over and on the few occasions that I was given a ride, I asked to be dropped off up the street in front of a modest single-family home, where I would linger as if looking for my keys until the car disappeared around the corner.

Even before she actually appeared, I would drop a mention of the maid in conversation, no doubt surprising my classmates since maids were commonplace to them and we might have been discussing something completely unrelated, like baseball. I imagined a woman in a starched uniform who would miraculously transform our home, turning the linoleum into wall-to-wall carpet, painting the kitchen a cheerful yellow, planting flowers in the nonexistent beds on the side of the house, and even sanding the pine floors of my bedroom in her spare time.

So it was somewhat disappointing finally to meet Daisy, a small woman, seemingly only a few years older than I was with marcelled hair and a ready smile that revealed one gold tooth in the middle of her mouth. What was most surprising about Daisy, however, was her body. Far from ever wearing the kind of uniform I had envisioned, she chose a series of tight sweaters with buttons missing in strategic locations due, I thought, to her full and insistent breasts. Her hips were encased in tight tube dresses that succeeded badly in camouflaging her large, round behind. Coming across Daisy bending over to clean under a bed was an event that caused me such discomfort that I frequently had to leave the room. She could have been young or old, a wife and a mother, and it wouldn't have mattered to me in the slightest. She was the most frankly sexual woman I had ever seen and since my interest in her was obvious, she was amused.

"What you looking at?" she'd say, and laugh uproariously. Then, "No, don't tell me, 'cause I know. Same thing any man looks at." And she'd laugh again.

My embarrassment at being so quickly found out was lessened by the fact that Daisy had called me a man and in doing so had granted me a new latitude. I had no idea how I was going to tolerate my frustration, for there was no question that I had to be around her, but I wanted to be less obvious. I took to coming home earlier on the days I knew she would be in our home and while she naturally spent most of her time caring for my father and tending to his needs, we would occasionally pass in the hall and I would smell her nearness, an intoxicating mixture of perspiration and old sex that I was too young to recognize but which nearly drove me crazy.

Daisy understood from the beginning. She toyed with me, laughing, flashing her gold tooth, enjoying my excruciating desire. And why not? What was I to her except another horny white boy? She displayed a knowing attitude that I imagined went back to the plantations in the South, a wily acceptance that must have enabled black women to survive for generations. And whatever my pretensions, why should it have been any other way? She enjoyed being in control for once in her life. When I could stand no more, I would say, "I'm going downstairs."

"Okay, then," Daisy would say. And I would retreat to the basement, where I would listen to her soft tread on the boards over my head, and wait for her, imagining the fantastic sexual character of our eventual coupling until she left for the day and peace of a kind descended for a while.

～

It was on one of these afternoons that I heard steps on the stairs and thought my dreams had been answered. When I turned to see Alfred standing there, my disappointment must have been obvious, as he had an ironic smile on his face. "Expecting someone else?" he said. I wondered if somehow he knew about Daisy.

"No, of course not." I rearranged some papers and cleared a place on the only chair. "Sit down?"

I hadn't seen much of Alfred since Paul's death and I attributed it to his innate good taste. He didn't want to seem to be mourning a man he hadn't liked; at the same time, out of respect to the dead, he had kept his distance. Now that I thought about it, Anna hadn't been around much either, or so I thought. The truth is that since Daisy's arrival I hadn't noticed anything else. But it seemed to me that after clearing out all of Paul's belongings, Anna had taken to spending most of her weekends in Chicago, I assumed with her lover. And while I thought this behavior was scandalous, that is, I disapproved, I still had trouble thinking of her in a sexual way, so in a sense I excused her. Now Alfred told me that she and Jesús were actually living together in a building he and Joe owned.

I wasn't sure how to respond to this since it was so far outside my experience, so I asked the only question that occurred to me. "Do you like him? Jesús, I mean, not Joe."

Alfred smiled again. "There's not really much to like or dislike, Danny. He barely speaks English and he's still on a diurnal calendar."

"Diurnal?" I had heard the word applied only to animals before and wasn't sure exactly what Alfred meant.

"He's really a peasant. Nice, but very simple. He was brought up in a mountain village in Guatemala without electricity. When the sun goes down, he gets sleepy and wants to go to bed, and then of course he's up at daybreak, like a rooster."

It was hard to imagine someone as thoroughly domesticated as Anna living with such a person, but this was the most interesting thing I had heard about Jesús. "You mean he doesn't use the lights?"

"For what? He can't read either. I guess he needs light to avoid running into walls if he gets up to take a piss in the middle of the night. Otherwise, the whole thing is irrelevant to him, except he likes to watch TV." I hadn't really heard Alfred talk this way before and I thought he wasn't being fair to Jesús, or for that matter to Anna, his great friend.

Behind the mocking tone, however, I heard something else, which even at fourteen I recognized as jealousy. While Alfred and Anna had no sexual relationship, I think they loved each other, and it was important to him that he always be primary in her life. When Paul was alive, this hadn't been a problem for Anna had no sexual relationship with her husband and she was excited by Alfred's intellectual gifts. But this new friendship forced Alfred to compete on a completely different field and one where he was at a disadvantage. It made no difference at all to Jesús how many books Alfred had written or was going to write. And at this moment, it seemed to be less important to Anna than it once had been. Yet the whole arrangement was a mystery to me. Anna had effectively sectioned her life between the two men: with Alfred she lived what she considered to be an intellectual existence, while her life with Jesús was completely physical. She and Jesús couldn't even talk with one another. The remarkable thing was that this seemed to work as well as it did, even if Alfred wasn't entirely happy. Still, while I liked him and didn't want to be disloyal, I was curious about this new man in Anna's life. "I'd like to meet him," I said.

"That's good because you're going to," Alfred replied. "That's why I came down, one of the reasons. Anna's bringing him here this weekend and you're invited to brunch on Sunday, your whole family is, I mean."

I wondered why my mother hadn't told me this before, perhaps because she was trying to avoid the minefield of sex. For all her liberal political beliefs, in this area she was both idealistic and a prude. If asked, she would talk romantically about the act of love being the most personal and privileged form of communication between men and women. Yet she was not in the least bit earthy herself, very careful about pulling her skirts close around her knees, and always on the lookout for vulgarity. Once, in a car, I had put my hand in my pocket for some reason and she snapped, "Daniel, don't masturbate."

I was only ten years old and hadn't yet begun to explore such things, but my mother's commandments had such force that I couldn't help but obey. And when in high school, the health teacher, in an attempt to put the class at ease, announced that 98 percent of teenage boys masturbated while the other 2 percent lied, I took grim exception to the rule and never mentioned it to anyone.

But Alfred was not here to discuss masturbation nor even Anna and Jesús, though that was the ostensible reason for his visit. Now I looked at him more closely and noticed an odd blue tint to his cheekbones as though his skin had somehow become translucent. Then, without warning, he began to cry silently, the tears leaking from his eyes and running off his nose and cheeks, and he seemed so unbearably lonely that I knew it had to involve something more than Anna's new lover.

I had nothing to say, no learned way of responding to his grief; indeed I had never before in my life seen a grown man cry, not even my father, who had good reason. It wasn't his style. Yet if I didn't know what to say, I could at least be useful. I handed Alfred a box of Kleenex and I didn't leave or show any sign of discomfort; I wasn't uncomfortable, or even very embarrassed at his display of emotion. Instead, I was interested.

After a few minutes, he said, "Joe brought someone else home the other night."

It was a simple statement and one that I didn't understand at first. I knew homosexuals were supposed to be promiscuous and that even men in ongoing relationships had many lovers. I would not have known how to pursue this with Alfred, but I had heard that homosexuals sometimes made love with two or three different people in one night, an idea that was both repugnant and fascinating to me. I had heard from Anna that Joe was openly contemptuous of the very idea of loyalty and often encouraged Alfred to cruise the gay bars in Milwaukee when he was in town to teach, to "go out and get laid" is what she had quoted him as saying. Alfred had tried, and had on other occasions parroted the party line to me, but I don't think he really believed it. As far as I knew Joe was the only man he slept with, and the only one he wanted.

But if this was an old argument, it didn't really seem right to point it out when Alfred was feeling so bad. Eventually, he added, "I mean, to stay."

"With you?" I asked, still not understanding.

"Maybe. Maybe *instead* of me." Then he started crying again.

I have always felt helpless in the face of tears since, like masturbation, crying is something I never learned to do. I've always envied the women I know for the access they have to their own vulnerability. But now I understood Alfred's grief. He had been able to tolerate Joe's previous infidelity because he knew he was the one Joe really loved; he was the one who remained when the handsome young boys left and they had always gone away before. If it had been true that he was what was being left, it was equally true that he had never been abandoned for anyone else before. Now that seemed likely to change. "Who is he?"

Alfred wrinkled his forehead and looked at the ceiling. "No one. Anyone." He paused, as if to gather his thoughts. I was an unlikely choice as a confidant and I wondered if he felt he had said too much. If so, he gave no indication of it. Instead, he took a deep breath and continued. "His name is Chuck, he has a name. And he's young and pretty and available. Which is why I'm here, in Milwaukee."

It hadn't occurred to me before to ask, but now I remembered that Alfred was usually in Chicago on weekends. If I had thought about it, I might have guessed he was here to ease Jesús' introduction to our society, such as it was. But it had nothing to do with that. He didn't even seem to like Jesús.

"I'm sorry," I said, and I was. The only ideas I had had about homosexuals before meeting Alfred grew out of my father's jokes, and vague stories I had heard of child molestation by teachers. If someone had asked me I would probably have said it was unnatural, but my friendship with Joey had forced me to change my thinking about that. Loving him had seemed completely natural at the time whatever I felt about it now. But my friendship with Alfred was different and in its own way more satisfying. He was quiet and decent and never laid a hand on me. He was neither a father figure nor a lover and didn't seem to want to be either to me. We were friends and now he was in the peculiar agony of love, which I had never experienced but recognized instinctively.

He looked miserable with his running eyes and red nose and now I rose and put my arms around him. Even then I knew that love was a necessity of life, like breathing or eating, and approval or disapproval of one's way of loving wasn't so much bigoted as completely irrelevant. Love, wherever and however one found it, was love. It was that simple; it was that difficult. I wanted to help my friend and so I held him.

Seven

A Friend of Kissinger

My mother had always been popular, in part I think because she modestly assumed that the worlds of her friends were more interesting and crucial than her own. She was a good listener, but she also spoke well and often; it was just that unlike the others who waited eagerly for a break in the conversation to tell their stories, she was actually interested in other people and seldom talked about herself. This led to people asking for her advice about everything from love to where to shop and I never came home without finding a few students or colleagues draped over chairs in the living room. No doubt there were people who didn't like my mother, but there could not have been many. Once she confided her secret to me: "Danny, it's very difficult to resist a person who really likes you." Though I never mastered the art of unreservedly liking everyone, I had to admit my mother was irresistible and in addition she had a Southern accent so soft and lovely that there were people who would call regularly on the telephone just to listen to her.

When my father was performing people had gathered around him too, but they were more sycophantic, hanging on the great man's words, laughing at his jokes, following his commands. Now that he was without a position, he was also suddenly without friends, if there had ever really been friends. In fact, in the past, part of what people admired my mother for was putting up with my father's dirty jokes and dictatorial manner. I never sensed that this cost her anything and she'd laugh politely at any story he told, no matter how often she had heard it. But to others this was the height of forbearance and one friend said unkindly that my mother had "to live with three adolescent boys."

None of this had changed. My father hadn't lost his commanding mien, or his ability to dominate any occasion. He was always the center of any gathering and my mother deferred to him in all things, but it wasn't the same and never would be again. A subtle changing of the guard was occurring in our household, and if my mother was too gracious to make anything of it for fear of offending my father, it would similarly have been impossible for anyone who knew us not to notice that things were different.

For all of her charm, however, my mother wasn't particularly nurturing or even if it came to that very maternal, at least in conventional terms. She hadn't especially wanted to have children and once told me that she had regretted her pregnancy up until the very moment that I made my appearance whereupon she fell in love. It made a nice story, but I was never entirely sure that she didn't in some sense resent the time children took away from her primary purpose in life, being an artist. It wasn't so much that she was absent-minded as that she was what I would call other-minded. She seldom thought about things that most women in our neighborhood would have taken for granted as their responsibility. Thus, I wouldn't have said that she forgot to wash the dishes, bake cookies, pack lunches, or do the laundry, but rather that these things were outside her frame of reference, as I sometimes suspected I was. I tried with little success just the same to make her conform to the model of my friends' mothers, tried that is to interest her in my own attempts to be conventional. But it was hopeless. When I asked her for pictures of Hopalong Cassidy or Roy Rogers to decorate the walls of my bedroom, for example, she responded by painting cubist designs in red and blue that were barely recognizable as cowboys at all. It wasn't that she didn't try, but that what she tried to do to respond to my requests had little to do either with me or with what I wanted. And when I asked one day if I should wear my galoshes to school, being mindful of the nagging mothers of my friends, who were on them constantly about their clothes, their homework, the state of their rooms, my mother responded reasonably by asking, "Is it snowing?"

What I wanted was for my mother not only to care but also to care *for* me, to know when I needed clean underwear and to sense when I was sick and do something about it. But from the first grade on, my brother and I were on our own. We made breakfast, prepared lunch, and made sure we had clean clothes to wear, which was sometimes difficult. Once my third-grade teacher discovered that I was wearing only a light jean jacket in January and called my mother, who, predictably, was unaware of the fact that neither my brother nor I were properly dressed for the Wisconsin winter. Yet, rather than feel guilty when notified of this, she resented the teacher's interference. This was typical: we were loved but not attended to, which gave me the sense ultimately that in a certain way I was not very important to my mother. This may not have been true, but I came to feel that my comfort really didn't matter very much. Hers was an odd style of parenting, if one could call it a style at all, if, that is, it was a conscious choice and not simply a random response to external stimuli. And while this made me independent and resourceful beyond my years, I always felt that I had been deprived of a real childhood.

That winter, along with the other improbable things that were happening, my mother and Anna became intimate and would remain so the rest of their lives. Oddly, the crucible of their friendship was an argument as vehement, and uncharacteristic, as I ever heard my mother have with anyone. She seldom made judgments on others. Not that she lacked opinions or was afraid to assert them, but she knew that hers were no better than anyone else's. Or perhaps it just didn't matter to her if the world adopted her attitude toward things. She would argue passionately for a while and then turn her hands up, smile and say, "I guess we're just not going to agree about this. Let's have some tea."

Anna had begun courting my parents shortly after we moved in. She would send over cakes with me or invite them for coffee. She seldom ventured into our apartment, however, because the disarray offended her Teutonic sense of order. My mother, never much of a housekeeper, had grown ever worse under the demands of her new job and Daisy's desultory efforts did little to right things. There were always dirty dishes spilling out of the sink, clothes on the bedroom floors, and newspapers strewn everywhere. One might have expected a kind of artistic charm in all this, given my mother's profession, an eccentric flair for design amidst chaos, but the sad truth is that it was all pretty squalid. And one day, this became too much for Anna. She arrived that morning armed with sponges, detergents, and buckets and spent the day washing and cleaning. By day's end, the transformation was remarkable. I hadn't realized before that the walls weren't gray or that the kitchen floor was yellow. She had cleaned the sinks and toilets, bought bedspreads for my brother and I, and as the coup de grace baked bread and cookies, which she left wrapped in cheerful gingham on the kitchen table.

Anna may have assumed that my mother had simply not known how to make a home comfortable and having been given a proper example would now adapt to the new order. This did not happen. When my mother arrived home from work, she took one look at the rearranged rooms and went next door. I had never heard my mother yell at anyone before, but it was more than twenty minutes before she returned and her face was still red. Neither she nor Anna ever told me what had passed between them that night, but the incident had two dramatic results: Anna never again interfered in the arcane order of our home and my mother and Anna became close friends.

They would talk on the telephone at six in the morning, before either of them had gotten out of bed and since Anna eschewed exercise, they would frequently go out to lunch, to Pandl's in Whitefish Bay or, if it was my mother's choice, somewhere less Germanic where one could get a glass of wine and a salad. They made an odd couple since they could hardly have been more different: my mother angular, Southern, and refined and Anna a squat refugee without formal education. And yet each claimed that no one could understand her like the other. So it was no surprise to me that my mother could have been as devoted as she was to Paul without condemning her friend, though I know she disapproved of Anna's behavior.

"I don't think any of us really know how we would act in a situation like that," she told me. "We know how we would like to behave, but that isn't the same thing. It's sad, Danny, but people always seem to think they know exactly how other people should live their lives and they're always willing to tell them so."

Of course, it would be easy to say something like that insincerely, and my mother was a Pollyanna. Platitudes rolled off her tongue like marbles, but her beliefs were borne out in what she did. So it made sense that when Jesús came to town, though my mother didn't like to cook, she insisted that he and Anna and Alfred come to dinner.

Given my mother's housekeeping, this could have been asking for trouble, but with Daisy's help, she restored order to our home. They found an old sheet that would do for a tablecloth and some dried flowers for a centerpiece. By the time the guests arrived, a table had been set up in the living room and things were as presentable as they ever were. My father surveyed the scene and commented, "Better have a couch available in case this guy nods off." But I could tell he was pleased with what my mother had done, even if his domestic requirements were minimal.

Whether any of this mattered to Jesús or if he even noticed would be impossible to say. A man of medium height, he had a broad unwrinkled forehead and round red cheeks beneath a mat of curly black hair. I noticed that he smiled constantly, whether he was being introduced or offered more of my mother's roast beef, but otherwise he said little, apparently because there was little he was able to say. Once, when Anna left the room, my mother leaned over and whispered, "I feel we should involve Jesús more. He must feel awkward."

I had no idea how Jesús felt, but he didn't look like he was in any discomfort and there was clearly nothing wrong with his appetite. "Don't worry about it," my father said. "He's happy enough.

Compared to where he's been, a warm place to stay and three meals a day must be heaven."

This made Alfred laugh and my mother smiled too. "Maybe, but don't forget Anna," she said. "Don't you want her to feel that she's done well?"

My father looked dubious at this, as if he wasn't sure what to think of Anna's new connection. But when he spoke, it was in a jocular tone. "I'm not forgetting her," he said. "On top of everything else, he's got love."

My mother didn't seem convinced, but then Anna returned and the subject was dropped. Moreover, it turned out that introducing Jesús to our family was only part of the reason for their visit, for Anna had news of a different sort. Once the dishes were cleared away and we were eating ice cream and cake, she announced that she was writing to Henry Kissinger, the advisor to the president, on a personal matter.

"Kissinger?" my father said. "You don't know him. You can't just write a presidential advisor because you're having some problem." He sounded impatient, as if he was giving a civics lesson to a recalcitrant student.

"Of course I know Henry," Anna said. "I've known him all my life. We come from the same town in Germany. It's true that he was a better friend of my brother, but we all did things together."

My father's expression changed at this. He was seldom surprised into silence, but this stopped him for the moment, and it was understandable. Sitting in our dingy living room with our guests—a holocaust survivor, a gay professor, and an illegal immigrant—it was hard to integrate the very idea of a man of Kissinger's celebrity into our reality. I had seen pictures of him, short, stout, and unmistakably Jewish, escorting starlets in evening dress as they attended some charity ball at the Waldorf-Astoria, and I had read of his taste for the finer things, of the private chef and dining room at the State Department. I knew that Kissinger had come from humble beginnings, that he had attended City College in New York before moving on to Harvard, and it was true that he had to come from somewhere. But

Anna's hometown? On the face of it, her claim of friendship with the great man seemed preposterous. Still, the possibility made my father uncharacteristically cautious. It was important to him to be right about things. "Maybe so," he said slowly, "but that was a long time ago. A lot has happened since then."

Anna shrugged. "Henry will remember me," she said simply.

What was remarkable about this to me was not Kissinger alone, but the apparently inadvertent extrusion of our lives onto the national stage. I would not have guessed that anyone in Milwaukee knew Henry Kissinger, much less our neighbor. Yet Anna talked about him as if they had had lunch the previous week. I had vague memories of the Kennedy administration and thought of them and everyone around them not only as royalty but also as being completely removed from us, and deservedly so. I wanted to think there was a glittering world outside that had nothing to do with our dirty little neighborhood. Like the English peasants who worshipped the king and queen, I loved to see pictures of the presidential party arriving somewhere in limousines or the portraits of the grand parlors of the White House. I liked the idea that there was a chief of protocol to tell everyone how to address the president and first lady. I liked the idea that there *was* protocol, that it was needed somewhere for something. None of that had anything to do with us, but Anna was suggesting a conjunction that seemed both impossible and somewhat disturbing to me.

"What are you going to write him about?" my father said now. "He's trying to resolve a war, after all."

"I know," Anna said. "And ordinarily I wouldn't bother him. But this is important and it won't take much of his time. It's about Jesús."

Upon hearing his name, Jesús perked up and started smiling again. But this had the effect of annoying my father. "You're going to write Kissinger about him?" he said in amazement.

My mother put her hand on my father's arm. "Take it easy, Sam," she said. "Let Anna explain."

"Of course about him," Anna flared up. "Why not him, or anyone else, for that matter?" Then she explained that Jesús had entered the country illegally and since they were now living together she felt responsible for him. Perhaps her friend Henry would help her find a way for Jesús to gain legal status so he could find a better job.

"I think it's a wonderful idea," my mother said, smiling at Jesús.

"I think it's nuts," my father said. "You haven't even talked to Kissinger since you were kids in Germany thirty years ago and now you expect him to forget about Vietnam and help Jesús get a green card?"

"You have to trust someone," Anna said. "And who else would I ask? Henry was always a kind person. I think he'll help if he can."

I found myself admiring her sangfroid and wondering at it. What in her life had given her such optimism? Born with a ruined face, pursued by the Nazis, and left a widow at an early age, she had nevertheless found love and was writing one of the most powerful men in the country in hopes that he would intercede in a personal matter and, incidentally, break the law, or help her do so. It might have been as unrealistic as my father said, but I was impressed.

After Anna and Jesús left, my mother said, "I think you were a little hard on Anna, Sam."

My father nodded. "Maybe, but you've got to admit it's a pretty crazy idea. I mean, Kissinger, for Christ's sake."

I wanted to see if my mother would agree, but she was noncommittal, and we all waited to see if Nixon's advisor would really remember his old friend from Fürth.

Eight

Suicide Season

Milwaukee was a great place to feel depressed. Something about the climate, the wet heavy air, the ornate architecture of the buildings on Prospect Avenue crowding in on one another, as if they were intent on blocking all light, always made me feel a midwinter low was not only inevitable but desirable. I never experienced that particular lethargy, the loginess in my limbs, to the same degree anywhere else, nor did I feel there was anything wrong with me, anything unusual about my unwillingness to make an effort to change things; change seemed like an abstraction as unreachable as the stars, which I couldn't see anyway in the fog. Of course, there were those with the money or time to try to escape, people who scheduled vacations in Mexican towns with unpronounceable names or, if that was beyond their reach, bought special lamps designed to lift their spirits or grew exotic plants in their living rooms in an attempt to convince themselves they were somewhere else. Anywhere.

This seemed absurd to me, and not only because in the eighteen years I lived at home we never went on a vacation. Trying to avoid depression in Milwaukee was a way of cheating yourself out of a grand, brooding experience. My mother called it the suicide season, though no one we knew there ever made an attempt, if you except a willowy schizophrenic named Dorothy Walters, who worked as a welder at Allis Chalmers and slashed her wrists repeatedly, though usually in the summer. The winter never seemed to bother Dorothy very much.

In the weeks that followed our dinner with Jesús, we saw little of Anna or anyone else. We kept to ourselves, moving slowly around the apartment in thick wool socks and sweaters, holding cups of hot liquid in our hands, not talking very much. It snowed and then it snowed again and then it became very cold. There were pictures in the papers of the mayor in what he now called his Command Post directing his troops, which in this case consisted mainly of the derelicts they rounded up at the Rescue Mission to clear street corners. But I liked the military image in our socialist city.

When I went outside, my cheeks would tighten in the wind, and I speculated that they would crystallize and crack if I were outside for too long—and what would I look like then with my face split open? I wondered idly if my eyes could freeze. But since failing to shovel your walk was a hanging offense in Milwaukee and there was no one else available to do it, the snow, along with keeping the furnace stoked, became a major preoccupation. A significant part of my day was devoted to chores after school, but now I imagined myself a part of the mayor's legion in the battle against February, standing shoulder to shoulder with freezing winos and sharing a bottle of Thunderbird around a blazing trashcan fire to ward off the blizzards. I welcomed the cold as nature's mirror to my state of mind, and it had the secondary advantage of making me think less about Daisy, who had inexplicably become rather aloof during her visits to our home and seldom teased me anymore.

My brother and I amused ourselves during this period by clipping disaster stories out of the newspaper, such as articles about people who had frozen to death in their cars or had their furnaces explode. Someone's Christmas tree had gone up in flames destroying their house, and a pipe fitter in Greenfield reported that his socket wrench had broken in half one subzero day. Although children were warned about wearing hats and not staying outside too long, inevitably some were brought to emergency rooms after having their tongues frozen to metal. There was never any explanation as to why they were licking the poles in the first place. And while my brother and I were caught up in the weather's drama, our parents seemed blithely unaware of it or of us. One day, I asked my mother if I should wear my boots and she looked at me uncomprehendingly and asked why.

"It's fifteen below," I said. "It's in the paper."

"Is it?" she said, as if she seldom ventured out. "Then I guess you should." As usual, my life was my own and she refused to intrude, even when I wished that she would. I came and went unfettered by rules or curfews like other kids.

The only real difference the cold made in our lives was in the constriction of social activities, even going to the movies. No one wanted to take the chance of having the car stall out in another part of town and it was too cold to wait for a bus. Rather than hanging around Campus after school, I came right home to tend the furnace and, if necessary, break up the ice on the walk.

It was February. We drew in upon ourselves, though I remember a picture someone took of our family then that has taken on the quality of a frieze in my mind. My father was smoking a pipe and laughing with delight at my brother, crew-cut and chunky, who had done something brilliant. My mother and I were on either end of the gate-legged table upon which the chessboard was arranged. My father wore a short-sleeved shirt because the arthritis made buttons an unnecessary challenge and he avoided cuffs; my mother was in a gray cardigan, hunched over in an attitude of concern. I was unaccountably wearing a what-me-worry smile that I recognize now as one of desperation, though God knows what I was thinking then. My mother and I were both strikingly thin, me in a boyish gangly way, but my mother suggesting nervous exhaustion at the task before her. I ask myself the question Paul asked on his deathbed: *Warum?* Why? Why her, why him, why any of us? But there is of course no answer. There can't be, anymore than there would be if something wonderful had happened to our family instead of illness. The great challenge of life, my mother used to say, is accepting it, even being grateful, no matter what happens, because it will be over soon. And more often than not she succeeded in talking herself into this, but in this picture she seems to be having trouble following her own advice and my heart goes out to her over thirty years. As always I want to help but I am able to do no more for her now than I was then.

I was wakeful. My brother had been sleepwalking again and I would lie awake hoping to catch him at it. I wanted to know where he went when he walked in the night, but he was stealthy in his psychosis. I envied him his peculiarities, not only his intellectual accomplishments but even his madness. I was on the contrary distressingly predictable, or so it seemed. I wanted to surprise someone with my idiosyncrasies, preferably my parents, but in this I was an utter failure. And while my mother worried constantly about Charles and spent hours on the phone talking to his various therapists, I never knew her to spend a moment worrying about me. In our house, neurosis was currency and I was bankrupt. Yet my nocturnal efforts to shadow Charles were unsuccessful; it was as if he knew somehow when I was awake and refused to walk then, outwitting me in this as he did in most other things.

Once awake, however, sleep was impossible for me and I would stand alone in front of the large leaded windows in the living room and watch stately snowplows going by in the street, a filigreed hail of snow in their wake. I wondered then what would become of us all, how sick my father was going to get, and if I would ever escape the net that seemed to be tightening around me. When I thought of the men I knew—my father, Paul, Abe Goodstein, Alfred—growing up didn't seem very attractive. I didn't necessarily see a cause-effect relationship between adulthood and disaster, but it was suggestive. I was drawn only to the past, which never changed. Neither the present nor the future held much allure for me.

Which made it all the more surprising that it was at about this time that my luck changed in an extraordinary way. I was sitting in my basement office, having dispatched my chores, reading one of the Bronk Burnett serials. The blue light of dusk was coloring the dirty windows when I heard something behind me and turned to see Daisy standing there, hip cocked to the right. She looked at the books, though I am not sure she could read, and then came close and put her hand between my legs. When she smiled, her whole face was alive, and though her lips were gray, her red tongue limned the edges of her mouth. I started to protest, since even for Daisy, this was extreme and provocative behavior, but I found I couldn't speak and I was having my usual involuntary reaction to her nearness.

"I think you like me, Dan," she said. "'Fact, I know you do."

This was not exactly accurate. Daisy and I had never had what one would conventionally call a friendship. We had never had long talks in which we exchanged information about our family backgrounds, our aspirations, what we hoped to get out of life. I didn't know how old she was or whether she had gone to school. I didn't know these things because I had absolutely no interest in them just as I assumed she had little interest in my world. I didn't know what bands she liked. I didn't know her favorite color. Still, there seemed no point now in denying my feelings for her. She rotated her hand, massaging my throbbing penis expertly, and I knew I would have exploded in seconds had she not suddenly turned away. I was embarrassed but oddly defiant. "Hey," I said.

Daisy looked at me and laughed and I couldn't blame her. I was in love and my pants were strained with desire. Then she turned serious, though at first I didn't understand why. "I get five bucks," she said. "Sometimes ten, but five's okay."

I looked at her, not understanding. Was she talking about her salary for cleaning? It would have been an astronomical hourly wage at the time. "For what?"

She looked at me as if I was demented, and in a way I was. "Straight or half-and-half," she said, assuming a shared vocabulary.

Then she smiled again. "And for fifteen, I'll take you around the mother-fucking world."

The word *fucking* jarred me, yet if the terms she used were unfamiliar, I now understood what we were talking about. Daisy, the object of my desire, was a prostitute and this made me sad because I doubted that anyone did that kind of thing because they wanted to. The idea of sex being work, like everything else, was depressing, but paradoxically the effect of this realization was just to inflame me more, to make my lust practically unendurable. It seemed unbelievable to me that I was actually in a small room with a sexual professional negotiating the price of her services. How many of my friends could have said such a thing? Who among them would even think of it? It was amazing. I jammed my hands in my pockets but came up with only a few quarters. "I've got seventy-five cents," I said.

Since we were talking business, Daisy's face had taken on a more serious expression than I usually associated with her, but now she looked at me with what I could only call pity. "You want me to do you for that?" she said.

I didn't know what to say. I still hadn't gotten used to the fact that we were discussing such things openly. The terminology was fascinating but unfamiliar to me. Yet, it would have seemed the height of gauche to ask Daisy to explain exactly what she meant by half-and-half or going around the world. Explanations would have to wait. Even if I understood the negotiation imperfectly and hadn't actually solicited her, there was no question about what I wanted and my good fortune astounded me. Ten minutes before I had been minding my own business, reading Bronk Burnett, and now I was on the verge of a sexual experience past my wildest imaginings. Beyond vocabulary, I was at another disadvantage since I had no idea of the going rate for the things Daisy had mentioned. I decided not to challenge her prices, however; it didn't seem appropriate to question her about it. I believed in a free-market economy; she had the right to charge whatever she wanted.

"Maybe I could get more," I said, thinking wildly of additional chores I might do for my parents or for Anna.

Daisy took a moment to think this over, then she pushed me backwards gently with her open hand and I collapsed onto the chair. "This is just 'cause I'm a nice person," she said. "'Cause I feel sorry for you." Then, with an efficient, practiced movement, she had my pants undone and my penis in her hand. She hiked up her dress to her waist and I discovered she was wearing no panties. Her smell was unbearably exciting. Then she straddled my legs and put me inside her.

Her vagina was slick and warm, but even then I would not have called this making love, though I flattered myself that it was not business as usual either. Daisy closed her eyes and leaned back, changing the angle, then she stroked the back of my neck for the few seconds it took before I ejaculated. I would like to say this was poetic, mind-altering, even decadent, but it was none of those things. Daisy was affectionate and I was appreciative, as I should have been considering the alteration in price. She moved from side to side, giving me a little extra, then she removed herself as deftly as she had gotten on top of me, though now she left a small puddle of semen behind on the dusty floor. I was too astonished by what had just happened to be ashamed of my eagerness or the fact that I was naked in front of a woman. I knew from reading magazines that it was supposed to take longer than this, that women were supposed to scream in ecstasy and tear your back with their fingernails. None of this had happened, yet Daisy didn't seem disappointed.

"That your first time, right?"

I nodded. I didn't think Joey Goodstein counted. The brief time with Daisy not only superseded my previous sexual experiences, but went far beyond any thoughts I had ever had on the subject. Daisy was in a class by herself and I was speechless.

Then she did a kind thing. For all her tough talk about her prices and, by implication, what other men paid her for the same thing, Daisy took my face tenderly in her hands and kissed me on the cheek. "First time's free," she said. "You keep that six bits." And then she was gone. I heard her steps this time, light on the stairs, going back into our apartment, and alone in my basement office, I smiled,

85

and then I laughed because I was lucky and I knew it, and I thought I deserved to get lucky for a change.

That afternoon was a defining moment for me, not just because it was exciting but because of the odd combination of desire, embarrassment, and generosity that characterized those few moments with Daisy in the basement. That was unique. One could say, I suppose, that it was little different than the relationships between masters and slaves on Southern plantations, except that Daisy had been in charge from the beginning and our union would produce no mulatto child. Indeed, our sex produced nothing at all except a new sense of ease that I had never experienced before. I felt lighter, more relaxed, and if I would discover later that love adds immeasurably to sex, sex alone seemed wonderful in its own way. No one had been hurt; I had been graciously introduced to a world of mysterious pleasure that I knew little about but I knew I wanted.

I was a man of the world now, even if I had to keep my experience with Daisy entirely to myself. Telling anyone would have broken the spell, or more seriously, led to my mother's asking Daisy to leave her job. At school, I listened tolerantly as the other boys bragged about their conquests and tried not to appear smug when the conversation turned my way. But the boy-girl parties we all attended now seemed childish. It was hard to get excited about kissing games when my fantasies tended more toward oral sex. And when I was swaying pointlessly in some girl's embrace to Johnny Mathis, I thought only of Daisy and when I might see her again. Our afternoon together had functioned in much the way a businessman's introductory offer might—and left me feverishly wanting more. Having had a free sample, I was eager to try Daisy's entire line at full price, though I still had no way to finance my obsession and I suspected the days of loss leaders were over.

Nine

The Over-Under

Though I saw less of Joey than I had during the fall, in some ways our friendship had deepened since his father's return. There was the accumulated common knowledge of things that we both considered too important to talk about. The weekly jaunts with Al and Pete had ended as they returned to their other responsibilities, whatever they were. Joe and I played basketball on an outside hoop and ate hamburgers at Riegleman's. Yet while he didn't say anything directly, I understood that life had become tougher for him at home and I sympathized. I had the feeling that my being around buffered things for Joe, which was little enough for me to do for a friend.

Joe's older brother Larry, a stolid, beefy boy, had unaccountably been Abe's favorite growing up and was spoken of now in the glowing terms a Catholic family might reserve for a son who entered the priesthood, though in this case Larry worked as a CPA in Chicago. Often, Abe would make invidious comparisons between Joe's slight physique and Larry, who had played guard on the football team at Whitefish Bay High School before going off to the University of Michigan. Not that either Abe or Mrs. G. were really neglectful of Joe's own talents. Intelligence was valued in most Jewish families and theirs was no exception. They attended functions at school and tried to encourage their younger son, but this didn't come naturally to Abe, who stood out at PTO meetings in his expensive haircut and cashmere overcoat. There was no way around that.

Still, I liked Abe Goodstein, and somewhat to my surprise, he liked me, perhaps more than he did his own son. When I visited in the evenings, Abe and I would chat and I soon learned that his time in Terre Haute had not had the desired, rehabilitative effect. Abe was, in fact, openly contemptuous of the efforts of the prison system in this regard. "I already had a law degree so I decided to pass up their GED program," he told me. "And what else was I going to do there? Make a career doing laundry and making license plates?"

Instead, just weeks after his return, he went back to gambling, openly and without apology. Often, when I visited I would find Abe in his silk bathrobe wearing a pair of thick glasses and studying crabbed newspaper columns or a loose-leaf notebook he had apparently put together himself. Inside, there were thumbnail summaries of every college basketball program in the country, which made for interesting reading for me. Colleges with exotic names like Gonzaga or Leheigh were included along with the national powers everyone had heard of. Abe noticed me looking and far from minding my curiosity, he sat down, put his arm around my shoulders, and asked, "You like basketball, Danny?"

I nodded. "I'm on the team at school, but we're no good."

Abe was sympathetic. "That doesn't matter. You're having fun right?"

It did matter and I think Abe knew it, but this was more interest or approval than my father had ever shown in any sport I had pursued. He thought exercise in general was a waste of time and tried to encourage more intellectual interests. He liked to quote Robert Hutchens, who was then president of the University of Chicago, who claimed to get his exercise serving as pallbearer at the funerals of his friends who exercised. But I didn't play basketball or baseball to extend my life or otherwise improve my health so the lesson had little effect and served only to further distance my father and me. I appreciated Abe's interest in what I was doing, but I was still cautious. "I liked it better in my school in Madison. There were more good players."

Abe took this in without responding directly. "I was too short for basketball," he said. "But I was a varsity wrestler." Then he looked me over critically. "You look like a pretty strong kid. Maybe you'll wrestle, too. Jewish kids are usually too short for basketball."

This was a little deflating since I had no interest in wrestling, but I was talking to a professional and I assumed that Abe knew what he was talking about and was merely stating a fact with no intention of discouraging me. I changed the subject. "I like your book," I said. "I like reading about all the teams."

"No kidding," Abe said, with the pride of authorship common to all writers. "You know what this book's for, what I do?"

I said that I did, surprised that we could actually be having this conversation since Joey had told me that his father rarely spoke to him about such things. But sons are rarely interested in their fathers' work. When had I asked my father about his concerts? Indeed, when in the second grade I had been asked by my teacher what my father did, I had replied that he drank coffee with my mother, which caused a flurry of activity resulting in my forced attendance at several evening concerts. After that, I learned to keep my opinions to myself. But talking to a professional gambler was different. I had heard about the mafia tradition of *muerta* and wondered if in some way this conversation would serve as my initiation into organized crime.

Abe had other things on his mind. "You got to ignore what you read in the papers," Abe said, flattering me, since I seldom opened the *Journal* and then never ventured beyond the sports or comic sections. "It's all lies," he said meditatively. "All of it."

I nodded, as if I too had been the victim of scurrilous reporters. "What do they lie about?" I asked.

Abe ran his hand through his hair and looked away. "Me," he said simply. "I'm a big gangster tied to the mob and all that shit." He shook his head to dispel the memory.

I didn't want to be rude or push too hard, but this interested me. I wanted to keep him talking. "The mob," I said in what I hoped was an encouraging tone.

"Okay," Abe said as if I had accused him of something. "Okay, I knew some people, so what? We do business together sometimes. We go to dinner together, take a trip to Vegas for some sun. What's wrong with that? Is that some kind of crime now?"

I hadn't suggested anything like this nor would I have known how to do so, but it was common knowledge that Abe had just spent three years in a federal prison. Still, I was fascinated by what he was saying and wanted him to continue. "Business?"

Abe looked at me quickly. "Okay, so some people wouldn't call it business. I do because to me that's what it is. It isn't fun and games, guys in short pants bouncing a ball or hitting one. It's more than that; it's my profession." He hesitated for a moment, apparently having confused himself since of course his profession, as he called it, wasn't exactly sports at all but betting on them. But rather than expatiate further on this, he continued in the same vein, shaking his finger in my face now. "And let me ask you one question, Danny. Who ever got hurt because of me, whose legs got broken, who got killed?"

I guessed. "No one?"

"Damned right, no one," Abe said. Now, he sat back and breathed heavily through his nose. "I'm very good at what I do, that's all." His tone indicated that he expected to be misunderstood about this, but I said nothing and he continued. "There's no one better. I'm at the top of my field. It's just illegal, that's all."

This seemed like a significant consideration given my limited experience in the world. But my father was always harping about the importance of excellence so I assumed that being the best at anything was noteworthy and I was always grateful for shared confidences. Most of what is interesting about anyone remains out of sight to others. Now, Abe sighed heavily and seemed to relax. "You're a good listener, Danny," he said. "That's a good thing in life."

I don't know what Joey was doing during this conversation nor why Abe had decided to confide in me, but it was the beginning of a friendship that would continue long after I had lost touch with Joey. Without my ever asking, Abe took me under his wing, explaining apropos of nothing the arcane calculus of gambling, perhaps because I was, as he said, listening. I came to understand over time that the reason he was good at what he did had nothing to do with knowing who was going to win or lose a specific game; this wasn't even what interested him. He didn't have favorite teams or players and was a completely disinterested observer of any individual game. He was in this way like my father, who far from having a love of music would never tolerate records being played as background music at dinner or in the morning. He didn't even really like to play, but he loved to perform, he loved to win over the audience.

This was roughly equivalent to Abe's passion for gambling. Abe's calculations revolved around oddities like the over-under or point spread, his ability to predict the number of points a team would score on a particular night in combination with another team, who would win the first half, or if a team won or lost, what the margin, the point spread, would be. This, he told me, was where the important money was to be won and this was the reason his services were in demand. Because of his ability to forecast such things, Abe was in charge of establishing the spread on a myriad of games all over the country for, as he put it, some important people who paid him well. Which meant among other things that your team could lose and you could still win—if you had taken the points. Indeed, Abe's particular specialty was to find games in which an underdog would fight harder than expected and beat the spread, thus winning money for his employers. Abe approached this task with a zeal that I could only compare with religion, and I could not help but feel that his enthusiasm had something to do with his having been the underdog so often himself.

The country may have condemned betting; the official fiction was that such activities took place only in Las Vegas. There were no state lotteries, offtrack betting or barges floating in rivers for the purpose of helping working people lose their pensions. Indian reservations were not using tribal lands for casinos and the morning line was not published in the newspaper. And exclusivity had its price. If you wanted to gamble, Abe Goodstein was practically the only game in town. Any town.

While I was drawn to Abe, the allure of gambling was a mystery to me from the beginning and remained that way. I had never bet on anything large or small and didn't even like playing cards for matches. Compulsive gambling made as much sense to me as alcoholics drinking cough syrup in the company rest room, and the idea of co-dependency hadn't been invented yet. What interested me more than Abe's business was the world in which he and Al and Pete moved, which was as complicated and stylized as any other subculture, but completely different from that of my parents. I liked the flash and toughness of these men, their willingness to say how things were and take the consequences. In its own way, on its own terms, everything the high rollers did was just as it appeared, and in that context, Abe was scrupulously honest. We weren't talking about sleight of hand here or a three-card monte game on Upper Broadway. If you wanted to lose your house by making a sucker's bet on a long shot, he would help you with alacrity. But he would never call at dinnertime, like a stockbroker, and promise to double your money in six weeks. He didn't believe in cold calls, in part because he had no need for them; people came to him.

I don't mean to be an apologist for Abe, or for gambling, only to say that like any other vice it depended on human weakness to survive. From Abe, I learned many things that have served me well in life, including a disbelief in sure things. "If something seems too good to be true, it is," he said. "Trust me on this. There's never a free lunch, even if you don't have to pay for it. And always put your wallet in your right front pocket."

Despite the conventional wisdom about organized crime, Abe never bribed anyone, never paid a fighter to take a dive, or tried to fix a basketball game, because it would have constituted an insult to his intelligence, a suggestion that he couldn't do what he did without help. He prided himself on knowing which star forward had a groin strain and how it might affect the outcome of a particular game. He knew who was tired, or having personal problems, who had a girl-friend on the side and an angry wife, who had a drinking problem, and who was in the process of trying to renegotiate his contract. He knew these things because he judged it his business to know them, part of being well-prepared, not because it gave him special advantages he neither needed nor wanted. It would have made what he always called his profession less demanding, less interesting, and, would obviously have affected the commission he could charge his clients. How could he be the best if they were betting on a sure thing? *Res ipse loquitur.*

Whether it was convenience or because he sensed a sympathetic relation between us, Abe took me on as a kind of apprentice that year, taught me the business as if I were a clerk in his law firm. But my duties were specific and limited. Though he derided the federal authorities, he had no desire to return to Terre Haute and he had a healthy suspicion of telephones. Sometimes he would ask me to run an errand, to go to the pay phone on the corner and place a call. He lived only two blocks from Downer Avenue, where there were several supermarkets and a drugstore, all of which had public telephones. It would have been impossible for the FBI to tap them all. I would choose one and dial a memorized number whereupon a voice, neutral but with something Eastern about it, would answer, "Ideal Grocery Company."

"I'm calling in an order," I would say. And then I would ask for, say, three lamb chops, four pork steaks, and ten pounds of hamburger. I never knew what the messages meant, of course, or what the coordinates were, but something about the numbers or meats must have signaled that it was Abe calling in his weekly choices. And if it seems ethically questionable to involve the fourteen-year-old friend of your son in such an activity, I would reply in Abe's defense that it was no more wrong than using underage help in a family drugstore. I didn't know if the phones in his apartment were actually being recorded or not and no one ever stopped me to question me on the street about my errands, but I felt intuitively that I was being observed. Invariably, when I returned Abe would already know my mission had been successful and slip a couple of bills folded upon one another into my hand. Then he would say, "Thanks, kid," and neither of us would mention it again, until the next time.

Initially, I saw the earnings from my new job as a means of being able to finance spending more time with Daisy, but in fact my wardrobe improved more than my sex life, though not dramatically enough for anyone to notice. I was able to buy a pair of sneakers I had coveted and two warm sweaters. More important, the family dynamic had changed subtly—Abe's family, I mean. Al and Pete now drove me the few blocks from Abe's apartment to ours and would sometimes show up unbidden to take me out for burgers on a Saturday afternoon, usually without Joey. After all, in a manner of speaking, we were all colleagues now while Joey was just a kid. I had risen in the world.

But the greatest surprise occurred one weekend when my mother and I were shopping on Downer Avenue and ran into Abe coming out of the supermarket. I thought of avoiding him out of an instinctive feeling that I should try to keep these worlds separate, but that was impossible as he immediately walked over and introduced himself to my mother. They were a study in contrasts, my mother tall and thin in her black cloth coat and beret and Abe, elegant as always, in cashmere with a silk muffler at his throat. "Nice to meet you, professor," he said to my mother, flattering her as he must have flattered women all his life.

My mother seemed completely at ease and unembarrassed to be talking to Abe in a place where the whole neighborhood shopped. She bowed her head slightly and smiled. "I wanted to thank you and your wife for being so nice to Danny, Mr. Goodstein," she said. "It's made everything much easier for him."

Abe ducked his head in such a way as to indicate that he knew what *everything* might refer to without alluding to it specifically. And I was impressed that my mother actually seemed to realize that moving to a new place where I had no friends had been hard. "Danny's a special boy," Abe said now. "He's never a bother. We love having him around."

They talked for a moment longer and Abe told some lies about art that my mother tolerated with grace. He said he'd like to see some of her work, that he was buying some art to decorate his new office, and he handed her an engraved business card. But that was the end of it, except I noticed that my mother's face was flushed as we walked home. Though I had never met my grandfather, I knew he had been short of stature and a romantic. I remembered that he had joined the Rosicrucians for a brief period and wrote poetry. I wondered now if Abe Goodstein, different as he was from her father, could have reminded my mother of him. One thing I valued about my mother was her ability to surprise you, to go against whatever expectations you might have had of her. I knew that what the papers said about Abe would make no difference to her at all, that she'd trust her own instincts in this as in all other matters. She had the upper-class sense of entitlement that allowed her to completely disregard the opinions of others who were socially inferior, which was almost everyone. In any case, I now felt vindicated. Even if my mother didn't approve of Abe's activities, I knew she saw what I saw in him and, like me, I could tell she was drawn to him. Which meant she wouldn't object to my frequenting the Goodstein's apartment and running the occasional errand.

We were quiet on the way home, but when we reached the steps to our house, my mother stopped and turned to me. "Mr. Goodstein is a charming man, Danny. I can see why you like him. I do, too." Then she paused and looked up the street, her eyes focused on something distant that I couldn't see. "But there's no need to tell your father about this," she continued. "I don't think he'd feel the way we do. I'm not sure he'd understand."

Ten

The Middle of the Night

Shortly after she accepted her new position in Milwaukee, my mother had been told the rules by some kind soul: though there was no available studio in which she could work and no likelihood of there ever being one, she was nevertheless expected to produce and show her art if she wished to advance to assistant professor and eventually receive tenure. A high value was placed on gentility in academe and it would have been judged to be in bad taste if my mother had interpreted this as a threat of any kind or reacted vehemently. It was only, as her colleague might have said, a word to the wise, an attempt to help her get oriented to her new position. There was no mention of my mother's need to support a crippled husband and two young sons and no suggestion as to how she was supposed to accomplish any of this with a full teaching load. That was her problem, or as the euphemists might have had it, her opportunity. The implication was clear: produce or leave. It was an easy choice since my mother had a one-year contract and no place else to go.

There was of course no room in our apartment for her to set up her easel, but luckily a more fortunate colleague had lately departed on a Guggenheim Fellowship and she assumed his lease at a rent so reasonable that even we could afford it. The payments were low, we discovered, because the studio was on Hubbard Street, on the edge of the ghetto, and except for a Syrian grocery on the corner, my mother's was the only white face on the block. Yet this didn't seem to bother her. She had grown up surrounded by blacks in Kentucky; they had cared for her and her family for generations. My mother was always surprising me and now I was impressed by the ease she felt in the presence of people who terrified all of our acquaintances, to the point that I noticed her voice resumed a more pronounced Southern accent when she was at the studio, which made it even more musical than it had been before.

If she was not concerned about the possible dangers of the neighborhood, however, my father was, and since the only time my mother could visit the studio was in the evening after work, he often insisted that she take me along. I was flattered by the implication that I was to be her protector, but would have been completely ineffective had someone actually attacked us on one of those dark nights. As it happened, however, no one on Hubbard Street was even rude to us. Indeed, my mother and I proved rather to be interesting to our new neighbors who soon developed a proprietary attitude about her art, and by extension toward us. The neighborhood children would often crowd the narrow doorway, eager to see what the art lady, as they called her, was doing now and I discovered that a high school acquaintance worked in the grocery and we would while away the evenings playing Hearts for a penny a point in the back room of the store. But if I was useless for protection, those visits provided an opportunity for my mother and me to spend more time together, something, it turned out, which was necessary for both of us.

It was on such a night that she patted the cushion next to her and said, "I need to talk to you." This usually signaled some criticism of my behavior, but in this case she wasn't interested in that. "Your daddy's getting weaker, Dan," she said. "He can hardly walk at all anymore."

I was immediately ashamed that I hadn't noticed this, that to a great extent my thoughts and energy had been divided between

97

Daisy's sweet urgency and my work for Abe. And I hadn't thought of my father's illness in a concrete way before. The idea of being unable to walk at all, of being sentenced for life to a wheelchair at the age of forty, now took on meaning for the first time. Previously, I had understood that he could no longer work, that his career as a performing artist was over, but since I had neither worked nor performed in my life, those were abstractions, serious but not personal. And if I took walking for granted, as everyone does, I now thought of it as I would if someone had told *me* that I would never do it again. I shivered involuntarily and my mother took my hand. I didn't know why she was telling me this, but I knew it wasn't small talk. She would have a reason. Then she began to cry softly and I reached out awkwardly to comfort her. It seemed that we were always trying to comfort each other.

"Maybe I could help him?" I said.

My mother seemed grimly amused by this. She wiped her eyes with a paper towel and said, "No one can help him. That's the trouble. He's scared to death and so am I and I can't talk about it with him and we've always talked about everything. He's afraid I'm going to send him away and the awful thing is that sometimes I'd like to, not because of him, but just because I don't know how I'm going to take care of things." Then she looked at me and added quickly, "Of course I won't, Danny. Don't worry, your daddy's not going anywhere."

The vagaries of health escaped me then. Whenever I went to the doctor for a checkup and saw the enormous books on his shelf full of descriptions of various illnesses, it seemed remarkable that I had so far avoided contracting any of them—and for that matter it was only a question of time before I would inevitably fall ill with something. Now this feeling intensified as my father's condition induced a kind of fatalism in me. He had done nothing wrong and had become so ill that his whole life had disintegrated before our eyes. Who was to say that this wouldn't happen to any of us at any time? But thinking about that was useless. It would have been like planning for the eventual car accident you will have. And in youth, health is the natural state of things. I had known children who became seriously ill and even one who died of leukemia, but these things were rare and had nothing to do with me. My father's illness did and not just because of heredity. I realized vaguely that his growing incapacity would serve not only to increase my household responsibilities, but also to narrow my options. And I knew that I couldn't resent him for this, that it wouldn't be fair because it wasn't his fault. My mother didn't say this, but I knew it. Still, I had other concerns at the moment, though it didn't really bother me that my mother had confided in me or that she was crying. I was flattered by her confidence and knew she had no one else to turn to in a new city. "What are you going to do?" I asked, since her tone implied that something had to be done.

My mother was thin to the point of being gaunt and had become more so with the difficult winter. When she had been crying, her large eyes became swollen, and she looked even more bereft than usual. "I don't know," she said. "Daisy does the best she can but she's not trained as a nurse and she won't be able to do some of the things we'll need to do soon."

I was unaware then of the arcana of the sickroom and knew nothing of catheters, Heuer lifts, and subcutaneous injections. I had never emptied a bedpan or given a sponge bath, largely because of my parents' desire to protect me from all this, but the mention of Daisy's name made me blush. My mother may have noticed, though what she could have made of it is a mystery. "So you're going to fire Daisy?" It was unthinkable and against reason, I felt responsible.

My mother looked at me, as if my feelings were completely transparent, and I suspect they were. She may have smiled slightly. "I wouldn't go that far," she said. "We all love Daisy. It just might become too much for her, that's all."

It was already too much. Just the move and my father's illness had stretched all of us to the limit. I had no idea what new things there could be to accomplish, but I doubted my mother's ability to deal with them. She was right: we needed help, but there was none readily available. Which was why she was crying. Sitting there, I became aware of the real poverty of our situation, which had little to do with money. What I saw in my mother's face was loss, though I didn't recognize it as that right away. Her parents had died when she was in her twenties and her only brother had died of heart failure during an appendectomy two years before. Her Kentucky relatives had disowned her when she had the temerity to marry a Jewish musician from New York, and now the loss of her long romance with my father—which had been her palliative for the injustices of life— had made all the other losses she had suffered seem trivial.

Like most children, I hadn't been aware of my parents actually having a relationship in the way people talk about such things today, but I knew they loved each other passionately because it was impossible not to know this. Whenever my father returned from even a short trip, they would fall into each other's arms with gratitude for his return. Now that was, if not over, then ending slowly. My father would need a nurse and he would have to go to a home if we couldn't care for him adequately ourselves. And while that would be terrifying for him, it would be equally so for my mother who would also bear a burden of guilt and responsibility, thinking somehow that she had failed, that she should have been able to cope.

I took the word invalid literally: to me, the illness had invalidated my father, as a man, as a husband, as a person. And while I knew he was blameless, I would be lying if I said I wasn't angry as a result. I was—I still am—because I needed him to push against and to guide me. My anger scared me because I thought in some deep way it would destroy my father and sometimes it seemed as if this were the actual case. If it was unfair to be angry with him, I knew it was also ignoble, so I tried to keep my feelings to myself, which was probably a mistake. Yet my anger, while understandable, was also perfectly useless since there was really no one to be angry with. That was the trouble.

"Maybe I could get a job," I said. Though I didn't want to tell her about my work for Abe, it seemed likely that he could find something more for me to do.

But this only made her cry harder. "Oh, Danny, that's not what I want. For you to go to work at Neubauer's carrying groceries or something. I want you to have your life, like we did, like everybody should. That's why I'm working so hard instead of just giving up and going on relief. I want you to grow up and be a man and go out into the world and *do* something with yourself." She said these words fiercely, with a growling intensity that even now makes me shiver, but it was oddly reassuring at the time. I knew with certainty that my father would get sicker in ways I only dimly understood, but I also realized that my brother and I would be all right because my mother wanted that so passionately and it would be impossible for us to deny her.

I don't know now if my mother took me to the studio that night with the express purpose of telling me all this or if the opportunity simply presented itself, but our conversation marked the time when I started taking my family responsibilities more seriously and left Madison and my idyllic childhood behind for good. Nor would this be the last time that anxiety would force my mother to seek me out that year. Sometimes, I would awake in the middle of the night and find her sitting next to my bed dry-eyed and staring, like a mad woman in a Greek tragedy. I never knew exactly how to respond in these situations but after a while I learned that there was really no correct response, that my mother neither wanted me to do nor say anything. She only wanted me to be there with her in the middle of the night, and I could do that.

Periodically, Abe would leave town and the understanding in the household was that while some travel was necessary in his business, it was equally important that the family not accompany him. "It wouldn't be good for them," he told me. "Not much to do and no one else has family there." It seemed odd to speak of what the newspapers might have called mob conclaves as if they were Kiwanis conventions, but a peculiarity of Abe's was his insistence, at least in conversation with me, on the appearance of a middle-class life. There were the candy dishes and family pictures on every surface in his apartment. He gave regularly to the temple and the Jewish Home for the Aged, and twice a week he and Mrs. G. invited friends in for dinner and an evening of bridge. It was only that when he wasn't doing these things, he was the oddsmaker for some serious people on the East Coast.

Abe explained that the gambling world rotated, with Las Vegas as its axis. He and his associates gathered in Toronto during basketball season and then in Miami during spring training. I suppose the purpose of these meetings must have been to scout new talent and exchange intelligence, but this would have been unnecessary for Abe, who was always prepared and had it in his head already. I've forgotten where he was off to this time, but he intimated shyly that I might join him on some future trip. "I mentioned it to your mom," he said casually, though I was unaware that they had seen each other since our chance meeting on the street in front of the grocery store.

"To Las Vegas?" The idea of a neon city rising in the desert west appealed to me since the dominant colors of my world were gray and rust. And I was aware that Joey had never gone with his father alone anywhere. My enthusiasm seemed to amuse Abe.

"Sure, Vegas, if that's what you'd like, but the weather's better in Miami." He reached over and patted me on the head affectionately, as a scout leader might have done in other circumstances. "Next time, kid," he said. "It's a promise."

"What about Joey?" I said. I didn't really want to include my friend, but loyalty made me suggest the idea.

Abe's eyes clouded now. "I don't think Joey'd want to go on a trip like this," he said in the tone a doctor might use when asked if his delinquent son was joining his practice. I was pleased because it made me feel I was Abe's anointed heir, more favored even than Larry, the CPA in Chicago. But I also felt guilty, as if I had made up for the loss of my father by stealing my friend's, and in the process doing a disservice to both my father and Joey. Yet of course nothing had happened, beyond the fact that Abe and I had recognized our mutual loneliness by becoming companions. And if it was an odd friendship, or at least one that would have seemed odd to others, it seemed to have earned my mother's approval in some way, which pleased rather than puzzled me. I had already learned that the geography of intimacy is extensive enough to accommodate a great deal of eccentricity.

Eleven

Piano Lessons

The comment I heard most often as a child from others was that I was lucky to have such interesting parents, to grow up, as was universally assumed by others, in such a stimulating environment. After all, my father was an internationally known concert artist, my mother was a painter, and for good measure, my small brother was a chess genius. The fact that by these standards I was nothing, or nearly so, did not seem to matter to anyone but me. I basked in their common reflection. The process of osmosis would presumably render me remarkable as well eventually; I had plenty of time. Teachers, family friends, and the parents of the children I played with were all in awe of our family to some degree and though I took this as empty flattery, the reality was still somewhat disappointing. For while our friends and acquaintances seemed to think the family round would inevitably take on the form of an artistic or intellectual soiree, my parents seldom talked about either art or music in our presence. My father did not even seem to like to listen to music unless it was a recording of Schnabel, Horowitz, or Casadesus, and he would not allow anyone else to do so except in a kind of tomblike silence that did not permit conversation or even movement. "Do you want to listen to this or not?" he'd snap, and then, quite often, get up and turn off the phonograph.

And yet, my parents were artists and art was undeniably what was important to them above everything else. In fact, their absorption in what they were doing and their complete trust in their own instincts—and their consequent lack of concern for received values— might have been the most important things I learned at home. That and their devotion to one another. My mother learned to read scores because my father said only imbeciles would attend a concert without knowing what was being played. And while my mother never achieved equal fame, her commitment to her work was if anything more pure than my father's. After long hours in the studio, she would bring home her oils and stand them against the wall in my father's study for his inspection. He would look them over carefully, often asking my mother to move the painting from one side to another so he could look at a part of a picture. Then he would always say the same thing with absolute conviction: "Honey, I think this is even better than the last one."

Without making any protestations of special gifts, my parents were unusual, even eccentric. They didn't wear funny clothes or contrive any particular kind of behavior, but they *were* peculiar, and probably without meaning to they gave me their implicit permission to find my own way too, whatever that might have been. Still, when we were sitting in our gloomy kitchen sampling the Chef Boy-Ar-Dee entrée my brother had prepared, I envied my friends in their cozy homes, whose mothers had looms in their kitchens and spent their days baking bread and cookies.

Neither of my parents was eager for me to follow in their career path, and my father held forth frequently on the perils of a musician's life. "There were eight thousand musicians in New York," he would say. "And two thousand jobs. I had one of the best and it was still lousy. Do you know that people would sit and knit while I played?" He said this last with a kind of wonder, as if the idea that anyone would consider music to be anything other than an exclusive activity was the most outrageous thing he had ever heard. Still, my parents felt compelled to expose me to the various arts. In succession, I had been given lessons in drawing, dance, acting, voice, even the clarinet, but unfortunately the only area in which I demonstrated any talent was piano, and this put me in direct conflict with my father. Not because he feared competition. This would have been absurd; in his view he had no competition from me or anyone else. Rather, the problem was my father's knowledge and experience of his instrument.

Someone had told him not to make the mistake of trying to teach his son and, for reasons that remain mysterious, he took this advice to heart. Instead of teaching me, he took it upon himself to teach my teachers, which in its own way was worse. Two of my early instructors were former students of his whom my father bullied to such an extent that each quit before making much of an impact on me. By the time we arrived in Milwaukee, I had been playing in a desultory way for three years and looked forward to now being able to join my father in retirement. The huge black piano sat in our small living room, looking more like a casket than something anyone could conceivably enjoy, and for months no one touched it except the piano tuner who arrived faithfully every three months by previous arrangement. This vestigial remnant of my father's career really had nothing to do with me, however.

Then, just when I had gratefully forgotten all about my musical education, my father announced that he had made arrangements for me to study at the Wisconsin Conservatory of Music. Though he had a low opinion of music teachers in general, feeling that teaching was an implicit admission of one's failure as a performer, a friend had recommended a Professor Braun at the conservatory and after talking to the man, my father decided that the professor would be adequate to teach his son. After all, the conservatory was the most prestigious school of its kind in the area and Professor Braun would have the assistance of my father in his task, whether he wanted it or not.

The conservatory was housed in a large building made of pink stone with pillars that fronted on Prospect Avenue not far from our house and I climbed the steps for my first lesson with a sinking feeling in my stomach. There was not only the actual experience of playing, which was seldom a pleasure for me, but what I imagined would be the inevitable disappointment on the part of my teacher when he discovered that I had been oversold as a talent. Whether they ever said so or not, I always believed that my successive music instructors took me on in the belief that my ability must in some way approximate my father's and that in time they would become known for having nourished a prodigy in his early years. Such was the extent of my father's legend in the area that my failure to demonstrate brilliance could never be accepted as a simple failure of genetics. It must instead be understood that I hadn't worked hard enough, that I wasn't really serious, that I didn't understand what was important in life as I went about playing basketball and listening to rock and roll. All these things were true, but the relevant detail was that none of it would have mattered had my father been someone else.

I had a certain modest talent, probably more than most people. I was musical and had long arms and large hands for a boy. Left alone, I might even have developed affection for the piano and a degree of mastery. I might someday have performed with a minor orchestra, given recitals in high schools, and taken students of my own. But, of course, I was never left alone. That was the problem.

Still, I shouldn't have worried about my new teacher, for Professor Braun proved to be a comrade-in-arms, at least where my father was concerned. Short, with gray hair and small black eyes behind wire-rimmed glasses, the professor had come to Milwaukee from Vienna during the war and was not easily intimidated. He struck me as being formal but not unfriendly in his vest and tweed jacket, which was out at the elbows. Now he shook my hand and said, "Your papa is not an easy man, Daniel. Yes?"

This was so direct and so true that I had to smile. "Not for me," I said.

"Ja," Professor Braun replied. "Except not for anyone, I think." Then he laughed a short, harsh bark and had me sit down at the piano.

From the beginning, the professor and I got on well and for the first time I began to make some progress, even within my father's strict requirements. He had told Professor Braun, for example, that I was not to waste time practicing scales. When the professor protested that scales were the basis for all music, my father said that this was his point. Instead of practicing scales, I should just start in on Mozart and then I would learn scales along the way. After all, he said, who ever went to a concert to hear scales? The fact that I wasn't playing any concerts did not seem to occur to him as being relevant. He also forbade any light pieces; that is, these were not to be your ordinary piano lessons with gold stars pasted on books full of easy arrangements of old favorites and a recital at the end of the year with other students. For my father, music was serious, all music, and Professor Braun said he agreed, but he said this with an ironic smile. We understood each other right away.

I was given a Mozart sonata and Professor Braun and I began work immediately. My progress through the piece was slow, but that didn't seem to matter. "To improve fast, practice slow," the professor told me approvingly. "Don't worry about mistakes, Danny. You can't be so afraid to be wrong."

Unfortunately, my father didn't share the professor's attitude toward imperfection. He would sit in the next room as I made my plodding way through the Mozart in what I imagined to be an agony of frustration. Periodically, he would call out, "It's too slow," or alternatively, "It's F-*sharp*, Daniel." And, of course, he was always right, which just made things worse.

Sensing my discouragement, Professor Braun came to our apartment one afternoon and the three of us had a meeting. My father had put on a coat and tie for the occasion and his jaw was set, as if he were expecting trouble. Professor Braun rubbed his hands together and made some remark about the weather, to which my father didn't respond. In his opinion, Braun had about as much right to discuss music with him as Daisy did, but I was glad to have an advocate.

"Your son is very talented," the professor began, in what had become the leitmotif of all of my teachers. But such flattery was really only reflected praise for my father; after all, I could claim no credit for inborn traits, for genetic gifts. Whatever I had in the way of musical ability came directly from him and no one ever told my father the truth anyway, about this or anything else.

It would have been better if someone had said, "Despite your genius, Mr. Meyer, Daniel has very modest abilities." But if any music teacher thought this was the case, no one had thus far had the temerity to say so. Yet Braun surprised me. "Daniel is talented," he repeated. "I wish to emphasize that, but he is not so good that he can improve without hard work and practice. No one can. I doubt that you yourself were that good, Mr. Meyer, as gifted as you are."

My father didn't respond directly to this, though the suggestion that he would have to work at something would almost certainly have seemed insulting to him. He loved to tell stories about his laziness, his inattention to various teachers and conductors, which had been followed by brilliant triumphs in the concert hall. "He practices," my father said now. "I've heard him. He drives me nuts sometimes with all his mistakes, but he does practice."

Braun nodded. He rose and walked to the window. Then he turned to face my father. "Perhaps Daniel would practice more and practice better if it did not drive you so much nuts," the professor said, and I was impressed with his bravery. "A plant cannot grow without water and few of us can improve at anything without a little praise now and then. Did you ever think of that, Mr. Meyer?" Now the professor grasped his throat, as if he thought he had gone too far.

But instead he had elicited something I had never known existed in my father who flushed but then shook his head slowly, as if the lowly piano teacher had actually told him something of value. His whole expression changed. His jaw loosened and I imagined that his cheeks were suddenly full and soft. Finally, he spoke. "I think you're right, Professor Braun." Then he turned and addressed me directly. "Your piano teacher is right, Daniel. I was wrong to criticize you so much and I'm sorry if I discouraged you by doing that. It's the way I was taught, but it's probably not the best way. God knows, I hated all of my teachers."

My father had never apologized to me before; in fact I had seldom heard him apologize to anyone for anything. But it seemed to be a relief to do so now and it occurred to me that always being right about everything could be both a responsibility and a burden. "Maybe it was the best thing for you," I said.

My father smiled ruefully and shook his head again. "I didn't like it either. Who would? I still avoid practicing and I've always been a lousy rehearsal pianist. I make a virtue of necessity, but the truth is it's neither true nor necessary. Just an excuse."

The fact that he used the present tense made me sad. It was as if my father nurtured the illusion that he still played, that he was still a concert artist. And now I understood that this had been the real problem all along. "I can't be you," I said. It was probably the most honest exchange we had ever had.

My father's eyes were red and he reached out to me. I smelled tobacco and aftershave on his coat as I held him and I knew that he was crying. "You don't want to be me, Danny. No one should ever want to be me anymore."

There was a moment of silence and then Professor Braun spoke. "So," he said. "Now we have a new understanding, yes? Daniel must try to practice more and you, Mr. Meyer, you must to encourage him, not too much, just a little bit."

I was once more impressed with the professor since my father was not only a well-known musician but the one who was paying his fee. Yet, it was clear that this was less a request than a demand. These were the professor's terms if he was to continue as my instructor. My father just nodded his head and there seemed to be no need for him to say anything else. Then, after reminding me of my next lesson, the professor left us alone in the apartment.

In the aftermath of the meeting, my father and I sat silently for a few moments. Then he said, "Play something for me, Danny."

It was the first time he had ever actually asked to hear me play the piano and I was both surprised and nervous. "Can it be something besides that Mozart?"

My father smiled. "Anything you like," he said magnanimously.

So I pulled out a contraband book of folk songs Professor Braun had given me and then for an hour I played songs of the Kingston Trio and Woody Guthrie for my father.

Despite our problems and my mother's growing anxiety about having to support the family, we had never spent so much time together. In Madison, my parents had been busy and my brother and I had different groups of friends with whom we spent most of our free time. Except for dinners together, which occurred only infrequently, we were seldom all in the same place at the same time. Now, however, since none of us had developed circles of friends, we tended to collapse inward for support, company, even entertainment. I often thought it was as if we were some frontier family huddled together in our prairie sod house, except, of course, we were actually living in a large city with all the diversions that such a place can offer.

Ironically, the first to take advantage of Milwaukee was my brother Charles, who was otherwise a recluse. He had read in the newspaper about a chess club and quickly discovered that the chess scene here was much more vibrant than anything he had known in Madison, though as a group the chess players were among the oddest people I had ever met.

Charles and my father became habitués of Hawthorne Glen on Sixtieth Street, where all the best players belonged. Charles immediately established himself among a talented group of juniors and began to enter both local tournaments and those scattered around the Midwest. Though a haze of smoke seemed permanently in place just below the ceiling of the club and it seemed an unusual place for children, he had never seemed as much at home anywhere else and was universally recognized as a player of brilliance and promise. And while my father never rose above class A level, he enjoyed my brother's success enormously and it gave them a place to go twice a week. It was a long drive, however, and it made little sense to turn around and go back to the East Side, so often my mother and I would go to the movies on these evenings. On other occasions I would just stay and read a book.

On this particular night, I had been invited somewhere and wasn't planning to make the trip to Hawthorne Glen. As I was getting ready to leave, however, my mother came in to my room and sat on the chair next to the desk. I could tell by the set of her shoulders that all was not well, though she didn't say what had happened or if anything had. She just said, "I wish you wouldn't go out tonight, Danny. I kind of need you to be with me tonight."

I wanted to go out with my friends. I always wanted to go out, even if there was nowhere in particular to go and nothing interesting to do. I would often walk around the neighborhood in the dark looking in store windows in preference to staying home. But something in my mother's voice made me hesitate. Certainly it wouldn't have been her tears, since she cried often, and if I wasn't inured to her sadness, I don't think I would have been alarmed by it either. More likely it would have been the fact that on this night she didn't cry, that instead she simply stated a need.

"Okay," I said.

She didn't seem especially pleased or vindicated by this. She just nodded and smoothed her skirt on her lap. "Just tonight," she said.

I don't remember what we did beyond driving to the chess club. I would like for that evening to have been memorable, for us to have finally visited Louie Bashell's jazz club, for example, or gone to another Garbo festival. But that isn't what has stayed with me. Rather it is that my mother asked me to stay home. Over time, I have wondered if it was fair to me, whether my mother was in some way expecting me to fill a role her husband should have assumed in listening to her fears, and whether in its own way this wasn't as seductive as Daisy shaking her behind in the kitchen while she cleaned. But I don't think so. In her whole life, my mother might have made such direct requests three or four times. I don't remember when this took place or what she asked for the other times, but I'm glad I recognized her urgency that night and skipped the party. There are pivotal incidents in life, times that provide the impress for the people we will become and often they are inconsequential, or seem so at the time. Memory reveals itself slowly and in increments; this was one such moment for me.

~

The weather slowly improved. It wasn't so much that it became pleasant to go outside, but it was no longer as much of a struggle. Dirty piles of snow lined the streets, which were coated by the city with sand and salt. And though the winds weren't as bad as before, they were still insistent, insinuating themselves through our drafty windows and finding their way into the most tightly buttoned jacket.

Once I awoke convinced that there was a ghost in the room and that the sound I heard was its mocking cough. I was not normally very imaginative in this respect and the image scared me enough that I got up and went down the hall to the kitchen where I found my mother in a blue chenille bathrobe drinking tea. She looked up, her eyes huge and dark, and put out her arms. Instinctively, I went to her and she rubbed my back until in time I calmed down, my fear replaced by an all-encompassing guilt. I felt like confessing, for in my mind there was a great deal to confess to: my encounter with Joey, lusting after Miss Harmon, having sex with Daisy, running errands for a known gambler. All in all, it had been quite a year and it was only half over. But in the end, I mentioned none of these things, knowing somehow that confession would be a blind for something else and that in time I would regret having spoken. Instead, to my surprise, nurtured in my mother's arms, I whispered, "I don't want to die."

My mother did not laugh. She nodded her head and then sat back and looked at me seriously. "I'd be concerned if you did," she said. "No one I know wants to die. I used to worry about it when I was younger, too."

The idea that this was something that would eventually cease to bother me was attractive. "And now? Don't you worry about it anymore?"

She thought this over. "It's not that I want to die," she said. "I wouldn't want to leave your daddy, and I wouldn't want you and Charles to have to grow up alone. That would be hard. But I'm not scared of it the way I was. Life takes an awfully long time, Danny, unless you're very unlucky. I think that's supposed to make you ready for it to be over when it's your time."

I didn't mention the obvious: that she and my father *had* been unlucky, that there hadn't really been very much in her whole life that one could call lucky. I was grateful for her grace and warmth and love and I knew that death would never get any easier for me, that I would never get used to the idea of losing the people I cared about. For that matter, I doubted that she had, no matter how she might rationalize it now. But I appreciated the fact that this wasn't what was important to her that night in the cold kitchen, that in the end she cared more about comforting me than she did about answering my question honestly.

Twelve

News from Washington

Because of Alfred's personal crisis I had seen little of him for some time; our contact had recently been limited to short conversations in the back hall. Although I was interested, I had little idea how to broach the subject of his love triangle without sounding naïve or intrusive, or both. Even his life in Chicago was a mystery to me, intriguing but somehow unimaginable. All I knew of the city was Lake Shore Drive and that impressive Lake Michigan skyline which I had seen on various trips with my parents to visit the Museum of Science and Industry. Alfred's descriptions of life with his lover in their shared lodgings on the North Side seemed at once illicit and mundane. I might have conceived of such things going on in darkened hotel rooms or even public restrooms under the cover of anonymity, quickly accomplished and as quickly forgotten. But putting it together with shopping, dishes, and taking care of a house was new to me. Yet here were Alfred and Joe, teachers and homeowners, carrying on in the open without apparent outcry from the neighbors. After several months of tension, however, a kind of equilibrium had apparently been achieved in his relationship with Joe and he felt free to resume his pattern of spending three days a week in Milwaukee, one of which was generally devoted to some kind of outing with me.

I thought of Alfred as an uncle, since I had no uncles, and he liked to indulge me. Often we would simply go to the Oriental for a matinee or early evening show, but if one or both of us was feeling ambitious we might go downtown to the museum or travel to the geodesic domes at Mitchell Park, where they were able to replicate various world climates, such as the Amazonian rain forests or Arabian deserts, something which could be desirable in the frozen north. It was on one of those trips that I asked Alfred with some hesitation to tell me about his work. I hesitated not because I wasn't interested, but because the general pattern was for adults to interview me and before I met Alfred I hadn't known science had a history. As far as I was concerned, the two subjects were worlds unto themselves.

Alfred seemed pleased that I had asked. "It's not really history in the sense you probably think of it," he said. "I don't keep track of when Newton was born and things like that. It's more a matter of how people thought about things we would now call science, and maybe about how we think about it now. I think of it more as philosophy. I'm a philosopher."

My perplexity must have been obvious. I didn't even know what philosophy was. "Think of it this way," Alfred continued, sounding like a teacher. "The Greeks didn't think they were inventing astronomy when they named the stars and the constellations and made up stories to go with them."

"What did they think they were doing?"

Alfred smiled. "Put yourself in their place. Imagine you're in this strange and frightening world and you don't know how you got there or what will happen next. You look around and you see other things on the ground, animals, trees, and so forth. What could be more natural than to assume you're all somehow connected, that there's a common root. This idea of humans *not* being connected to the rest of the natural world is really a pretty modern idea, and not an attractive one." He stopped, his small intelligent eyes looking intent, as if he wanted to make sure I was following. "Well, anyway, the natural thing for the ancient peoples was to try to provide explanations for all this. Maybe it's one way to fight the natural anxiety anyone would feel in that situation."

"I still feel afraid sometimes," I said. "I think about the universe not ending and it scares me, that it just goes on and on. I want it to be inside something."

"That's interesting," Alfred said. "Would that make it better, if it were contained in something?"

I hadn't really thought before why that would be better, but I thought it would. "Everything else is inside something," I said. "Milwaukee is inside Wisconsin and Wisconsin is inside the United States, and the United States is inside the world and the world is inside the solar system, until you get to the universe."

Alfred was quiet for a moment. "And that makes you feel insecure, right?" He nodded and patted me on the shoulder. "Well, that's how the Greeks felt, and the myths and legends made them feel better about where they were, even if they couldn't control anything. Their stories make it clear that something could, and that was the gods. The Olympians."

I could see that, but it didn't seem to have much to do with science. "Why is it history?" I asked. "Were the stars different then?"

Alfred laughed at this. "No, at least not in the way you mean. But it's like I said. People thought of them in different ways than we do now. For example, we think of all the planets in our solar system revolving around the sun. Ptolemy thought the sun and moon revolved around the earth."

"But we're right, aren't we?" I asked. This seemed like an important distinction.

Alfred sensed my anxiety. "Sure," he said. "Don't worry about that. But that isn't what I'm interested in. I don't really care who's right." This seemed remarkable to me, but I didn't interrupt because he was absorbed in what he was saying. "Ptolemy's way of thinking about things was elegant, much more so than the way people think today with their computers and lab coats. And he wasn't even necessarily wrong; he just lacked certain data, not to mention a telescope. The thing is, it's all a great mystery, isn't it? I mean, here we are, all of us, and all of these natural phenomena that we spend our lives trying to control, but *why*? Scientists tend to devote their research more to process, to describing the mechanisms of nature, observing them. How things work together. Philosophers, like me, are more concerned with the meaning of the whole thing, so we spend our time looking at the questions people have asked over the history of civilization and then analyze the ways they found to answer those questions, or not to answer them." He paused and smiled at me. "So, that's about what I do, Danny. Does any of it make sense?"

The truth was that some of this was over my head, but no one had ever spoken so eloquently to me about science before. Certainly neither my parents nor my teachers ever had. It made me feel differently about Alfred. Not that I liked him more or less, but he now presented a more complicated picture to me than before. Without thinking about it one way or another, his homosexuality had previously defined him in my mind. Of course I had known he was a professor; I even knew he was well known in his field. But I now saw his troubles with Joe and his jealousy of Paul and Jesús within the context of an intense and productive life. This would have been nothing new for him, of course, but it changed the way I would think of him.

Like Paul, Alfred didn't drive and by the time we got home on the bus it was almost dark and I was cold. Surprisingly, Anna was leaning out her window as we approached and now she waved excitedly at us. "I have to speak to you," she said in a commanding tone. I assumed she meant Alfred and continued up our steps. But then she said, "No, Daniel. I must speak to you, not to Alfred."

This caught us both unawares, I think, but I went next door where Anna took me into the living room and shut the door. The inevitable kuchen was on the table, but I wasn't particularly hungry. Now Anna held up a piece of paper and waved it before me in the air. "I wanted you to see this," she said mysteriously and passed the sheet to me.

The paper was thicker than I was accustomed to and embossed in blue ink with the words "The White House." Below that in lighter blue ink was "Henry Kissinger, Foreign Policy Advisor." I had scarcely had time to read this before Anna snatched the letter back. "You see," she said triumphantly. "Henry wrote back."

I had forgotten all about Anna's friends in high places or why she had written in the first place, but I did recall that my father had been skeptical. "That's amazing," I said. And it was, but I wasn't sure what else to say about it. "What does he have to say?"

But Anna was in no hurry to surrender the moment. "Sit down," she said, pointing at the tufted couch. "Have some cake. I have something important to ask you." Then, as if anticipating a protest, she said, "It is all right. I spoke already to your mother."

The room we were in was reserved for ceremonial occasions and was both overheated and crowded with furniture. There were matching mahogany end tables that went with the coffee table and a loveseat and easy chair to complement the sofa. On the walls were reproductions of Dutch masters, along with a few prints by Milwaukee artists, including my mother, and a large mirror in a silver frame to reflect everything back onto itself. There was a small bookcase in the corner filled with German books in crumbling leather bindings and two small oriental rugs lay incongruously on the floor, elegant in their colorful complexity. Anna reigned supreme, sitting in her royal blue caftan, her head wrapped in a burgundy turban, her short, fat fingers gripping a tea cup in one hand and cake in the other. I could tell she was pleased with herself and it was hard not to share in her enjoyment.

Irrationally, I wondered if she had called me in to talk about Daisy, but when Anna spoke again it was clear that my sexual initiation in the basement was not on her mind. Her friend Henry had not only written, she told me, but he had given her the name of a man in the State Department who would help her. Henry was too busy with the Vietnam War to handle it himself, but he had told her how to go about things. Anna had already spoken with the man in State, being careful not to mention Jesús by name, and this man had told her that since Jesús had entered the country illegally, as far as the government was concerned, he didn't exist, unless he was arrested or died. The only way for Anna to solve her problem, he said, was to have Jesús leave the country and then come back in legally, with a green card.

"You mean he has to go back to Guatemala?" I asked. I knew nothing about the intricacies of immigration law, but this seemed risky. What sense did it make to draw attention to yourself by leaving and then trying to get back when you couldn't get in legally in the first place? "What if they won't let him past the border?"

Anna shook her head and pushed the cake in my direction as if this would solve something. This time I took a piece. "You think like a peasant, Daniel. The truth is, you think exactly like Jesús. He said the same thing." She smiled in a patronizing way as if the complexities of foreign policy were nothing to her. Then she continued. "Henry has worked it all out with this other man. Even though it's practically impossible to get a visa from Central America, Henry says he'll find a way to do it. But Jesús has to go back first."

My disbelief must have shown, but I couldn't help it. It was one thing for Anna to know Kissinger, who was in the papers every night for one thing or another; we had doubted that and she had proven everyone wrong. I was impressed by that, no question. But whether Anna knew him or not, I couldn't understand why Kissinger would go out of his way to help Jesús, why he would take an active interest in his case. Even if he knew Anna, he didn't know Jesús—and what was one more illegal immigrant considering the difficulties he had to face every day? "It's hard to believe," I said.

This seemed to irritate Anna, who now shook her large head from side to side as if she had gnats. "Jesús won't believe it either," she said. "And since he can't read, I can't show him Henry's letter."

From all I could tell, Jesús didn't think he had a problem. He was happy with things as they were. He had a job, a roof over his head, and a woman to love. How many of his friends could say the same? What difference did it make to him that he was in this country illegally? It would only matter if someone was trying to send him back and so far that hadn't happened, though he might suspect that was Anna's actual intention with all this talk of going back to Guatemala. I didn't blame Jesús for being cautious, but there didn't seem to be much more to say. I had eaten the cake and seen the letter proving Anna right. "I guess I'd better get home," I said.

"I'm not finished," Anna said in a magisterial tone. "Jesús says he'll go if I go with him. That way he thinks if he can't get back in, we'd both be stranded there. He doesn't seem to understand that I wouldn't be stranded, that I could come back whenever I wanted, with or without him."

This was true, but it still seemed like a reasonable plan to me. "So you'll go and come back with him, like Kissinger said?" I couldn't bring myself to call the president's foreign policy advisor Henry, though oddly that was the way I thought of him now. Little Henry. *Kleiner Heinrich,* in lederhosen, from the old country.

"It's not so easy," Anna said in a tone of voice that suggested I knew nothing of life's difficulties, of the burdens she shouldered every day, which was nearly the truth. "I can't go to some half-savage place with ten words of Spanish. That would be insane." This seemed a bit histrionic to me, though I knew nothing about Guatemala. I thought it was near Mexico. But I assumed there were cities there and people who spoke English. And I felt it was instinctively unfair to characterize them as savages.

I said as much to Anna, who responded, "There is a revolution going on in that country, Daniel. There is something they call the EGP, the Guerilla Army of the Poor, fighting the government. The man from the State Department knew all about it. He says they're very dangerous."

I didn't understand what this civil war had to do with Anna and Jesús, but I decided not to challenge her. Like most adults, Anna really had little use for the opinions of adolescents, assuming we hadn't lived long enough to have any thoughts worth paying attention to. Beyond this, however, revolution sounded romantic to me, much more interesting than life on Frederick Avenue. I thought of George Washington and Thomas Jefferson. "They probably wouldn't be where you're going," I said, having no idea where she was going or where the guerrillas were. I still didn't understand why she had called me over.

Anna sighed heavily, her huge breasts rising and straining the material of the caftan. "There is no choice. I have to go, but I can't go alone."

"You'd have Jesús," I said.

"That's the same as being alone," she said, dismissively. It always amazed me how Anna referred to her lover as if he was hired help despite his being slavishly loyal to her. "You can't talk to him. I mean, really talk."

This seemed unfair. Jesús could have said with equal justice that you couldn't talk to Anna because she didn't know Spanish, but he wasn't complaining. "How about Alfred?"

Anna looked incredulous. "Alfred would be worse than useless. He'd get sick and then I'd have to take care of him. Besides he doesn't like Jesús." She looked at me. "I think you must go with me, Daniel."

This caught me by surprise and not for the obvious reason that on the surface this affair had nothing to do with me. What possible help could I be to Anna in Guatemala? At the same time, the idea had a certain appeal. The idea of escape was essential to me and that was the way Guatemala presented itself at the time. We would travel halfway around the world and then perhaps be stranded in a world of passion and revolution. But I felt a duty to protest just the same. "How could I help?" I said.

"You take Spanish in school," Anna said, which was true but the approach to languages at Campus, as in every other subject, was student-centered. Miss Harmon was afraid we'd get discouraged if we were confronted with all those strange tenses so we spent most of our time reading translations and speaking English. Still, I probably knew more than Anna did. "You'd talk to me," Anna continued, "and I'd talk to you. Aren't we friends?"

I hadn't thought of it that way before, but I could see her point. "Sure, I guess," I said. "But I have school."

Anna waved this away as if it were smoke. "That's nothing," she said. "I'll speak to your teacher. You can do some kind of report, or take some pictures. What would you miss in that school anyway?"

I had to think, since at Campus every day was its own creation. It wasn't that we never studied anything but that the teachers didn't believe in chapter tests or any other conventional methods of measuring growth. In fact, the idea of expecting students to progress at all was currently under review. Was progress the same as learning, that is, the same as education as it should be? The more enlightened minds at Campus were afraid that emphasizing goals would tarnish the experience, and implied that there wasn't really much point in studying if the only reason for it was to do well on tests. Anyway, Anna was right. I had been reading about the Depression recently, but it would be there when I returned. And I had no doubt that Anna would bulldoze any objections Miss Harmon might raise to the plan. She had already decided what was going to happen; she was just informing me of my part in the whole mosaic.

"Who will do my work?" I asked, remembering the clinkers and shoveling.

"Your mother and I will work everything out," she said with finality, letting me know I was dismissed.

"When?" I asked, standing.

"As soon as you get a passport we leave," Anna said. "I pay for everything."

Thirteen

Guatemala

One of the formative experiences of my mother's life was a trip she had taken at fourteen with her father, who was an engineer and had been invited to inspect sewage systems in Germany, just as the Nazis were taking over. With little or no encouragement, she would carry on at length about the beautiful gardens and friendly people she met while her father was inspecting the German sanitation systems. No one she met took Hitler seriously, and despite what happened later, for the rest of her life she would continue to think nostalgically about the trip, a tendency she assigned to travel in general. Of course, my mother's ability to see the bright side approached the pathological. She would describe anything that had happened, good or bad, as an experience and though she frequently talked of life as being a tragedy in the Greek sense, this somehow did not come in conflict in her mind with its also being a good experience. When anything bad happened, she would say, "Every kick a boost" and encourage us to move smoothly forward. Except, of course, for the times when she dissolved in tears leaving me feeling helpless and confused.

My father took a rather mordant view of all this and sometimes, when he was annoyed with my mother, he would talk airily about his illness as being an experience and speculate about all the good things that might come out of it. I suspect that if I had been old enough to be drafted for the war that Kissinger was trying to resolve, my mother's response would have been that Vietnam might be very interesting and that I should go.

Whether this was true or not, my mother's convictions about the value of travel led her to agree enthusiastically that I should accompany Anna and Jesús to Guatemala, though the similarities between her travels with her father to Europe and my going to a Central American country riven by earthquakes and insurgencies were hard to see. My mother was convinced this would be a wonderful adventure and immediately went out to buy whatever guidebooks and maps she could locate in Milwaukee. If she or my father were concerned about my safety, they said nothing about it; my mother's only stated concern was that Guatemala may not have been the most interesting country I could have visited—she might have preferred Brazil or even Chile. But as my father sensibly observed, Jesús couldn't help where he had been born and certainly there must be interesting Aztec ruins or something to see in Guatemala. Anna had not mentioned any such thing to me, but my parents were already sketching out the trip *they* would take, if they were going, and mine quickly became of secondary importance.

Anna's approach to our journey was more strategic. Assuming that she would be in a country with no civilization worth talking about and one which in addition would be innocent of Western medical advances, she not only insisted on being inoculated against typhus and diphtheria, but also purchased large quantities of diarrhea medication, aspirin, antacids, unguents, vitamins, and a bewildering variety of trusses, wraps, and heating pads. Jesús, from all I could tell, made no preparations at all, but then Guatemala was home to him. Jesús' idea of exotica would more likely be Milwaukee and Chicago.

There was a Guatemalan consulate in Chicago, and after my passport arrived, Anna and I took the train down to pick up our visas. This proved more complicated than we had imagined. Since our last names were different, the official on duty asked Anna to prove I was her son.

"He's not my son," she said indignantly. "What gave you that idea?"

The official was a young man with a low forehead in a gray suit, and while he said nothing overt to suggest it, I had the impression he suspected Anna of kidnapping me, an intriguing possibility that had not previously occurred to me. The official admitted it was a mystery, however, why, if she were doing this, she would go to the trouble of taking me to Guatemala, of all places? Anna took umbrage at the young man's hesitation and demanded to see his superior, whereupon she pulled out her now dog-eared letter from Kissinger and told the assistant consul that the young man had insulted her. The assistant apologized profusely but said that his colleague was unfortunately correct: Anna must go back to Milwaukee and then return to the consulate with a notarized letter from my parents authorizing her to take me out of the country. On the way home, Anna was out of sorts and I suspected she was questioning the wisdom of her plan, but it turned out that she was only annoyed with Jesús, who, she said, should have told her about this requirement.

Eventually, my mother cleared everything up herself. We took the train to Chicago together this time and she charmed the assistant consul by flattering him about some native artifacts in the lobby that neither Anna nor I had noticed. On the way home, she said it had been a very interesting experience, but my reaction was to start feeling anxious about being alone with Anna and Jesús in a strange country. I felt oddly responsible for them and at the same time doubted my own abilities. Whatever Anna might say, I didn't really know the language and Jesús, who did, seemed more like a brother to me than anything else. That left us with Anna as the responsible adult who, if things became difficult, would probably attempt to bully the Guatemalans and get us all thrown in jail. Still, it was too late to make objections as the tickets had already been purchased.

In April we left Milwaukee for Los Angeles, the main connecting point for Guatemala City, with my mother taking snapshots and then waving wildly from the gate. We made a rather odd traveling party that day, and I could sense people staring furtively in our direction, trying to decide who was related to whom. Jesús and I played checkers and pushed baggage around, while Anna either slept or gave orders. I felt, oddly, as if I had gained an older sibling, though one whose language and customs were foreign to me. On reflection, I decided this wasn't so different from my relationship with my own brother, a chess genius who walked in his sleep and invited Martians into his room at night.

We flew Mexicana, which seemed suitably exotic since I assumed there was no national Guatemalan airline. For several hours, the plane meandered along the Pacific coast and then veered crazily toward some mountain peaks before the pilot righted things and brought us to a higher altitude. Though I had never flown before and was nervous, I thought there was an air of inspired amateurism about the flight crew who gaily spread peanuts and soft drinks around the cabin, laughed frequently, and sat on passengers' laps. Bred on films of the fifties, I had expected there to be an air of solemnity about the whole thing, for the pilot to look like Randolph Scott, and the crew to be crisp and efficient as they followed his commands. Instead, we seemed to be in the middle of an airborne party. To retreat, I looked out the window at what I assumed must be either southern Mexico or Guatemala, but the thick rug of trees made the ground invisible except for brief patches of arable land and occasional mountain peaks.

What I knew of Latin America had largely been gained as a result of watching *The Cisco Kid* and *Zorro* on television and I had little idea what went on in these countries between gunfights and chases on horseback. It had not occurred to me before that there would be farmers in Guatemala, not to mention cities with neighborhoods, buses, offices, and shops. Indeed my sense of Central America was inextricably wed to the exotic, so much so that I could not imagine normal life occurring there. It seemed like a contradiction in terms. Just as the Iron Curtain in Eastern Europe was something that I thought of only in the most concrete terms, I could conceive of our destination only as a place of dusty streets, mongrel dogs, and indolent, brutal policemen. Though it was late to be coming to all this, it now seemed simple to me: we would be herded off the plane, our belongings confiscated, and then thrown into a packed cell where unimaginable things would be done to us until we mercifully died of gangrene or some other disease. Under the circumstances, why shouldn't the stewardesses have a party?

Surprisingly, we made it through customs with ease, but the crush of tourists in the terminal made it difficult at first to decide which direction to go. Along with people who were actually traveling, there were hangers-on and what seemed to be permanent installations in the middle of the corridors, stands at which one could buy fruit, gum, sandwiches, and sundries. Jesús, unaccountably, had perked up and now talked animatedly, pointing this way and that, pulling on Anna's clothes until she told him that we had to move on. Her irritation seemed to cut both ways, however, for at one point she confided to me, "I don't know why I'm such a bitch. I should leave him alone. Of course he's happy to be home. What's wrong with that?" This resolution was hard for her to maintain, however, and a moment later she would be complaining loudly about something Jesús had done.

It was an odd relationship, to say the least. I knew of course that she was going to all this trouble out of her feeling that Jesús shouldn't be living illegally in America without the privileges the rest of us enjoyed. Her face was bright red and she was perspiring heavily; obviously she would never have chosen to visit this place on vacation. As generous as this impulse may have been, however, it expressed itself in a myriad of gestures, raised eyebrows, and gruff commands that kept Jesús and I running to meet her desires.

Guatemala City, I was to discover, was a place of few tourist attractions and less charm, due largely to its having been destroyed on a regular basis by earthquakes over the last two hundred years. The streets were crowded with cars, buses, and bicycles and a humid cloud of exhaust hung over everything. Beneath the stink of diesel fuel, I was aware of some kind of meat being grilled and the sweet smell of rotting garbage. The sidewalks were as crowded as the streets, but the people were small and polite, saying *con permiso* like a mantra as they jostled for space to sell the fruits and vegetables they had brought down with them from the mountains. Though it was five o'clock in the morning, the crowd was constant and I was struck by the brilliant red of their shirts and by their beautiful clear skin, which seemed luminescent, as if light was somehow reflected from within. Even the men were no bigger than I was, yet they seemed almost to be of a different species. I had never felt so foreign and it made me feel anxious, alone. Not knowing why, I grabbed Jesús' arm and we joined hands as we made our way slowly down the street outside the terminal.

From the airport, we took a taxi to the Pan American Hotel, where Anna's travel agent had booked two rooms. As we drove, I noticed that the buildings were low with corrugated steel roofs and neither the neighborhoods nor the streets had names. Instead, the city was divided into zones, which made it colorless but easy to navigate. The hotel itself had a vast, high-ceilinged lobby and was only a few blocks from the Parque Central, but the rooms themselves were utilitarian, though they did have television, something that surprised me, in part I suppose because I had not thought of there being television available to the masses in Guatemala. Without discussing it, I somehow understood that Jesús and I would share one room while Anna would stay alone in the other, as if she were the parent and we were her children.

It was now close to seven A.M. and the trip had started for us at noon the previous day. Anna retired almost immediately, but I was much too excited to sleep. The warm humid air was intoxicating enough, since it gave me the illusion of being one of those wealthy Milwaukeeans able to escape to a warm climate during suicide season, but beyond that the scene unrolling before us in the Pan American lobby was the most exotic I had ever seen. Jesús and I deposited ourselves in matching armchairs to watch the parade while we decided what to do next. The hotel, I learned, was a center for Europeans, but mixed in were what I supposed to be Arabian sheiks in long gowns and Indians in native dress selling pottery and colorful rugs; there were stands selling mangoes, papayas, and three kinds of bananas in addition to plantains, which they cooked in milk over small fires. Jesús bought a small green fruit that seemed unpromising until he peeled it, revealing a beautiful pink core that was succulent and delicious. A parrot flew in among the peddlers cawing loudly in protest of something. Neither of us were in the mood to seek out whatever tourist attractions the capital might offer, but I wanted to be in the middle of things rather than trapped in the small hotel room watching reruns of old American sitcoms and Jesús didn't object.

A curious role reversal was taking place as Jesús was now becoming more jovial and outgoing, bantering with the peddlers and nodding at me occasionally in response to their questions. He and I communicated in a strange argot made up of English, Spanish, and hand and body gestures. It would not have worked in Milwaukee, in part because we would not have made the effort, but in Guatemala City Jesús and I were thrown back on one another and thus forced to be more inventive. As we walked around the Parque Central near our hotel I noticed that while most of the citizens of Guatemala were Indian descendants of the Maya, the people we saw seemed primarily to be Ladinos, the mixed-blood descendants of the Spaniards who ran things in the country. Jesús looked like a cross between the two groups, what was sometimes called an *indígena cadinazada,* an Indian who spoke the native dialect of his village but dressed in European clothes and lived like a Ladino in the city. I was struck by the Indians who wore the colors of their native villages, often embroidered with animal likenesses. Both men and women wore their heavy black hair in braids. As I walked close to them in the park, I recognized the smell of sweat, wood smoke, and sex, which reminded me of Daisy. Women lolled on the grass, nursing babies, their breasts like brown balloons, while their men sat on their haunches smoking and watching nothing.

130

None of this seemed exceptional to Jesús. We were simply part of the mix strolling in the park as the day grew warmer and moved toward noon. Jesús seemed content to be back in his native land, and to have returned better than he had left, even if ironically his purpose in coming back was to leave for good. He seemed to walk with a new confidence, his broad shoulders rolling rhythmically, his hands loose at his sides. I had no idea how long this promenade should last but we were in the park most of the day and when we returned the hotel lobby had quieted and exhaustion had overtaken us so we went up to bed.

━

The next day we visited the American Embassy, which was in a zone across town, necessitating another bone-jarring taxi ride in a Fiat made for people smaller than Anna. She was dressed rather formally for the occasion in a maroon suit whose seams and buttons showed the strain of enclosing her body. It was hot and dusty and a day of rest had not improved her mood, but I didn't care. I was imagining myself as a world traveler, dreaming that this would just be the first of any number of far-flung adventures, perhaps with my loyal friend Jesús at my side. And I was eager to see what my role was going to be in this drama. The consular officer was a thin, pinched man of about forty in a blue pinstriped suit who greeted us with a finger handshake and showed us into an interior office. He had a note about Jesús attached to a file, which was reassuring, but otherwise he seemed bored and unconcerned. Obviously, a directive from Henry Kissinger would always be important, but Washington was far away. There would be some delays in any case since there were papers that needed to be filed with the Guatemalan government, which was located in Zone One, near our hotel. As far as the embassy was concerned, Jesús had never left Guatemala, which meant that he now needed his government's permission to travel as well as the approval of our embassy to admit him to the United States. It was complicated, but Jesús was smilingly unconcerned as if he had nothing to lose.

On the way back, we were quiet, and I could tell that Anna was feeling a bit despondent. She had imagined we'd be in and out in a day and wasn't taking it well. She looked over at Jesús, whose face was blank, and said to me, "It's not his fault, but sometimes I yell and shut him out and what has the poor man ever done except devote himself to me? At home, he cooks, he cleans, and he draws my bath." She shook her head and then she began to weep silently. Noticing this, Jesús put his arm around her broad shoulders and pulled her toward him, though he couldn't have known what we were talking about.

Like all Latin American cities, Guatemala City had a large German population and Anna had arranged to have lunch at a restaurant where German was spoken, which seemed to cheer her somewhat. Her attitude toward her native land had always puzzled me. Though she bore an intense hatred toward all ordinary German citizens, whom she indiscriminately considered to be Nazis, she was equally scornful of so-called holocaust Jews as well, because, in her view, they should have known enough to escape when they had the chance instead of waiting around for the inevitable. She had walked out of a performance of *Fiddler on the Roof* in disgust, saying, "It's just like the Jews; they're all about to be killed and all they want to do is sing and dance." Still, she received a check from the German government every month, adored Bertolt Brecht and Kurt Weill, and loved heavy German pastries.

Though we were invited to lunch, it seemed to me that Anna preferred to be alone with her countrymen so Jesús and I struck out on our own, for he had been in the capital only once before, and that was years ago. I should have felt anxious being alone in a large, strange city with only Jesús as my guide, but what I felt instead was an almost tangible sensation of escape from everything that had previously limited me. Perhaps Jesús and I would just head out for the mountains and find an Indian village where we would wear native clothes and subsist on *comida típica,* the native diet of tortillas and beans. Milwaukee and all it represented no longer seemed to exist as Jesús and I wandered the dusty, broken streets. No one bothered us, though we must have made an odd couple, a squat Indian and a blond American, dressed identically in jeans and polo shirts. Yet Jesús was an ideal companion, uncomplaining and willing to do absolutely anything I asked.

From our hotel window I had noticed the Torre del Reformador, which was named for an ancient president, who had supposedly changed everything in Guatemala. It was in another zone, but I had had enough of taxis and we walked across town instead. When we got there, however, the tower wasn't much to see, a rusting filigreed spike in the sky, and we couldn't read the ceremonial plaques affixed to its base. So we bought ice cream from a man dressed in a *capixayo,* and then sat in the square and ate. I tried to engage Jesús in conversation about the reformer, whose name was Justino Rufino Barrios, but he had never heard of the man. Unlike children in our country who are told that anyone can become president, Jesús labored under no such illusion. The Ladinos were in control and always would be and everyone knew it. An Indian was lucky to find his way into the city and get a job, any sort of job. Yet this didn't seem to bother Jesús because unlike most Americans he didn't consider what he did for a living to define him, nor did he care about status. He was outside all of these systems, and outside politics, which made me wonder if Anna had adequately explained Kissinger's efforts in his behalf, but that wouldn't have mattered since Jesús would have considered such intervention to be personal, not political, which of course it was. Jesús knew that he had Anna to thank for his new opportunity, not the foreign policy advisor, regardless of who had actually made the call.

After inspecting the tower, we went to the Terminal Market, which shared space with the bus depot, where we ate peppers and some kind of grilled meat with beans. I gave the vendor a *quetzal,* and received change. Then we walked through the market itself where Indians fought for space and dodged buses. Inside, there were more stalls with vendors selling suitcases, saddles, hammocks and rope, *piñatas,* and even tropical birds and monkeys. I found myself wondering who was buying as the crowd seemed to consist largely of

Indians looking at one another, but the overall impression was one of deadening poverty. Though the people were polite they seemed at the same time to be without hope. Children in rags, apparently alone, circulated through the crowd begging. I gave one the change from lunch and we gained a following. Yet while the general ambiance was seedy, I didn't feel in danger and Jesús was happy, or seemed to be. While he held my hand when we crossed one of the busy *avenidas,* I couldn't be sure if it was for his benefit or mine.

The next morning, as we were finishing breakfast, Anna received a call. She was wearing an enormous purple nightgown and her hair was wrapped in some kind of terrycloth babushka, but as if she was ashamed of having snubbed us the night before, she had invited Jesús and me in for room service at eight. I thought she was in a better mood, but with her it was impossible to be sure. Now, she listened quietly, asked a few questions and hung up. She looked at Jesús and then at me. Her face had the expression of a bulldog, mouth in a grimace, and I guessed she was no longer happy. "We have to go to Jesús' home," she said.

"Isn't this his home?"

She shook her head impatiently, as if I were an idiot. "He didn't live here, Daniel. We have to go to his actual home, his village, in the mountains. They say he has no papers."

It seemed late in the day to discover this fact, but Anna did not have the look of a person who was open to discussion and it didn't matter anyway. The questions would not have come for either of us because we lived in what Anna called a civilized country, where our every movement from bassinet to casket was elaborately chronicled by a dozen governmental agencies. Though I had never seen such documents myself, I knew they existed and even parents as absent-minded as mine would have known where they were or been able to locate them if pressed. For Jesús, this was not the case. Neither his government nor ours had any reason to accept the fact of his corporeal existence without papers. It was at once absurd and alarmingly simple. Jesús may not have understood the situation perfectly, but he knew Anna was angry and now began a lengthy examination of his hands. For the first time it occurred to me that this was more than a pleasure trip to him and that we might actually be unable to get him back to Milwaukee.

"Are the papers in his village?" I asked.

Anna asked Jesús something in Spanish and he nodded. "He thinks maybe," she said with disgust. "How about that? He waits until we're here to tell us he has no papers and now we're supposed to get on a bus, go out two hundred miles in the mountains on a wild-goose chase, and at the end of all this *maybe* they'll be there."

I could see that she was considering catching the next plane to America despite her promise not to desert Jesús. It hadn't been an easy trip for her and it was not about to get easier. I wondered how many years it had been since Anna had been on a bus. At the same time, I sympathized with Jesús. How was he supposed to have known he would need proof of his existence when he decided to travel illegally to Chicago and get a job as a candy dipper? The reason he had entered illegally in the first place was that he didn't have papers. He hadn't intended to meet Anna, didn't know what social security was, and probably didn't care. But none of this was very helpful to us now. The fact was that we were stuck in an ugly city trying to retrieve documents that might not exist so that we could bring Jesús into our country by the grace of Henry Kissinger. Looked at in this light, it seemed an unlikely task, but I didn't want to go back home. "Doesn't he have a birth certificate?" I asked.

"Birth certificate," Anna said scornfully. "He doesn't even know when he was born, except that he thinks it was in the summer. Big help that is. Henry can't help us if we can't find something that will prove Jesús is Jesús."

"Who else would he be?"

But Anna wasn't amused. "That's not the government's problem. You've never been an immigrant, Danny. You believe all that bullshit they teach you in school about America's open arms. The truth is it's not easy to go from one country to another, and it's practically impossible to get into the U.S., especially if you're not rich or well-educated." She thought for a moment, then she said, "Maybe there's a baptismal certificate or something."

I was surprised to discover that Jesús had religion. I had assumed that Indians would go to shamans rather than priests. "You mean he's Catholic?"

"Not really," Anna said. "Not the way you think of it; he wasn't a choir boy or anything. But the priests in these villages work hard to convert the Indians, so it could have happened that they baptized all the children when they were born. Anyway, we don't have a choice. He's got to have papers or he can't go back, Henry or no Henry. And that village is the only place they could be."

For the first time since we had been talking, anger was displaced by her characteristic optimism. One thing I admired about Anna was her conviction that nothing was ever beyond her. She may have been tired and annoyed by the situation, but now that she was here she was determined to succeed and some junior officer at the embassy was not going to dissuade her. She looked at me and nodded her head. "His mother is still alive so we go and ask her. Pack your bag, Danny."

〜

Jesús' village had no name. As with birth certificates, it had apparently been considered redundant to name a place everyone already knew. There was a rough logic to all this. After all, if you were living in the village already, there was no need to say where you were; and no outsiders had visited since the Spanish invasion or were likely to anytime soon. Yet, surprisingly, the village's obscurity proved no hindrance to our plans. It was in the Cuchumatanes range, near Huehuetenango, so the travel agent in Guatemala City suggested we take a bus there and then figure out how to accomplish the additional kilometers to Jesús' home. Inasmuch as I had spent a good deal of my young life planning for contingencies that didn't occur, I admired

136

his sangfroid at the notion of taking such a trip with Anna, who considered traveling in a car without power windows and air conditioning to be a hardship. Our bus looked as if it had been retired by the Milwaukee public schools some years ago, but we had no choice, though Anna swore under her breath as she climbed on board. There was one rack overhead for baggage and every seat and the narrow aisle were packed with Indians, screaming infants, chickens, and goats.

"I don't know if I can do this," Anna said to me.

I patted her broad back, which was already wet with sweat. "Sure you can," I said, deciding my role was to sound more enthusiastic than I felt. I tried to imagine what my mother would say to her friend. "It will be interesting," I said. "And maybe we can get some things at the market."

The idea of shopping momentarily cheered Anna. She squeezed my hand and managed to maneuver her bulk into a seat. "You're just like your mother," she said when we were all seated. "She can find something good in anything."

On board we were reasonably comfortable, but the bus's engine noise resonated throughout the trip, seeming at various moments to be coming through the floor, the windows, or even descending from overhead. We made good time on the Inter-American Highway out of Guatemala City, but once the road narrowed from four lanes to two, our progress slowed considerably because of the local traffic, which often consisted of more bicycles and horses than cars. As we climbed the hilly terrain the driver was constantly grinding his gears, causing the bus to jump and roll from side to side like an angry animal. It seemed inevitable that eventually it would keel over from exhaustion and tumble down the mountain, killing all of us.

The weather, which had been described as eternal springtime by the travel agent in Milwaukee, had been warm enough in the city, but when we ascended the barren peaks, it changed radically, requiring sweaters or blankets, which we then discarded on our descent. Dense forests lined the road, broken only by small, cultivated patches in which farmers were growing maize and beans. On the horizon, I could see a line of perpetually erupting volcanoes, and periodically sulfurous steam would rise from the ground alongside the road, as if the whole country was a volcano only superficially covered with a skin of dirt and trees.

Despite her complaining, Anna had come prepared with warm clothes and food. She fed Jesús and me a steady stream of mangos, papaya, and tortillas filled with small bits of beef or chicken. And when we finished eating, Anna, ever fastidious, produced wet-naps from somewhere to help us clean up. As we traveled, she carried on animated conversation with two women who were sitting in front of us. "What are you talking about?" I asked.

Anna puffed out her lips. "What is there to talk about with such people? They are mother and daughter and both have lost their husbands, so they are going back to their village."

I tried to look unobtrusively at the women in their black capes, but it was hard to attach the concept of age to either of them. They looked equally young or old, their faces equally lined, their expressions equally dour. But mainly I was struck by the otherworldly nature of the group as a whole. I had heard only vaguely before this the term third world, and I had no idea what the second world might be. I assumed that America was the first, if only because it was the only place I knew. But sitting on that bus it became dramatically clear that we couldn't share the same view of life as our fellow passengers and, knowing nothing about them, I found myself envying what I imagined to be the certainty of their lives. Their clothing, language, food, customs, whom they would marry, where they would live and work all grew out of the village in which they had been born, in all likelihood a village in which their families had lived for generations before them. I, on the other hand, had no family connections worth talking about beyond my mother, father, and brother and for all the opportunities of my country felt adrift in the world. I knew that by any objective standard my life was better than

138

these people; that is, I knew that even in a family like ours, I was privileged compared to most of the rest of the world, if only I had consistently compared myself to impoverished peasants with a life expectancy of thirty-five. But it was that stolid sense of belonging so obvious on the Indians' faces that I wanted. Riding the bus, I felt as insignificant as air.

Frequently, the bus would stop for reasons that were unclear to me and we would all get out and stand around a lean-to where Indians sold pots and rugs. I would walk away from the group and stretch my arms and legs, drawing curious stares from the other passengers. What I remember of that trip is the smell of sweat and rain and wet dirt, the smell of fecundity. Things seemed to be growing everywhere. Then I would walk back to the group, wishing I were one of the Indian babies so tightly strapped to their mothers' backs. Sometimes there would be a kind of café under a tarp supported by long wooden poles. Silent women heated water for tea on a woodstove and sold little cakes and bottles of uncarbonated soda. It was impossible to guess what flavor these drinks were; they had no taste beyond being overpoweringly sweet. I imagined my teeth rotting as I drank. There were no bathrooms on or off the bus and up and down the road Indian women squatted, sending rivulets of urine down the hill toward us. Though we were traveling for hours, Anna never availed herself of the outdoor toilets and seldom even got off the bus, remaining alone in splendid isolation as Jesús and I mingled with the others.

It made me appreciate anew the journey Jesús had undertaken. I wondered as we shifted back and forth in the narrow seats if, despite all her complaining, Anna didn't appreciate this as well, if perhaps this was the reason she acted as she did. In any case, the fact that she was willing to go to all this trouble to try to locate his papers represented to me an earnest of her love for him and I was touched because I wanted it to be true.

Toward dusk, we had been ascending a mountain for about twenty minutes when the bus made an unscheduled stop, shuddering to a halt so abruptly that I thought we must have hit an animal.

Packs and suitcases fell to the floor and there was much commotion among the passengers as everyone craned his neck to little avail because of the ground fog that rose around the bus like smoke. Then what looked like a young farmer carrying a machete appeared in the doorway and ordered everyone off. What struck me immediately were the man's intense black eyes, which scanned the passengers as we walked past, though he said nothing.

Outside, more men appeared out of the fog and they were obviously not farmers as they wore bandoliers and carried an assortment of ill-matched rifles. Dressed simply in loose white pants and collarless shirts, some of the men wore straw hats with bandannas twisted around their crowns while others wore brightly colored turbans and looked like pirates. They all seemed as serious as their leader, but I had no idea why they had stopped our bus nor who they were. I assumed they were robbers, but the men were quiet and respectful as they made their way among us, helping the women and children to the ground, seeming somewhat apologetic for putting us out, but far from being annoyed by this the other passengers were frankly curious. No one seemed in any hurry to get moving again.

Three men in city trousers and flowered shirts who had been sitting together in the back of the bus were separated out of the group at rifle point and the leader spoke to them briefly in muffled tones. Then they were handcuffed together and led off into the fog. The leader moved slowly down our line, speaking to some of the passengers in what I took to be a reassuring manner, kissing children like a politician, and seeming completely at ease. When he reached our little group, he looked at Anna and me with undisguised curiosity, before engaging Jesús in conversation. Though they were not speaking a Spanish I recognized, I knew they were talking about us because occasionally the man would gesture in our direction or even turn back and look at Anna in wonder. I understood the word *patojo*, which Jesús had told me meant boy, but little else registered with the exception of Huehuetenango, perhaps because the man wanted to know where we were going. When they finished the man patted Jesús on the shoulder, apparently in approval. After this they examined our luggage in a casual way, picking up first one item then another, though they seemed unconcerned and didn't give the impression of being in search of anything in particular. Eventually, we were all allowed back on the bus and we continued on our way.

Later, Jesús told me that the men who had been taken were soldiers on leave who were returning to their posts in the mountains. The rebel leader had been curious about Anna, Jesús reported, and he was impressed that such a woman was not only with him, but that she would make such a trip since few white women had previously been seen in this area. Jesús blushed furiously as he told me this, but his pride was obvious.

The men were not what I would have expected guerrillas to be, but my knowledge consisted entirely of John Wayne movies and the occasional propaganda film. What I knew of revolutionary movements was that they flourished in countries in which the women weren't pretty and it was hard to find good shoes. Yet these men had seemed polite almost to the point of being deferential. It was confusing. Jesús said that in other countries, the revolutionaries were ruthless, but that in Guatemala people thought the army was unreasonably brutal and corrupt and so most sided with the rebels. The war between the two groups had been going on for decades and Jesús seemed to doubt anything fundamental would ever come of it. As we arrived in Huehuetenango that evening, however, I couldn't help but think of the young soldiers who had been taken from the bus. Under the circumstances, I might have sided with the rebels, but I had never been close to a war before, any kind of war, and I found myself feeling unreasonably upset by the almost certain prospect of death.

The bus swung through the nearly deserted town and stopped at what I assumed would be the market. Anna, Jesús, and I retrieved our luggage and stood looking at each other in the dim light of the square. While she had said nothing about it, I could tell that the encounter with the guerrillas had shaken Anna, too, despite the leader's admiration for her, and she was uncharacteristically silent. Jesús was quiet too. As I stepped down, I had the sense that a feeling of hopelessness pervaded the place we had come to, and I wondered how much farther we had to go to get to Jesús' village and how it could be any more desolate than this. But there was no turning back now. The bus had gone, leaving us alone here.

In the distance I saw a sign advertising a hotel in faded green light. "Why don't we see if they have any rooms?" I suggested. We couldn't stand out there all night and I thought we might feel better if we had at least arranged for our night's lodging.

Anna was crying. Her whole body was shaking and Jesús was holding her. Now she enclosed me in her capacious bosom and said, "Daniel, I'm sorry, but would you just take care of this, please? I can't move."

I walked the two blocks to the hotel where with some difficulty I made myself understood to the desk clerk, a swarthy man in a stained navy blazer and open-necked yellow shirt. A cart for our luggage was discovered and Anna, Jesús, and I were deposited in a large dank room on the second floor furnished with three single beds. I wondered if Anna would object to our sleeping in the same room, but the bus ride seemed to have robbed her of fastidiousness and she was in no mood now to complain about anything. She simply collapsed on the bed nearest the door and was soon breathing heavily in sleep. I considered trying to separate the room with a blanket and clothesline, as I had seen in movies, but under the circumstances this seemed like a rather quaint precaution. In the end, we all fell asleep in our clothes without eating dinner.

Fourteen

A Village with No Name

Things looked better in the morning. Though there was no bath in our room, Anna persuaded the manager to allow her to use his private apartment while Jesús and I made do with leftover wet-naps. After breakfast on the small patio, Anna and I went to the market while Jesús made inquiries about the next stage of our journey—for so I had begun to think of it—not so much a trip as a pilgrimage, open-ended with no destination in sight. After all, we had already been interdicted by a rebel army and seen soldiers led to their certain death. I now thought of the mission to acquire Jesús' documents as being heroic and possibly tragic.

As it happened, market day was every day in Huehuetenango and by nine A.M. the little square was filled. Brick archways sheltered the sidewalks and a run-down band shell loomed over the scene from the second floor of city hall. In one corner of the park was a relief map of the department, showing the road through the mountains to San Juan Ixcay and other towns on the way to the Mexican border state of Chiapas. I didn't know how far we were going, but it looked like an arduous trip, and considering the difficulty we had experienced getting here from Guatemala City, I wasn't optimistic about Anna's ability to make it.

When I returned to the market from the park, however, she was moving swiftly enough to belie her bulk, going inevitably from one stall to another and then doubling back to compare prices. She had enlisted a small boy to help her with her purchases and she was bargaining with great flair with several traders in an exotic blend of Spanish, German, and English, which surprisingly they seemed to understand perfectly. When language failed, Anna would make large sweeping gestures with her hands, but she had already discovered the key to shopping here, that a palmed *quetzal* would go a long way. It was clear to me from the expression on the Indians' faces that they did not often see a gringa like Anna, but of course that would have been equally true among our neighbors in Milwaukee. Anna was one of a kind. Watching her operate in this small out-of-the-way place, however, I was again impressed with her ability to reinvent herself effortlessly depending on the circumstances. She had had an incredibly tragic life, starting with her birth, but she seemed not to think about this and thus it seemed to have little effect on her. Despite having lost her family to the Nazis and her youth to Paul, despite having been deprived of educational opportunities she should logically have had, the result in Anna as we knew her was not depression but verve for life, for everything. It reminded me of the time I had learned she loved to swim. I had assumed that a person as large as Anna would have neither the ability nor the motivation to pursue sports, and that she would be reluctant to show herself publicly in a bathing suit. But she swam three times a week at the Jewish Community Center and seemed utterly without self-consciousness. She was buoyant in every way and unsentimental to boot, unwilling ever to pause to consider where she had come or what she had left behind. As much as she annoyed me at times, I loved and admired her.

By the time I persuaded her to leave, Anna had amassed an impressive pile of *huipiles,* the chemise-like shirts worn by the Indian women, along with bags, sashes, and serapes. Though I seldom saw such things at home, Anna felt obliged to return with gifts for Alfred and my family, at the least, and as she pointed out, everything she bought had cost less than ten dollars. Since Jesús and I would be responsible for transporting all of this, and since I knew that Anna was far from finished with her purchases, I was not as excited as she was with these bargains, but I was glad to see her smiling.

We found Jesús waiting at the hotel with a thin laconic Indian dressed in a UCLA sweatshirt. Jesús introduced us to Jorge, a friend from his village, only recently returned from the States, which explained the sweatshirt. Jorge would drive us to the village in his truck, Jesús said, for a small price, an incredible stroke of good fortune, which was leavened only slightly when we saw the truck, an ancient Chevrolet, whose passenger seat springs were completely exposed and whose blistered paint revealed large holes in the skin of the vehicle. I expected Anna to insist on some more conventional form of transportation, but she could be quite practical when the situation called for it and she understood without asking that Jesús' village would not be among the destinations of the large tourist buses idling in the town square. If we wanted to get there, it would either be with Jorge's help or walking. The choice was easy.

The only question was where we would sit, for in addition to the sprung seat, the bed of the truck was piled high with rusted junk and left little room for passengers. Taking charge, Anna ordered the truck emptied of the detritus that had gathered in its bed and Jorge knew well enough not to argue the point. Then Anna borrowed a large chair from the hotel lobby and had the men fasten it to the truck with ropes. When this had been accomplished, she climbed up with Jesús' help and sat like a monarch looking down on all of us. Jesús and Jorge looked at each other and shrugged. The arrangement would have to do. Jesús and I squeezed into the passenger compartment and thus we began the final leg of the trip to his village.

It would be generous to call our route a road. Barely wide enough for the truck, it was actually little more than a path for cattle, incredibly rutted and overhung with vines that crashed against the windshield as we moved slowly along. Any fellowship I had previously felt for those people who went south for the winter had faded quickly with the seedy reality of Guatemala City, and now it was replaced by a dull anxiety about the wisdom of our ever undertaking such a mission. I was not quite sure what I would tell my class if I managed to return, but I understood intuitively that this was not a place Abe Goodstein would choose for a vacation.

There was a sense of being completely removed from time, which might have been liberating to others but wasn't for me. There were of course no telephones and thus no way of contacting my parents in case of an accident. I thought melodramatically of being hacked to death by machetes when the guerrillas returned and then left to die alone in the jungle with no one ever knowing what had become of me. Of course, what difference would it have made to me if I was dead? Yet it did make a difference, or it seemed to at the time. Death, like life, seemed to require validation, ceremony, and now I was seized by the certainty that my life would end in this remote place, smelling of wet dirt and manure.

Jesús, too, seemed worried as we bounced along, though he said nothing. Only Anna, stoic in her lofty superiority and borne along like an ancient pharaoh in her sedan chair, was enjoying herself, and called out periodically, "Look, Danny, those purple flowers are so beautiful. I wish your mother was here." It was as if she were Lady Bountiful leading a group of faculty wives on a tour of the university arboretum, but this incarnation of Anna was surprising because she had never evinced the slightest interest in horticulture before and I wondered if perhaps she was nervous too and this was her way of showing it.

Mercifully, the distance to the village wasn't great, though because we had to stop frequently to clear the trail, it took us nearly three hours to get there. But then, suddenly, we emerged, sweat-stained and exhausted, from the forest onto a mountain plateau with the standing peaks of the Cuchumatanes rising overhead in the distance.

Directly in front of us was a collection of wood shacks with tin roofs circled around a community fountain and rimmed by a dirt road. Standing in front of the fountain, as if our arrival had somehow been announced, was an old woman dressed in black, wearing an elaborate lace mantilla, as if she were prepared either to pray or mourn. I wondered idly how long she had been standing there. Our time of arrival could not have been more uncertain and I had no idea how the news could have been communicated from Huehue. I thought of Indian drums or perhaps carrier pigeons, but this mystery was never to be explained.

Now, Jorge turned off the engine and, on cue, the old Chevrolet's springs relaxed bringing the truck to a level with the waist-high weeds that surrounded us. The old lady and her party of three approached slowly through the mountain meadow. No one had spoken, but now Jesús stepped forward and embraced the woman. She tolerated this, but her face was a mask with severe vertical lines running down either side, framing her impressive nose and dark eyes. "My mother," Jesús said, in explanation.

Jesús' mother had Anna at a disadvantage since despite the splendor of her throne, there was no dignified way to dismount the truck, but this didn't seem to bother Anna at all. Jesús and I understood that we were peripheral to this meeting, aides-de-camp to our respective generals, and as such, I helped Anna down from the truck bed to stand in the rocky pasture. In its own way, it was an impressive sight: the old woman in black from the native village and Anna, sweaty and bow-legged, but unbowed, with her ruined face and monumental physique. Though it made no sense, the image that came to mind was of two rams facing one another for dominance over the flock. This face-off seemed to continue for an hour as the two women examined each other with curiosity, but in reality it could only have been a few minutes. Then Jesús' mother said something unintelligible, though I recognized his name.

Anna and I waited for a translation and Jesús smiled broadly. We discovered that what his mother had said was: "I am at peace. At last, I can die. I have found a woman who will care for my son."

I thought this was an odd thing to say, if only because I did not then see death as a relief, a welcome destination. I wondered if my own mother was waiting expectantly for similar surcease, but the exclamation by Jesús' mother did not have the quality of a dirge and now she walked toward Anna with outstretched arms and the two women embraced. There was something momentous about this and I think everyone who was there felt it, though Jesús seemed somewhat embarrassed at being referred to by both as a kind of client to be cared for. Nevertheless, the tension was broken and now Anna walked arm-in-arm with Jesús' mother up the hill, leaving the rest of us to transport the bags since it was clear that the Chevrolet was finished for the day and perhaps for good.

—

Even to call Jesús' home a village would be a misrepresentation if one takes by the word those tidy collections of red-roofed houses, found on postcards, filled with cheerful peasants. What lay before us were perhaps ten dilapidated shacks with dirt floors and no windows. There were no municipal buildings, no church, no market, no shops. Rather than the colorful Indian crockery we had seen in Guatemala City and Huehue, these people cooked either on the open fire or used old kerosene and gasoline cans that had been cut in half. Children ran around naked and the adults were for the most part barefoot. Yet, the people did not seem discontented or sullen; as far as I could tell they were neither happy nor unhappy that we had arrived. We were just there, like weather. Still, it was amazing to me that Jesús had actually grown up here and that anyone chose to stay on, for there seemed to be nothing to stay here for, nothing to do. The village was situated at too high an altitude to grow crops and it was cold and windy. Sheep and goats grazed in the meadow but the people couldn't all be shepherds. As hard as it was to understand how the village endured, however, it was equally perplexing to imagine why it had been established in the first place. Who or what had inspired the founding fathers to settle here? What great battle had been fought, what valuable resource lay buried beneath our feet? There was neither water nor natural shelter. A few scrawny cows stood watching, but it was hard to imagine them being up to the task of giving milk.

In memory, our apartment in Milwaukee now seemed like the height of luxury, and for some reason I remembered my mother being concerned about including Jesús in our conversation the night we had met him, when he and Anna and Alfred came for dinner. Unwittingly, my father had been right then: after escaping from this place, conversation would seem to be the last thing one would crave. Indeed, language had lost a good deal of its urgency for me since I had virtually been without it for a week. The few times I had tried to communicate in Spanish had been futile and I understood little of the stew of words constantly flowing around me. Even if I could make my immediate needs known, there was no room for subtlety, no way, for example, of describing my feelings or reactions to things. As a result, I experienced an interior life, seeing more and saying less. Still, that wasn't all bad; at home, I sometimes thought too much was said, felt, analyzed. Now, practical matters edged into my mind. I wondered where we would sleep or if, somehow, we were expected to retrace our tracks to Huehuetenango for the night, which seemed impossible.

As we approached the fountain, the rest of the inhabitants of the village came forward. There were several women, a couple of men, and Jesús was greeted like a returning warrior: the men embraced and the women and children bowed their heads in respect. Though I had no way of knowing what they were thinking, the village was at such a remove from anything remotely resembling civilization, that it was hard to imagine anyone coming here. In all likelihood, people just left, for Huehuetenango, Guatemala City, Mexico, or, as in Jesús' case, the United States. From this perspective, his emigration would have taken no less courage than the voyages of Columbus or Magellan. And, of course, Jesús had not had the power of the crown behind him when he set out. In fact, he had no support at all.

With difficulty, a chair was found for Anna and with night coming on, she sat before the fire, holding a gourd of cider in one hand and looking oddly content in the wild mountain setting. She looked at me and laughed. "What do you think of this, Daniel? Isn't this unbelievable? I mean, can you imagine Alfred in this place?"

This seemed so absurd to her that it set off another round of laughing and coughing, but the truth was that I was more worried about the possible presence of wolves beyond the fire. The blackness outside our little circle was absolute and made me doubt the existence of light anywhere in the world. But I thought it better not to say anything about this to Anna. Let her be amused by the situation. "Do they have Jesús' papers?" I asked, changing the subject.

Anna had a vague smile on her face as she surveyed the mountain peaks, which were scarlet in the fading light. I wondered if she was drunk. "I don't know," she said. "I haven't asked anyone yet."

I found this mildly annoying. After all, this was the reason we had come and I had no desire to stay any longer than was absolutely necessary. But the royal welcome seemed to have gone to Anna's head and now I wondered if by some perverse turn of fate she would insist on staying on in the village. "But you're going to ask, aren't you?"

She nodded her head to some unheard music. "We don't want to be rude," she said quietly. "They're going to have a feast for us. Relax and enjoy yourself, Danny. How often would you find yourself in a place like this?"

It was hard to imagine how the rudiments of a meal could be scraped together in this place, much less a feast, but it seemed pointless to argue, given Anna's state of mind. Anyway, I reasoned, it wasn't really my problem. Still, I was surprised that Anna, so enamored of her spotless kitchen, could contemplate a meal around a campfire with such complaisance. At home, she wouldn't even go on a picnic for fear of ants. Yet somehow hygiene had become a forgotten science and she seemed completely unconcerned about rodents, bacteria, or anything else. Her mouth hung open slightly in a somnolent leer and her expression told me, if I needed to be told, that there was nothing to be done. We would attend the feast and sleep in dirt-floored huts and then tomorrow we would find what we had come for. And if not tomorrow, then the next day, or the day after that.

I have no memory of the feast or even of going to bed that night, but I awoke alone in a hut whose walls were covered with rugs woven in what looked like red and blue dyed rope. At first, I was disoriented; I knew where I was, that is, in Guatemala, in Jesús' village, without being able to place my surroundings in a familiar context, and this made me vaguely anxious. It was similar to the feeling I had expressed to Alfred about the universe being uncontained, except now I *was* the universe, speeding uncontrollably toward an unknown destiny.

I threw off the blankets, pulled on a sweater and went outside, where a huge fire had been erected. My first thought was that they were going to roast us in the manner of white missionaries in the Congo, as enormous cauldrons boiled on either end of the fire. But no one showed the slightest interest in me, and as I edged closer, I noticed that a pile of rugs and some liquid soap were arranged next to the blaze while over to the side two women were scouring a large wooden tub with horsehair brooms.

I thought this might be some sort of saint's day that required ritual cleansing, but then Anna appeared, austere and immense, with her short hair swept back in waves and Jesús' mother attending her. All the men were immediately dismissed to the other end of the village where I found Jesús drinking bitter coffee and eating hard biscuits, a meal he offered to share with me. Jesús smiled and said that Anna was having a bath and since bathing was unusual in his village, it required some preparation. The water had been boiling since dawn. Yet no one seemed to consider Anna's request unreasonable. Having been given the approval of Jesús' mother, she was being received with courtesy and consideration by everyone. While it might seem ridiculous to insist on one's daily bath in a place where electricity and running water were unheard of, Anna might have said it was ridiculous to contemplate the trip in the first place, and she would have been right.

I describe all of this with detachment, as an outsider, because that's what I was. I was, or felt I was, completely unnecessary to the accomplishment of anything. Ostensibly, Anna had brought me along because I studied Spanish in school, but the cursory knowledge I had of the language had proved useless and Anna and I had hardly spoken since our arrival. She seemed to want me there to fill out the traveling party, but that was all. Being without any familiarity with the customs of the country produced an odd kind of displacement that I had never experienced. I now realized that perspective is everything, not timing, and that no truth could ever be absolute. I was in awe of the path Jesús' life had taken, but watching the preparations for Anna's bath, which allowing for scale, approached the magnitude of the Allied invasion of Normandy, produced a conjunction, and these unlikely worlds were merged. Having lived my life so entirely locked into my own perceptions, the scene in the village made me nearly dizzy with disassociation. I not only could not see the continuum between my previous experience and this; I could not even frame the idea of there being one. My life in Milwaukee and this village perched on the edge of an unknown mountain seemed rather to be occupying adjacent worlds.

Yet the bath proceeded in its stately way, with frequent calls for hot water, more towels, and soap being attended to by teams of native women until, finally, the task was accomplished and Anna was clean and dressed in her caftan once more. Then we were all summoned to another, small fire, on the other end of the dirt street where a plank table had been set for lunch. Before we ate, however, Jesús' mother produced a small rectangular box of hammered tin that she now opened in a manner suggestive of a priest's attitude toward the sarcophagi of ancient civilizations. When opened, however, the box revealed neither jewels nor shrunken heads. The contents were ordinary enough: what looked like a dog-eared bankbook, some rusted photographs, and, in a plush purple sack, a rosary. I was about to be disappointed when Jesús' mother reached beneath these treasures and produced a small card with some Latin characters superimposed over the sign of the cross. She handed this to Anna with both hands, as if it were an amulet.

Whether she knew why we needed this certificate was never clear to me, but it didn't seem to matter. What was occurring was more in the way of a changing of the guard. Jesús' mother was ceding responsibility for her son to Anna, in a kind of inversion of the traditional dowry produced by the father of the bride in a conventional wedding. The fact that Jesús would need someone to watch over him and care for him seemed obvious and beyond discussion for the two women. And Jesús himself became ever more childlike, laughing and joking with friends as all this was going on, a foolish smile on his face. There was, of course, no ceremony or talk of marriage; given the lack of certification in this society, there might not even have been such a thing. But people here cared for one another, especially in sickness and old age, that was clear enough, and this woman had recognized a kindred soul in Anna, though as far as I could tell they had not exchanged a single word in a common language.

Anna accepted the baptismal certificate with appropriate seriousness, hugging it to her breast, but then she looked at me and shrugged, unimpressed as always with the trappings of organized religion which in a strange way this was. I examined the certificate as well, but neither of us read Latin, and since everyone else was illiterate, it was impossible to determine if this document, whatever it was, would be enough to win a visa for Jesús. Still, it was just as clear that this was all there would ever be to mark Jesús' passage on the earth and that his mother had entrusted it to us. Whatever the officials might say, it seemed to me that this should be enough. Moreover, the look on Anna's face said everything that needed to be said. With the certificate in hand, she would retrace her steps and launch her assault on the American Embassy and she would not be turned away. Which allowed me to feel an enormous sense of relief. The trip had been an adventure, I'd admit that. But there was no question at all that I was glad to be leaving the village and glad to be going home to Milwaukee.

Fifteen

Remission

I have said that my mother placed great value on what she called experience and this inevitably covered a multitude of things. For her, a determined optimism was not merely a way of rationalizing misfortune, though it was certainly that; more important, it was a means of ordering life so that things seemed somewhat less random than they actually were. She did not actually say, for example, that my father's illness and our subsequent fall in the world had been a good experience from which we might learn things that would help us in life's journey, but at times I wondered if she thought so.

There could be no question, though, about our trip to Guatemala, and my mother hung on every word when Anna and I returned triumphant with Jesús' green card in hand and reported on our adventures in Central America. She showed particular interest in the guerillas, and was somewhat more restrained when Anna showed her the handicrafts she had purchased in Huehuetenango. When we were alone she said, "What a wonderful experience, Daniel. This is something you'll have for the rest of your life."

I had enjoyed the trip, if one may be said to enjoy something as uncomfortable and arduous as the trip to Guatemala had been, but I was glad to be home. Moreover, the dissociation I had felt in the village with no name recurred in Milwaukee to the extent that once I was home it seemed impossible that such a place as we had visited could actually exist. The unreality of the whole thing produced in me an understanding that it was possible to be both in and out of the world simultaneously, whereas before I had assumed that what I saw before me was all there was or could be. I suppose I had Henry Kissinger to thank for this, and whenever I saw his picture in the newspaper, usually entering or leaving some function, I imagined an essential connection between us. In some dim way, I thought the time would come when I would appear in his Washington office and the great man would ask about Anna and Guatemala and I would show him slides from our trip. But if such a meeting was destined to occur, it hasn't yet and as time goes by it seems increasingly likely to me that it ever will.

Still, I was glad we had been able to help Jesús. Within a week, he had found a job paying more than the minimum wage at a potato chip factory and had moved into Anna's apartment, thus becoming a permanent part of our community. I would meet him early in the morning for coffee on the front steps or when he was returning home in his work clothes and he would always shake hands with me and ask, "How are you, señor?" I wondered if there was an edge of mockery to this, referring perhaps to my nonexistent Spanish or the possibility that our enforced intimacy in Guatemala had made him feel personally exposed, but if this was so Jesús never revealed it except for his greeting, which would never vary in all the years I would know him.

～

An unexpected benefit of the trip was that I was now seen as a kind of world traveler, perhaps a junior diplomat, by Miss Harmon and the others at Campus School. Dr. Patterson made me address a school assembly and bring in the native clothes and cheap gifts we had purchased, and since Anna had had the foresight to buy post-cards and slides of Antigua at the airport as we were leaving, I could now claim I had actually been there and carried on with some fervor about the difficulties of preserving a native culture in the face of the onslaught of tourism. In Miss Harmon's eyes this alone justified the time away from school.

A more tangible benefit arrived a few days after my presentation in the form of an engraved invitation, placed discreetly on my desk at school, by Madeline Zimmer, to come to dinner at her home. Madeline was not someone I knew well; indeed, I doubt that we had exchanged words during the year to this point. But I had admired from afar her firm buttocks and full breasts. She had a small mouth with bruised lips and deep-set eyes that made her look oddly like a raccoon when she wore eye shadow. I examined the invitation carefully since the only engraved stationery I had ever seen previously had come from the White House when Kissinger wrote Anna. The paper was off-white and expensive, or seemed to be, and on the front of the card there was a drawing of what looked like a mansion with "The Surf" printed below in scarlet. I had never received such an elaborate invitation to anything before and it had never occurred to me that adolescents would have their own personal stationery.

"She lives with her grandparents, I think," Joey said, when I asked him about Madeline. "There was some Schlitz money in the family I think and they live in this old dump on the lake, but no one except them calls it anything." He took the card in his hands now and examined it closely. "Maybe you can get in her pants," he said dismissively.

"Is it a hotel?" I was still focused on the drawing of the mansion.

Joey shrugged. "I guess you could call it a hotel, except no one they don't know ever stays there. It's not like the Schroeder or the Pfister."

"So it's a rooming house?"

He shook his head. "Not exactly. You'll see. I've only been there once myself."

I stifled the impulse to ask Joey if he had had any luck with Madeline because the truth was that I was pleased to have been asked. My only experience thus far with women had been with Daisy, and as exotic as that had been, you couldn't really call an assignation with your cleaning lady in the basement a date. This would be different, I thought. Besides, I was eager to capitalize on my new celebrity, such as it was. I wasn't sure of the protocol in such situations, whether I should write in reply, but I decided to do what seemed natural and just walked over to her desk and told Madeline I'd be happy to come to her house.

Social Milwaukee had grown in spurts starting with the large mansions on Prospect Avenue and then moving out along Lake Drive until the wealthy gradually accumulated in the northern suburbs. Some of the old places had names, or had been named by others, like the Pabst Mansion, but few really wealthy people lived on the East Side anymore. Many of the big houses had been broken up into apartments or offices and some had been destroyed to make room for high-rise condominiums. It was unique to Campus School that the kids would occasionally brag about the size of the pillars on their houses, their grounds, or stables, but to me it was all the same and represented an attractive if forbidden world that I had now been invited to enter.

The Surf was located on lower Prospect Avenue and the neighborhood wasn't as grand as it once had been. Nevertheless, considering where we lived, it was a definite step up. The building itself was solid and constructed of pink granite with two narrow pillars framing the entrance. A small brass plaque to the left of the door announced simply "The Surf," though some breakers filled out the panel and I thought perhaps a palm tree lurked in the background, which would have been extraordinary in Milwaukee.

Given Joey's description of faded elegance, I thought perhaps Madeline would open the door herself, but instead an older man welcomed me, took my coat and ushered me into a dim, wainscoted parlor. He was perhaps seventy, stooped with a spray of white hair. He offered his thin hand and introduced himself as Henry. Then he stood expectantly, as if he was waiting for orders. I didn't know what was appropriate in this situation, so said nothing and eventually

Henry bowed himself out of the room, leaving me alone to wait for Madeline.

The furniture consisted of several sofas, a loveseat, and an overstuffed chair, all done in burgundy velour. Bookcases lined the walls beneath several sailing scenes in ornate frames with small lamps mounted upon them to illuminate the pictures. I climbed onto one of the sofas to examine a group of fisherman pulling their boats onto a rocky coast. At closer inspection I saw that the portrait had been taken from a book rather than painted and there was a printed caption that read, "Home is the Sailor, Home from the Sea."

I almost fell off my perch when I heard a noise behind me and turned to see Madeline, who appeared to find nothing unusual about my standing on her couch. She was dressed in a purple velveteen dress and had applied so much makeup that I could barely see her eyes, but I was glad I was no longer alone in the room. Now she smiled and said, "Granny loves art."

She led me into a long sepulchral hallway that opened into a large dining room lighted by a dusty chandelier and some wall sconces. There were several elderly people seated already and now Madeline took my arm and presented me to her grandparents and two or three older men, who seemed to be members of the household, though I did not think they were relatives. When we were all seated Henry brought food at a stately pace, assisted by a sullen woman in a black uniform. Then we sat expectantly, waiting for the signal to begin. Finally, Madeline's grandmother lifted her fork and everyone fell onto his or her food in an attitude of prayer.

Madeline's grandparents barely seemed to notice me, nor did the other guests; indeed, considering the lighting and their hearing aids, they might not have known I was there. Every so often they would direct a question to Madeline, or Maddy as she was called, but I ate my roast beef undisturbed. I liked the dim grandeur of the room, but the Surf seemed like an odd place for a young girl to grow up and I wondered how Madeline had landed there. Our move to Milwaukee had impressed me with the general helplessness of children before the whims of their parents. People had children with no apparent idea of what would happen or where life would take them, and then, when whatever happened did, they acted as if the disruption to the child's life was incidental, even unimportant.

After dessert, Madeline and I excused ourselves and went downstairs to what seemed to be her apartment. She talked incessantly about kids at school and Miss Harmon, with whom she apparently had trouble, and about the Surf. She told me that her parents were on an extended European tour and had been gone for five years. There was the faint suggestion of an association with royalty, but she was vague about the details. Then she asked me about Guatemala, after which we sat looking at each other, wondering what came next.

At length, Madeline took action. She came over and stood in front of me. "You're cute," she announced. Then she pushed me backward onto her bed and fell on top of me, pressing her red lips determinedly against mine. After Daisy, Madeline seemed somewhat inexperienced as she moved my hands busily over her body, but she was purposeful and I have always admired women who know what they want.

The primary emotion I experienced under Madeline's assault was confusion. As she fumbled with my belt, I tried to work my way through a welter of foundation garments, keeping an eye on the door as I did for fear Henry might charge in with a posse of octogenarians in his wake. But we were alone and soon Madeline became frustrated with my incompetence and sat up long enough to reach behind and unhook her bra leaving pendulous breasts free to dangle in my face like ripe melons. Given the situation, it seemed completely natural to fasten my lips around her nipple and this was clearly what Madeline had in mind since a series of high-pitched cries and panting followed. I was still limited in my movements, however, pinned by Madeline's large body with her breasts nearly suffocating me. Finally, she pulled back and said, "Do you want to do it?"

What I really wanted was to catch my breath, but this would have seemed churlish. There was only one honorable way to answer her question, so I nodded my head in the affirmative. As if this was what she had been waiting for, Madeline lifted herself off me, adjusted the stack of Johnny Mathis records on the stereo, and was out of her dress in what seemed no time at all. I don't know why I didn't hesitate, why the myriad consequences of making love to Madeline didn't present themselves to me as a caution, but they didn't. I took off my pants and then we were writhing in the warm passion of youth on her bed and I had forgotten about Henry, her grandparents, or anyone else. It wasn't love; I had cared more for Daisy. But it was enjoyable and I wanted it to last longer than the few minutes it did, after which Madeline emitted a small squeak of satisfaction and fell asleep in my arms.

Unaccountably, I was wide-awake, but I wasn't sure what was expected of me now. In the movies, people always smoked, but Madeline was dead to the world, so I waited, examining her dimpled ceiling and listening until the records ran their course. An hour later, I extricated myself from Madeline's sweaty embrace and retrieved my clothes. She was lying, legs spread on the bed, her sex still dewy with love, which made me desire her again. Rather than wake her, however, I got dressed and returned to the front hall to look for my jacket. The vestibule was deserted and there was no sign of Henry. Apparently, bedtime came early at the Surf. Eventually, I found my coat in a closet and let myself out, pleased to leave but not unhappy that I had come. I thought I would see Madeline again.

꜒

My lessons with Professor Braun had resumed upon my return and while he continued to praise me, we both knew that I would never be a musician. I was reasonably musical and reasonably talented, but from watching my father over the course of my life, I realized without anyone ever telling me that reason had little to do with success in art. This did not stop Professor Braun from taking me seriously. Before entering what he always called his studio, I was required to remove my coat and boots and wash my hands. Then he would inspect my fingernails, and if all was in order, I was allowed to approach the gleaming black Steinway parlor grand that he called his jewel. Despite the professor's fussiness, however, I began to enjoy the piano for the first time and I admired his devotion to his craft.

We had worked through the elementary books quickly, and while I could still play the occasional folk song, for some time I had been making my way slowly through one of the less complicated Mozart sonatas. As it happened, Professor Braun had no substantial disagreement with my father in this; it was only that he disliked being told how to teach.

Often I would practice at home in the afternoon after school and now, as an earnest of his resolution to change his attitude, my father would often come out and sit on the couch and read while I played. I can only imagine what self-control this took, but my father betrayed neither irritation nor impatience, and while I was made self-conscious by his presence at first, I soon gained the confidence to plunge wildly on with the Mozart, making many interesting mistakes along the way.

One afternoon, several weeks after our return from Guatemala, I was mired in the second movement of the sonata when my father entered the room and leaned against the piano, an interested expression on his face. When I paused, he said, "Let me try that, Daniel."

He hadn't played publicly in over a year and not at all for several months, so I had assumed the disease had taken that from him forever. Now he sat down, adjusted the dials on the seat easily, and laced his fingers together and pushed them out toward the ceiling in a stretch. Though it seems strange to say so, what I felt then was a mixture of suspense and fear. He had never interrupted my practicing before to play and I was afraid that he'd be unable to perform and that we'd have to share his embarrassment.

I need not have worried. My father's long fingers blanketed the keys and the sound that came from the piano had no relation to what had gone before. It would be comic to say that he was better than I was, or even that he played the Mozart better. The truth was that as musicians we did not occupy the same universe, for the effortless grace with which he moved through the piece suggested another activity entirely. It was as if he and the composer had collaborated as the notes, previously labored and overstressed, now took on substance and meaning, alternately languorous and playful, inevitable. As my father played, he bowed close to the keys, his expression serene, eyes closed, with an occasional sigh. In his playing that afternoon, he communicated not so much what he had lost but what music could be in the right hands. For him, it had never been a tired succession of lessons, assignments, and recitals, but rather a way of being more completely alive than most people ever know. And if I was not completely aware of this that afternoon, I sensed it then and was touched by him.

When he finished, he said simply, "That's what it's supposed to sound like."

Professor Braun had played the sonata for me, but my father without even looking at the music had driven that performance out of my mind for good. It was more effective than any argument my father would ever make on the subject. "I'll never be able to do that," I said.

"Probably not," my father said. He could withhold criticism but false modesty was beyond him. "But so what? You'll do other things with your life, better things perhaps."

Emboldened, I said, "I didn't think you could play anymore."

My father nodded slowly. "It's a funny thing," he said. "The last few weeks I've felt stronger, more energetic. I've even been taking short walks without my cane."

I had noticed this without noticing it. Children rarely enter their parents' lives without invitation. "Are you cured?" I asked.

My father laughed, his large teeth flashing in the somber room. "Let's hope so," he said. Then quietly, "It doesn't do any harm to hope." Then the smile faded. "I doubt it," he said. "I went to the doctor and he told me that this is a remission, that it happens."

"What? What happens?"

My father looked at the ceiling and then down at the piano again. "Suddenly, for no reason, the disease stops progressing. Not that you're back to normal, but for a while you're not getting worse anymore."

I thought this over for a moment. The idea of remission seemed to me to typify my life: I would be going along from disaster to disaster, then improbably, something wonderful would happen and all the misery would be behind me and forgotten. Except my father hadn't said he felt wonderful, only that the disease had stopped progressing. In his world of small triumphs, that might be noteworthy, but he remained cautious, still expecting the worst, and who could blame him? "How long do they last?" I asked. "Remissions."

My father puffed out his cheeks, and then exhaled. "No one knows. Not everyone even has them, but for some people it lasts their whole life."

"So they're cured?" It seemed like a miracle.

He nodded. "Sort of. They're not the way they were before they got sick, but they don't get any worse. I'd settle for that."

It was something to hope for, something far preferable to what had seemed like an inevitable progression from cane to walker, walker to wheelchair, wheelchair to nursing home. "I'll bet you're having one of those," I said.

Then we sat enveloped in optimism on the tufted leather piano bench with Mozart in front of us. Finally, my father said, "You used to be a baseball player, didn't you? Back in Madison, I mean."

"Sure," I said slowly. This was usually a prelude to a lecture about my misspent life. Perhaps I had done something wrong without knowing it, broken a window, who knew what? The possibilities were endless.

"Why don't you go and get your mitt now," my father said. "We'll have a catch."

I wondered if his medication had induced hallucinations. He had never played catch with me before, never come to my games, never evinced the slightest interest in the idea of sports. His usual position was that America was a country of hobbyists, perennially in search of fun, and that our obsession with sports and the media's preoccupation with it was the most dramatic illustration of this. "You want to play catch?" I said.

He shrugged. "Why not? Who knows how long this warm weather will last?"

So my father and I left the piano and went out on the rutted front walk and threw a baseball back and forth. I remember him standing stiff and tall, wearing an old Yankees cap. He didn't use a glove or otherwise protect his hands, as he once would certainly have done. His hands were no longer what was important to him. But when he threw to me, the ball had perfect loft and carry and nestled softly in my mitt as if he had as thoroughly perfected this new art as he had the Mozart. We played for over an hour, neither of us wanting that time to end, and only went inside when it became too dark to see the ball.

During this period, I was only dimly aware of the inherent contradictions in my life, that is, the sense of being expected to assume the responsibilities of a man while still being occupied with the confusing apparatus of boyhood. What seemed most peculiar to me was my parents' passive acceptance of this. There was never any feeling, or none that I knew of, that perhaps I should be spared, for example, full knowledge of my father's condition, including the fact that it often had the effect of making him incontinent and impotent. Much of this, I think, was due to my mother's need to talk to someone, but it seemed odd that she considered me to be the appropriate person. Not that I was alone in this; certainly she talked to Anna as well. But what my mother saw as the tragedy of her life was so omnipresent that in all likelihood, if she had thought of my needs, she would have decided that they were necessarily subservient to the greater good of the family, and in this she may have been right.

Whatever her reasoning may or may not have been, each day I rose, got dressed, prepared my own breakfast, and walked the eight blocks to Campus, where the talk was of parties, vacations, and the various schools others were considering for high school the following year. Because none of this seemed very crucial to me, I would float on the edge of conversations and in so doing gained the reputation of being somewhat superior and aloof. This was ironic since I actually saw myself as being socially inferior to everyone, with the possible exception of my friend Joey Goodstein, whose father was a well-known criminal.

It was probably more significant that I did not consider myself to be an active force in my own life. I was not aware, for example, of choosing what I wanted to do in the future or even of there really being a choice. It seemed to me that there were large forces of which I could only be dimly aware and that they would invariably push me in one direction or another. And I thought this was true of everyone. If you were rich, it followed logically that you would find it easier to acquire the necessary education and connections that would allow you to remain rich. If you were poor, however, a new path needed to be broken if you were to be successful. My mother had once been rich, but that was before my time. She became poor, for reasons I didn't fully understand but which had to do with love, an overpowering force. Something would eventually happen to me, I thought, but in the meantime I saw myself as a passive recipient of my fate, not an actor in life's drama. I was surprised, therefore, when one day Miss Harmon told me she had put in my name for a scholarship at the Country Day School, a preparatory school that channeled the rich and powerful into the Ivy League. I had not previously considered the possibility of my attending this school or any like it; in fact, I didn't really know that one could apply for admission. I assumed that a select few were chosen by some arcane formula, but that whatever it was would remain forever mysterious to me. And while I didn't want to reveal my ignorance I had no idea what putting in my name meant, or to whom I had been submitted.

Miss Harmon sat back at her desk, waiting for my reaction, her huge horse-face being finally so fascinating as to disallow any disagreement with anything she might wish to say. I felt an erection begin to form and this made me blush.

Confusing my sexual embarrassment with pleasure at her announcement, Miss Harmon patted me on the shoulder. "Your interview is on Saturday," she told me. "I'll be there, of course, and we should meet ahead of time to help you prepare. I've already shown them your work and they were very impressed."

Without telling me, Miss Harmon had previously submitted some autobiographical stories I had written to a contest and they had been published in an anthology she had brought to class. I assumed this was what she meant by my "work," but I didn't know what preparations might be necessary for the interview. Still, I was touched by her efforts on my behalf. Not for the first time, I realized that there were things a parent might properly do but which never occurred to my parents, so Miss Harmon had acted for them. "Maybe I should tell my mother about this," I suggested.

This produced a physical reaction in Miss Harmon. Her mouth twitched involuntarily and she seemed to have been pushed back abruptly in her chair. I think she was remembering their last encounter, but she couldn't very well expect me to keep something like this a secret from my parents. She nodded grimly. "Just make sure you're there on time," she said briskly. "And wear something nice."

This last comment was thrown off in the manner of a person speaking of something that was clearly beyond me. I suppose she might have been referring to the fact that I owned only two pair of pants and two shirts, besides the sweaters I had purchased with Abe Goodstein's tips. Now, three-quarters of the way through the school year, my clothes had lost whatever luster they might once have possessed, and since I had grown, the sleeves were too short and the cuffs on my pants were ragged. Yet Miss Harmon had never criticized my dress before and I had naïvely assumed she hadn't noticed. Of course, she might have thought this would play to my advantage with the Country Day people. Why give a scholarship to a boy who could afford nice clothes, after all? But given the importance fashion obviously played in her life, I doubt that she was being ironic. Certainly, I didn't take it that way, though I had no idea what to do to improve my wardrobe in a couple of days.

When I spoke to my parents about the interview, however, a new suit was the last thing on their minds. I had expected them to be pleased, particularly since I remembered how happy my mother had been when I was admitted to Campus at the last minute. After all, many of the kids in my class would be joining me if I won the scholarship. Instead, she sat quietly listening to my description of my conversation with Miss Harmon. Then she said, "Do you really want to go to a school like that, Danny?"

I had not really considered this. Volition was foreign to me. Miss Harmon had nominated me for the scholarship and I assumed that if I got it I would go, plain and simple. I'm not sure I had realized I could demur. Now, however, there was a conflict or potential conflict. "I don't know," I said. "Miss Harmon thinks it's a good idea."

My mother nodded and looked away. I didn't understand what possible objection she could have, but it was plain she had one. "I grew up with people like that," she said now. "That's why I went to New York and married your dad, to get away from them."

I had an incomplete understanding of what she had been escaping, or how the people she had eluded could have mysteriously appeared in Milwaukee thirty years later, but it was hard to see how whatever she had known as a child could have been worse than what we had. At the same time, the romantic image of the two of them in flight from my mother's aristocratic ancestors had an undeniable allure. I looked around the dingy room, at the dust devils in the corner and the peeling linoleum, and a familiar feeling of gloom crept over me. "Where do you want me to go?" I asked.

"There's a public high school nearby, isn't there?" she asked, as if she had never investigated the neighborhood on her own. "If you went there you'd meet all kinds of people and you wouldn't be the poorest boy in the school."

I knew that the only kinds of people I'd meet at Riverside High School would be the poor whites in the neighborhood tinctured with a smattering of black kids from the other side of the river. "I'm the poorest one now," I said, pointing out the obvious. "I'm used to it and you think Campus is okay, don't you?"

"Yes," my mother nodded. "That's true. I think it's worked out well, all things considered, despite that social-climbing teacher."

My father hadn't said anything to this point. He had been sitting quietly to the side, drinking coffee. "Does it seem like an interesting idea to you, Danny?" he asked me now.

I was glad he had spoken, that he cared what I thought. "I was surprised that Miss Harmon did it," I said. "I didn't know you could get a scholarship to a place like that."

"And pleased, too? Flattered?"

I knew that my father's musical education had rested entirely on scholarships, that he had moved to a strange city away from his family at the age of fourteen for music school. He was an unlikely ally, but a promising one. "Sure. Wouldn't you be?"

My father smiled and nodded. "I would, no question about it." Then he turned to my mother. "I don't see any harm in Danny going to the interview, Marie," he said. "If he gets the scholarship, we can visit the school and make a decision then. He's excited about it now, why shouldn't we let him be excited?"

I could tell my mother wasn't entirely won over, but it was the only time my father had asserted himself on a question involving my education and I could see she was impressed. "If you think so," she said.

"In the meantime we can look at all the socialist day schools in the area," my father said, which brought the small concession of a smile from my mother.

"That isn't exactly what I meant," she said.

My father persisted. "I know," he said. "But close?"

My mother laughed at this. "Close enough," she said.

Sixteen

Haircut

I got my hair cut at a shop on Downer Avenue owned by a man named Andy Silverman, who was legendary for underachieving even among the significant collection of Jewish failures in Milwaukee. Universal disappointment, I would discover, had a direct relationship with the community's degree of expectation, and everyone's hopes had been high for Andy. Now around fifty, he had been tall and good looking when he graduated from Riverside High School in the thirties and received a scholarship to the University in Madison. Andy had not only been valedictorian of his class, but had won the state prize in mathematics, sang in *The Mikado,* and played on the baseball team. Beyond this, he was dating the daughter of the owner of a large meat packing business where he worked in the summer.

It was the Depression and Andy's parents, who owned a small grocery store on Center Street, had three younger children at home, so sending Andy off to Madison was a hardship, scholarship or no scholarship. Still, like all Jews, the Silvermans revered learning as a secular religion and they loved their oldest son. He would become a doctor or a professor and make them even prouder than he had already.

No one knew, or at least no one who did know had ever said, what happened to Andy in Madison, but there were theories. Some said it involved alcohol, which would have been unusual for a Jewish boy; others said Andy had gotten involved with a shiksa, since despite his alliance with the girlfriend Andy was known to have an eye for women. The shiksa, so the story went, had then humiliated and deserted Andy and he had never recovered from this traumatic experience. Such was the xenophobia of the time that the way in which this mysterious gentile might have accomplished all this was deemed to be self-evident. In any case, Andy had no heart for his studies after this. He came home, married his girlfriend, and then joined the army to fight Hitler, hoping, so rumor had it, to die a glorious death.

Such was not to be the case, however, and when Andy returned home it was revealed, in the way such things are, that there was nothing distinguished in his war record, in fact that he had not even seen combat, that he had spent the war working as a clerk-typist in Birmingham. Still, he was alive, praise God, unlike many other boys, and only in his twenties. Though he had lost his scholarship because of the shiksa, he now had the GI Bill of Rights and this would enable him to go back to Madison and complete his education. Time remained to realize his dreams and make his parents proud and now, as a married man, there would be no foolishness with women to distract him.

Somehow, though, the energy and charm that had been so much a part of Andy when he had been in high school seemed to have been bled out of him over the intervening years. Listless where he had been passionate, cynical where he had been romantic, fatalistic where he had previously oozed optimism, instead of studying he would now spend hours sitting in Maimon's delicatessen holding forth on the arbitrary nature of existence, even directing rhetorical questions to me on occasion. Andy possessed the kind of self-importance that assigns philosophical significance to all of life's petty misfortunes. What had happened to him was simply evidence of the random nature of life, but since everything *was* random there was no point in getting your hopes up. In the end, instead of returning to

Madison, he received an associate's degree in fine arts from the technical college and a barber's license. His father-in-law had died and there were now two children. With his wife's share of the meat packing business, Andy opened the shop on Downer and he had been there ever since. I had seen his wife only once or twice but she impressed me as a bitter, disappointed woman who had suffered the consequences of her husband's philosophy of life without sharing it.

Andy, however, remained entertaining, a raconteur who played opera at high volume in the shop and was rumored to provide a venue for various illegal activities in his back room. Whether this was true or not, I did not know, but often men would appear with faded blonds on their arms while I was getting a haircut, nod at Andy, and then disappear into the back room, not to return. This was accompanied by much winking and nodding between Andy and the men who habitually filled the shop's four chairs and read magazines. But nothing of a scandalous nature ever happened out in the open, much to my chagrin.

My father disapproved of Andy, whom he had known slightly in Madison as a hanger-on in the music scene, but Andy had an almost reverential respect for my father, whom he always referred to as "the real thing, an artist." Whether this was for my benefit or as a means of establishing his bona fides for the regulars I never knew, but Andy felt quite differently about Abe Goodstein. He and Abe had grown up together on the East Side and both had gone to Madison, but Abe had avoided the army, pledged ZBT, and made law review, which seemed only to increase Andy's contempt for him. He seemed gratified by what had happened, by Abe's misfortunes, and his pleasure in the other man's downfall could be only partially explained by envy.

"Smart Jewboys are a dime a dozen," Andy would say referring to Abe. "What's it ever got him? Time in federal prison, that's what." He would nod with satisfaction and then continue in the same vein. "Mr. Bigshot, Mr. TV star. Too good for his old friends, his old neighborhood." Then he'd shake his head and mutter. "A *goniff*, no more, no less. You'll never see him in this shop, Danny. Oh, no, he's downtown at the Pfister getting a facial from some bimbo." Then he'd laugh derisively, as if the idea that there was a better haircut in town was too ridiculous to talk about.

Thus it was surprising that on this day, when I was getting my hair cut in preparation for my Country Day interview, Abe appeared in the doorway of Andy's shop flanked by Al and Pete and looking vaguely lost. It was hot and Abe was wearing a silk jacket and an open-necked shirt. The shop wasn't large, but it was not so small as to require the shuffling of chairs among the regulars that now took place. Miraculously, seats were made available for Abe's entourage, though I was still confused about the purpose of the visit. My first thought was that Abe had heard what Andy was saying about him and had come by to settle accounts.

Now he approached the chair. "How are you, Andy?" Abe said, his tone genial and condescending. "It's been too long. How's Bev?"

"Fine, Abe," Andy said, all the bravado gone now from his voice, replaced by a kind of brittle hysteria. "How are you?"

Abe didn't bother to answer. The clear implication was that the details of his life were of no possible concern to Andy Silverman. "Andy," he said now, "I need to talk to Danny." He looked vaguely at my neck. "You're done, aren't you? There a place we can talk here?"

This was a rhetorical question. The whole East Side knew about Andy's back room, but the idea that whatever Abe wanted to say couldn't have been said in public amazed me. Andy nodded, eagerly, "Sure, Abe. I guess so. Use the back." He whipped the barber's cloth off with a flourish, as if he were auditioning for something. Then he brushed my neck with a talcum brush. "You're done, bud," he said. Andy looked expectant, but like many important men, Abe seldom carried money or paid for anything himself. He slapped some Lilac Vegetal on his cheeks and examined his handsome face in the big mirror. Then Al placed a bill in Andy's hand and Abe and I went in back by ourselves.

After the build up, the room was disappointing, consisting only of a poker table, some chairs, and a roll-away bed in the corner with a faded spread thrown over it. I had expected more, but Abe didn't seem to notice. He was smiling, truly delighted, and said, "I heard about that interview, Danny. Mazel tov." Then for the first time since we had known each other, he pulled me to him and squeezed my head in the vice of his forearm. "I'm proud of you," he said, his voice hoarse, as if he were my father and I his son.

I thanked him and stood shifting my weight from side to side because I didn't know what to say next. "Look," Abe continued. "I talked to your mom. I'd like to buy you a new suit for the interview. It shouldn't matter how you dress, but it does. Why shouldn't you look as good as any of those phonies? We can go over to the Colony Shop. You pick out whatever you want."

This was a tempting offer and not only because the Colony Shop occupied a place in local society that I had only imagined before. It was as if I had been transformed from an urchin hauling out cinders to a prep school boy in expensive clothes without doing anything myself to effect it. But even if Abe had discussed this with my mother, I knew my father would not approve. I also wondered about the question of looking needy. "I don't know," I said, and I could almost see Abe deflate before my eyes. He had come over and made the big gesture and now I was rejecting him, and why? Because my father, who hardly knew whether or not he was wearing shoes, might object? It made no sense but that was how I felt and I couldn't help it. I wanted to say, "It's not because you're a gambler," but I couldn't do that because in a way that *was* the reason, as irrational and unfair as that would have seemed to him.

Now Abe stepped back and patted his pockets, as if he was looking for something. "Sure," he said briskly. "You're right. That's better. It was just an idea, forget about it."

It was a moment freighted with moral ambiguity for me, a moment in which what was right was obscure, in which right and wrong were dominant values but also oddly irrelevant. What was surprising to me was that it mattered to Abe, that I did. I knew he had made no such offer to Joey or that if he had it would not have had the same meaning. And now I was sorry I hadn't accepted him for I knew that in some way I had misjudged him and the situation. To me this represented a conflict between Abe and my father, and not only them, but what their lives stood for. I was grateful to Abe for his kindnesses, but when I thought a choice had to be made I hadn't hesitated. And yet, Abe had never said anything derogatory about my father, never tried to undermine my love for him; he had only offered to buy me a suit, something I needed but which I had found compromising, whether it really was or not.

So Abe left with Al and Pete and we never talked about it again. And later that day, my father took me to downtown to Gimbel's and we bought a gray gabardine suit that I wore twice but which hung in my closet until I went off to college four years later.

~

The Country Day campus was located in Whitefish Bay, a suburb north of the city, which my mother's university friends sometimes called Whitefolks Bay. Except for a commercial strip on Silver Spring Drive, which bisected the village and ran into the lake, it was a community of palatial homes with long winding drives, ornamental gardens, and an army of servants who arrived daily by bus from the Inner City to care for it all. There were seldom any people in sight, though sleek sedans moved silently through the wooded streets, and I imagined them all cavorting behind the Gatsbyesque façades doing whatever rich people did. Nothing in my past had prepared me for Country Day and as I entered the half-timbered administration building, I thought of it not as a real place but as something like a movie set, and myself as an actor playing a part.

Al had driven me out in Abe's Lincoln, a sort of compromise gesture to make up for the suit, but now with uncharacteristic reserve he decided to wait in the car. "Don't you want to come in?" I asked.

He shook his head. "Better this way," he said.

I straightened my tie and glanced in the mirror. My sandy hair was slicked back, as it had been when I left, but I knew I didn't look like the prep school boys I occasionally saw at the tennis courts in

Lake Park. I was trying hard and it showed; I lacked their studied dishabille, the tie slightly askew, the raincoat with a torn pocket. But I would always lack this, no matter where I went, in school or out. I looked presentable, which was as much as I could hope for. "Okay, then," I said. "If you're sure."

I felt vaguely guilty, but I was glad Al was staying behind, just as I was glad my parents hadn't accompanied me to the interview. Now, he patted me on the cheek. "I'm sure," he said. "Knock 'em dead, kid."

Inside, there was a dark vestibule that ended in some leaded glass behind which sat a gray-haired woman, who smiled when she saw me and offered her hand. I wasn't used to shaking hands with women, but I supposed that this was the way they did things in Whitefish Bay. "You must be Daniel," the woman said now. "I'm Mrs. Richards. They're waiting in the library."

I was unable to speak, but the woman's manner helped. She took my coat and brushed it in what I guess was a motherly way since my mother never did such things. "You look so nice," she said. "What a handsome young man."

What I wanted at that moment was to return to the car or, failing that, stay in the vestibule with Mrs. Richards, who for her own mysterious reasons seemed to think I was handsome, but that was not an option. I had to go into the library and face people whom I didn't know but who were in control of my fate. Now, Mrs. Richards propelled me through the door and I found myself facing two men and a woman. Miss Harmon sat off to the side wearing a long burgundy cape and a beret, which reminded me of Marlene Dietrich. Her face was a ghastly white and her red lips only intensified the impression. When she smiled I expected blood to leak from her lips, but I knew I should be grateful since she was the only reason I was there.

The small gray-haired man who seemed to be in charge stood and shook my hand. "Good morning, Daniel," he said. "I'm Dr. Eccles, the headmaster. Welcome to Country Day. Please sit down." He indicated a chair and I sat.

In addition to the strangeness of Whitefish Bay, I had never before been in a room like this. The three interviewers were seated behind a table made of some dark wood that I assumed was mahogany. Behind them were floor-to-ceiling bookcases filled with leather-bound volumes in red and green. There was a thick green carpet, oil paintings of various prosperous people whom I took to be patrons of the school, and a bank of leaded windows that looked out upon the most verdant meadow I had ever seen outside of a movie. The idea that I might actually attend such a school seemed incredible, and yet here I was, facing my expectant inquisitors, who were apparently waiting for me to say something.

"The playing fields of Eton," I said, surprising myself since I had no idea what this phrase meant, where I might have heard it, nor how I had known to repeat it.

Oddly, however, this led to much approving clucking and seat straightening on the other side of the table. Dr. Eccles then said, "Well, that's an apt association, Daniel, though of course we have no royalty in this country."

There was a good deal of chuckling and throat clearing at this, but of course I knew better and not only because of my recent association with Dr. Kissinger. If the people who lived in Whitefish Bay and went to this school weren't royalty, they were close enough. I wondered what they would think of our neighborhood, of the people sitting out on their tiny porches in ratty folding chairs on warm nights; what they would think of Jesús and Anna or Alfred or Abe and Al and Pete; I wondered what they would think of Daisy and everyone else in my life. But I knew better than to express any of this. In fact, I didn't know what to say, what was expected in such a situation. I had never been interviewed for anything before. But I needn't have worried because Miss Harmon took over now and it was clear that Dr. Eccles and the others were as cowed by her as I was.

Miss Harmon stood and walked around the room, one hand on her skinny, cocked hip. Her head was tilted slightly toward the ceiling as she ran through the many reasons they should give me what apparently was called a Founder's Scholarship, though it would have seemed more appropriate to call it a foundling scholarship, given the cast of characters. She referred to my writing, the trip to Guatemala, which had now become a "diplomatic mission," and my academic gifts. What she said was replete with "brilliants" and "superbs" and bore little resemblance to anything I had previously recognized in myself, but I enjoyed her performance just the same. After ten minutes of encomiums, she sat down and quiet descended upon the room.

At last, a thin man with ginger hair who had been introduced as a trustee found the courage to speak though not to disagree with Miss Harmon's characterization of me. He looked hopefully in my direction, as if he was expecting me to help him along. "Do you have anything to say, Daniel?" he asked. "To expand on Miss Harmon's account of your academic background or any questions you'd like to ask us about life at Country Day."

For me to elaborate on what had been said would have seemed like an implicit criticism of Miss Harmon who sat with a grimace on her face, as if she was suffering intestinal distress. My primary concern was not to interfere with what was obviously her strategy. She knew these people and I didn't, and obviously she had gained their respect if not their affection. "It's a nice campus," I said, just to have something to say.

The man nodded. "Thank you," he said. Then he looked around at the others. "Perhaps someone else has questions? Miss Dunphy?"

Miss Dunphy was probably in her mid-thirties and had once been pretty. Her brown hair was cut short and she wore a brown suit with a boxy cut that seemed designed to hide her body from sight. I wondered if she had been a nun in a previous life, but her smile was open and friendly and I liked her immediately. Now she said, "I enjoyed hearing your father play, Daniel. I used to go to his concerts at Music Hall when I was a student in Madison. I was sorry to hear about his illness. How is he?"

I never knew what to say in situations like this, and I could feel my throat closing up. Miss Dunphy meant to be sympathetic, interested, but I was simply incapable of discussing my father's health in a casual way with strangers, regardless of their good intentions. I felt myself becoming hot and hoped desperately that I wouldn't begin to cry. Fortunately, Miss Dunphy rescued me by interrupting herself.

"Do you play?" she said.

"Play?" I thought perhaps she meant basketball, though it would have seemed like an odd question in these surroundings.

She nodded, encouraging me. She looked at a sheet of paper in front of her. "It says on your application that you're a pianist."

She pronounced it *peeonist* and I thought of flowers, but in any case this was stretching things. Miss Harmon had handled the application and God only knew what she might have written on it about my musical ability. "I take lessons," I said.

"At the Wisconsin Conservatory," Miss Dunphy said, apparently for the benefit of the others in the room. "And from Professor Braun, no less." She looked up. "He's written us a letter about you. So those are not just any ordinary lessons, are they, Daniel?" I recognized that she was trying to help me, but it was like pulling a boat through shark-infested waters because I was close to paralysis and almost unable to respond.

"Yes, with Professor Braun," I managed to say. Then, "I like Mozart."

This was of course both stupid and untrue. Mozart was the bane of my existence, but as with the playing fields of Eton, my response elicited much head nodding and more coughing after which Dr. Eccles said, "Does anyone else have any questions for Daniel?"

Then everyone stood and we all shook hands and said how much we'd enjoyed meeting one another. Dr. Eccles said, "Daniel, could you step into the hall for a moment. I'll be out shortly."

I wandered the hall and stood looking into the trophy cases at the darkened plaques inscribed with the names of now-forgotten boys who had once done something for the school. There were trophies for football and basketball and tennis but also for forensics and chess. Yet for a school the place seemed oddly dark and empty to me. Despite this, however, I had somehow in the preceding hour conceived a desire to win this scholarship that was so fierce that for a brief moment it made me dizzy. I now thought that if I were allowed to come here everything that had seemed tragic and confining in my life would be overcome and, conversely, if I were turned away and sent off to Riverside as my mother wished, I would never escape the clinkers and ash heaps of the East Side. I felt, that is, as if this were a defining moment, a turning point in my young life, that everything rested on what these strangers in the next room would decide in the next few minutes.

The door opened behind me and Miss Dunphy beckoned me to come in. She was smiling and they were all standing now, red-faced, as if they'd been either arguing or toasting themselves while I waited outside. Only Miss Harmon remained seated by the windows, though she had a contented look on her face. Dr. Eccles looked around at the others then settled his gaze on me. Again, he offered his hand. "Congratulations, Daniel," he said. "We've decided unanimously to offer you the Founder's Scholarship for this year."

Then the other man shook my hand and Miss Dunphy hugged me, pushing her breasts into my face and saying, "I'm so glad you'll be coming here. I think we'll be great friends."

I hadn't thought of teachers as being my friends before, but now I supposed that perhaps Miss Harmon was, so I surprised her by going over to the window and squeezing her. "Thanks, Miss Harmon," I said. "I know I wouldn't be here if it wasn't for you." She looked a little stunned by my gesture, but she smiled and with a soft hand ruffled my hair, obviously pleased by what I had said. Then I thanked everyone else in the room, surprised but pleased that my lackluster performance had somehow enabled me to win the scholarship. Still, I knew nothing was settled yet about my attending Country Day. My mother was waiting at home.

—

Al was leaning against the Lincoln with a cigarette in his hand when I came out. "How'd it go?" he asked casually.

"Good, I guess. They offered me the scholarship."

His eyebrows went up at this and he puffed out his cheeks. "No shit. What's that worth?" He looked back at the school. "A couple grand, at least?"

I shrugged. I had no idea what the tuition was at Country Day. Without the scholarship it was only an abstraction and didn't concern me. My parents wouldn't even buy me new tennis shoes. Just then, Miss Harmon came out and hesitated on the steps lighting a cigarette. It was an oddly intimate moment, as she sheltered the match with her hand, if only because I knew so little about her. Then she straightened from the waist and looked over us in the direction of the lake. "Who's the broad?" Al asked, visibly impressed.

"That's Miss Harmon. She's my teacher, Joey's too."

Suddenly, Al slapped me on the head. "So why don't you offer Miss Harmon a ride for Christ's sake. Where are your manners, kid?"

It hadn't occurred to me to wonder how Miss Harmon had gotten to the interview, unless by divine intervention, or how she might return to her apartment. I was so taken up with my own life and problems that Miss Harmon's life outside of school was a mystery to me, just as she was. But Al was right so I approached her and she replied, "Thank you, Daniel. I would like a ride. I want to speak to your parents anyway."

Panic struck. When I left, our apartment had been in its usual chaos and I didn't even know if my parents were home now. But there was no denying Miss Harmon, so I followed her swaying back to the car where Al held the door open, a big smile on his face. I introduced them and got in. Miss Harmon dropped onto the cushioned front seat, showing a lot of leg in the process, which I could tell Al noticed. He was on his best behavior, offering another cigarette, and switching the radio station to something he imagined Miss Harmon might like. It was hard to tell what effect this had on her, or whether in fact there was an effect, but she seemed comfortable with Al and I could tell he liked it when she cradled his wrists in her hand when he offered her a light. I felt oddly like a matchmaker, though I

would never have thought of the two of them together as we continued down Lake Drive toward the East Side. When we reached our
apartment, Miss Harmon said, "Please wait for me, Al," as if something had been settled between them during the trip. Then we went
inside.

Perhaps they had discussed this visit beforehand without my
knowledge, but whatever the case my mother and father were waiting for us. My mother had done her best to make the place presentable. There was a colorful throw covering the daybed and she had
put out a dish of cookies, but the contrast with what we had recently left in Whitefish Bay could not have been greater. My mother
seemed tense, my father withdrawn, as we sat around the little coffee
table. I thought of saying something about Miss Dunphy's admiration for my father to break the ice, but I knew it would mean less
than nothing to him, so instead I plunged right in. "I won the scholarship," I said.

"That's very nice, Daniel," my mother said. "Congratulations."
My father said nothing.

"There were more than fifty candidates from all over Milwaukee," Miss Harmon said now. "They interviewed eight finalists this
morning before Daniel, but it only took them five minutes to decide. You should be very proud of him, Mr. and Mrs. Meyer."

I knew my mother wouldn't appreciate anyone telling her what
she should take pride in. "I've always been proud of Danny, Miss
Harmon. I always will be proud of him. But not because someone
has decided he's good enough to go to school with a bunch of rich
kids."

I expected Miss Harmon to be taken aback by this, but she just
nodded her huge head. I was used to my mother's socialist tenden-
cies, her general suspicion of the rich. For while she had been raised
in an aristocratic family, she lost no opportunity to point out that
she had left Kentucky of her own free will and had not gone back. I
knew it was more complicated than that, but she had never gotten
over knowing communists in New York when she was in her twenties, or organizing against Joe McCarthy. For her, it was all of a piece.

Dr. Eccles, Miss Dunphy and Tailgunner Joe were all trying to subvert her son and only she stood in their way.

"So your objection to the Country Day School is that it's elitist?" Miss Harmon said, and I sensed some anger under her deep, drawling voice. "Is that it, Mrs. Meyer? I mean, you have no academic objections?"

My mother gave an exaggerated shrug. "I'm sure it's fine academically," she said. "Small classes, advanced methods, individualized instruction." She threw these off as if only an imbecile could really think they were important in a school.

"A lot like Campus, then?" Miss Harmon suggested.

My mother gave her a superior smile. "Please, Miss Harmon. We both know Campus is a *laboratory* school, sponsored by a university, where the teachers are all professors, like you. It's hardly the same thing."

The way she said laboratory made me think of Frankenstein's monster, but Miss Harmon was undeterred. "That's true," she said. "Nevertheless, we have a number of wealthy children at Campus. In fact some of Daniel's classmates will be going on to Country Day next year as well, but without scholarships."

"Which makes my point," my mother said. "In addition to learning the wrong social values, my son would be a poor boy in a rich kids' school."

Miss Harmon brushed this off easily. "Oh, I don't think that would bother Daniel," she said. Then she hesitated for a moment, changing her tack. "Let me ask you, Mrs. Meyer. Where did you go to high school?"

My mother flushed, caught off-balance by a question she hadn't expected. "I went to a girls school in Kentucky," she said.

"Would you call it a rich kids' school?" Miss Harmon persisted.

My mother was red-faced now. "I suppose so, but this is different."

"No doubt," Miss Harmon said, boring in. "But it wasn't a public school, was it? And may I ask where you went to college?"

"Bryn Mawr," my mother said quietly.

Ms. Harmon nodded. Then she turned to my father. "And you, Mr. Meyer?"

"I never finished high school," my father said. "I went to Juilliard when I was fourteen."

"And I wonder if you had a scholarship," Miss Harmon said, in the manner of a prosecuting lawyer who already knew the answer to her question.

"My parents were immigrants," my father said. "There was no other way. It was the Depression." His voice had taken on a pleading tone, as if he was desperate to be understood, but Miss Harmon was merciless. She was on a mission.

For a moment, she said nothing, letting all this settle between us in that small room. When she finally spoke, though, there was an edge to her voice. "I don't want you to think I don't respect your social concerns, Mrs. Meyer," she said. "And I don't necessarily think everyone at Country Day is admirable, but they offer an outstanding education as well as opportunities beyond high school for Danny. In a sense, all of this is settled very early for most students, and trying to break out of the mold later on becomes harder at every stage. Like Mr. Meyer, I was raised during the Depression. My father was a machinist and out of work most of the time, so there was never any talk about my attending any private schools even though I was a good student. I went to the Normal School and became a kindergarten teacher, then continued at night working for my master's. It took me six years going part-time and summers. There was no money to send me even as far away as Madison." Miss Harmon didn't mention Bryn Mawr, but the irony of my mother preaching social values to her was obvious. Now she leaned forward and took one of the cookies and ate it, chewing thoughtfully before continuing.

"I don't know if Daniel will like the other children at Country Day," she said. "I don't know if he'll feel self-conscious because of his clothes or where he lives; I don't know if he'll form close friendships or feel inferior because of the differences in family income. But I don't care. I don't think he likes most of the other boys at Campus, to tell the truth, but that doesn't seem to bother you. I remember you telling me that you didn't care what kind of impression he made as long as he got a good education, and you were right about that." She stopped and took a deep breath. Then she looked directly at my mother. "But I believe you're wrong about this. I hope you don't let social stereotypes or your political beliefs stand in the way of your son getting what is really a tremendous opportunity. It's very nice that you had a family with the money to send you to a good college, but I'm afraid that if Daniel is going to follow your example he's going to have to continue to win scholarships and the simple fact is that he has a better chance of doing that if he attends Country Day than if you send him to Riverside." Then she leaned back in her chair, apparently satisfied with what she had said.

The argument was over, even if my mother couldn't bring herself to concede completely. "I understand that the public school, Riverside, is very good," she said weakly.

"No, it's not," Miss Harmon said, and I was surprised by the fierceness of her expression. "It's not good enough for Daniel and I don't know why I have to sit here and tell you people this. Your son is unusual. He has talents other children don't have and this committee of strangers out in Whitefish Bay seemed more willing to acknowledge this than you do, which amazes me. Daniel deserves a chance in life. Now he's got one and all you have to do is let him take it."

At this, my father broke in. "I don't see why we have to argue about this, Marie. It's wonderful that Danny won the scholarship. Why ruin it by acting like it's a problem? Going to school with some rich kids isn't going to change Danny if he goes on living here and I don't think anyone has suggested he should leave home and board in Whitefish Bay. Miss Harmon is right," he said mildly. "If Daniel wants to go to this school, I don't see what harm it can do."

I was impressed with my father's speech, but a little disappointed since my hope was that Country Day would not only change me but my whole life so that I could leave this place and never return. My father looked expectantly at my mother who hadn't replied. I knew she wasn't convinced but apparently she had decided there wasn't much more to say.

Miss Harmon stood, wobbling a bit on her high heels. Then she did something surprising. She held out her arms and hugged me tightly to her breast. "I'll call Dr. Eccles on Monday," she said, "unless I hear from you, Mrs. Meyer." Then she smiled. "I have to go," she said. "My ride is waiting." I had to stifle the impulse to laugh at the thought of Miss Harmon and Al going off together in Abe's Lincoln, but then she swept out the door, leaving the three of us alone with the cookies to sort it all out.

Seventeen

Flooded

There was a time then, in the darkness before morning, when I would awaken, disoriented, convinced that my dark, cavernous bedroom was the dank hotel room in Huehuetenango, and that far from escaping, Anna and Jesús had returned to America, leaving me to negotiate a new life with the Guatemalans. I would imagine the stone floor of the room, the bored hotel clerk outside the door, the life of unrelieved poverty, and shiver in my bed. It is hard now to suggest the absolute terror of these moments, harder still to rationalize or explain them, but I think in that long-developing spring I had some of the feelings I should logically have had in Guatemala when, in retrospect, I had been in a state of shock, sleepwalking, like my brother, through that wet, oppressive country. Now, like depth charges, true and powerful, those sensations returned in a visceral way in the night, making sleep unimaginable.

After tossing for an hour in bed, I would get up and go into the kitchen and sometimes I would hear Jesús moving slowly in the back hall, and I would go to join him, though in those early mornings I never asked him if he remembered his native country in the way I did. We would sit on the back steps and drink strong coffee, saying little but enjoying our friendship as the day began. At those times, I would remember standing together around an open fire in the Village With No Name waiting for Anna to finish bathing but firm in the illusion that Jesús and I were men together, drinking coffee, and thinking thoughts only men might think.

Except for rising early, Jesús had begun to resemble the other men on our street in his work clothes and peaked hat, but I sometimes wondered if things had worked out as neatly as Anna had hoped. Alfred was around less now, spending only the requisite days in Milwaukee when school was in session and seldom appearing at any other time. I knew that Anna had thought she was compartmentalizing her life with Alfred on one side and Jesús on the other, but this had apparently not been so easy for Alfred. I missed his presence, but my life had changed, too. I spent less time in my basement office and more with Madeline and her friends, something I expected to continue when I began Country Day in the fall. Yet, that stopped neither the early morning nightmares nor the heart-stopping terror when I awoke convinced I had been left behind to fend for myself in Guatemala.

It was on one of these mornings, as Jesús and I were sharing coffee, that Joey Goodstein appeared unexpectedly, his hair disheveled, his eyes wide with excitement. I immediately thought something must have happened to Abe, since Joe was not usually an early riser, but he was saying something about the Mississippi River and the Red Cross. It did not make sense to me right away because I still found it exotic to think that river, perhaps it would be more accurate to say the River, formed the western boundary of our state. It was probably the most cosmopolitan thing about Wisconsin to my way of thinking. "It's flooding," Joey said in wonderment. "The whole town is under water."

Since the Mississippi flooded every year and the town in question, Prairie du Chien, was two hundred miles away, I didn't see what this had to do with us, but Joey was insistent. "The Red Cross is calling for volunteers," he said. "I heard it on the radio. They need people to build dikes."

"Now?" I asked. I had a rather unformed idea of what a dike was exactly, though I certainly knew about the Dutch boy with his finger in one. And while it was attractive to think that we might be involved in something important enough to be newsworthy, it was barely six A.M. and the whole house was asleep. I still couldn't get over the fact that Joey was there. Jesús offered him some coffee, but Joey shook him off with irritation.

"Of course now," he said. "The flood doesn't know what time it is. Come on, Al's in the car. We can be back by tomorrow night; my mother will call the school."

As far as I knew, Joey had never before evinced any interest in the vicissitudes of nature or rivers, but the idea appealed to me, though it might only have been because getting away always held some appeal. I went back into the darkened apartment, thinking I suppose that I should ask my parents if I was going to go to an area that was flooding and was potentially dangerous, but I didn't want to wake them for something they would surely consider ridiculous. The door to their room was ajar and I stood there for a moment, uncertain what to do. Then I heard labored breathing and it became clear to me that they were not asleep. In the blue light I could see only the outline of their bodies, but my mother was sitting astride my father as he caressed her hips, pulling her down to him. They were making love, but something was clearly wrong and I couldn't tell what it was. The rocking movement continued for a few minutes until I heard my father mutter "Shit," and then my mother began to sob quietly.

I retreated from the door. Something about what I had seen was deeply disturbing, but it wasn't the sex, which I found interesting and compelling. Rather, I felt like an intruder in a scene so intimate and tragic that what I had done seemed unforgivable, even if my parents didn't know I had witnessed it. I picked up a sweatshirt and a jacket from my bedroom and went to the kitchen where I wrote a note telling my mother where I was going and asking her to call the Goodsteins who would always know where we were. I knew this wasn't the right thing to do, but as Joey said, the flood wouldn't wait, and I needed desperately to get away.

We stopped for breakfast in Tomah, where each table had a small ashtray in the form of a beaded tom-tom, a nod to the town's Indian heritage, but we still made it to Prairie du Chien by eleven. The sky was overcast but so far the rain was holding off, a good sign. As we approached the town, the landscape varied little from what had gone before—stretches of prairie broken periodically by drumlins and the other glacial remains common to southwestern Wisconsin. There was no way for the casual viewer, which certainly would have described everyone in our car, to know there was a crisis of any kind at hand—no roiling waters, no streams of grief-stricken refugees, no field hospitals. There was only the gently rolling landscape under the gray sky. I began to wonder if we had come to the wrong town.

As we drew closer, however, I saw that the gray mass I had mistakenly taken to be the river was actually the town itself. What had seemed in the distance to be bluffs were actually the tops of buildings and the trees were not usually alongside the river at all, but in drier times lined the streets of the town. Now we were stopped at a Red Cross checkpoint and directed toward a parking lot, from which we could survey the area.

Below us, people floated in rowboats, with men and boys ducking into second-story windows from which they then emerged with arms full, though whether they were homeowners or looters was impossible to say, just as it was hard to tell where the river's banks ordinarily stood, that is, what had been lost and what was left to protect. It was eerie standing there and I felt a little like the spectators of the Civil War must have felt as they took their picnic lunches out to hilltops in Virginia to watch the boys of the North and the South kill each other. There was no noise and nothing communicated urgency; just the slow rise of the river and the small boats making their way along the watery thoroughfare.

Al was impressed. "That's a lot of fucking water," he said, cutting to the heart of things as usual. "I wonder whose idea it was to put a town there." It was the kind of thing my mother said, but it hadn't occurred to me before that the locations of towns were actually planned, that some thought might actually have gone into it. I had always just assumed they *were* there, and that it could be no other way.

"Before they had cars and trains, the rivers were like highways," Joey said now. It sounded like something he had read in a book, but Al and I were impressed. Encouraged, Joey went on. "They had all kinds of forts on the rivers, too," he said. "During the Revolutionary War, if you controlled the rivers, you controlled the movement of food and guns and everything else so the armies couldn't get supplies to their soldiers without the rivers."

Now it was clear that the history lesson had gone on long enough for Al. "Great," he said. Then he pointed off to the right. "You guys want to build dikes, whatever, there're some people down there probably know what's going on." He pointed in the direction of a group of tents and trucks. Then, "I'm going to take a nap. See you later."

The ranger at the far end of the parking lot seemed mildly surprised that Joey and I were there without adults, but we didn't really want to introduce him to Al and under the circumstances no one was going to check IDs. Now the ranger pointed to a church steeple rising out of an eddy of dirty water perhaps a block away. "Yesterday, that was the high ground," he said. "If it doesn't rain, we might be able to hold it here; if it rains, we'll all be underwater. Why don't you boys go on over there and help with the sandbags?"

Considering the publicity the flood had received, there were relatively few people around. A Red Cross tent was off to the side with a picnic table and folding chairs arranged around it. A few other tents dotted the clearing and there were about ten people standing in a pit silently filling burlap bags with sand. Joey and I got in line and spent the morning transporting sand bags to the dike itself, which was simply a double row of the bags six feet high that stretched perhaps thirty feet in either direction.

There was something essentially futile about the whole thing that I found oddly appealing. The idea of doing something simply for the sake of doing it, and not because it would necessarily succeed or make money for anyone, seemed right. Anyway, filling sandbags was better than waiting passively for the water to rise over us and I admired the perversity of people who would choose to live in a floodplain knowing that each year nature would force them out of their homes and require them to live in tents until the waters receded. We all knew that the dike we were building would be useless if the waters rose enough, but we couldn't help building it any more than the water could help rising. It was the yin and yang of life on the river, and though I didn't live there, I began to feel I would like it if I did. I knew that in ancient Egypt floods were important for farming, but this had nothing to do with agriculture. This was all about stubbornness and extending your jaw in expectation of the blow. It reminded me of my family, of my father's refusal to act like a cripple and my parents' lack of concern about the normal expectations of middle-class life. This was not what I would have wanted, but no one gets to choose his parents and with all their shortcomings, I loved them.

I remembered once asking my mother whether they would have had children if they had known my father would get so sick. She hesitated for a long time and finally nodded her head yes. "We wanted a life," she said. "And there are never any guarantees, even if people act as if they're entitled to live to be a hundred. No one can ever tell when he's going to die or if something awful will happen. You have to live in spite of it. You're part of my life, Danny. I needed to have you, no matter what."

Escape had been on my mind, but as I lifted sandbags that gray morning, I realized that in essential ways there could be no escape for me, ever. I could go to Country Day and then on to Yale and have a successful career, but in the early morning bleakness of the years to come, I would always be flooded with the detritus of my family life, of poverty, illness, and neglect, and there was nothing to do about that. Like the boys in the rowboats retrieving the necessities of life, I would always be going in and out of the windows of memory, trying to retrieve what would be necessary for me to live.

Al showed up in time for lunch, which was Kool-Aid and bologna sandwiches in the Red Cross tent, and then we spent the afternoon piling sandbags together. Al removed his shirt and I was impressed again with his rippling muscles and intensity as we worked side by side. "Looking good, Danny," he said at one point, and I was unreasonably pleased by the approval of this large violent and gentle man who had become my friend in this odd year. There were cots available in a high school gymnasium nearby, but Al had taken a room for us at a motel instead. "Abe don't want you kids sleeping in no gym," he said in explanation.

Then Al made me call my mother, who, predictably, wasn't in the least worried and wondered where we were in Minnesota. When I told her that, further north, the Mississippi formed the border between the two states and we were now across from Iowa, she said that this was very interesting and that I should have a good time with Al and Joey. It was an odd conversation, considering the fact that the governor had just declared most of western Wisconsin a disaster area, but my mother was right in a limited sense. It was fun to be out there in our mud-caked clothes, eating in field kitchens, and playing poker with Al at night in our motel room. He had taken us to an army-navy store and bought us boots and field jackets and I imagined that no one could tell us from the National Guardsmen who had arrived during the night to fortify the dikes.

I wondered why my mother didn't worry about me, why she didn't have the natural concerns that any parent might have about a young boy far from home in a potentially dangerous situation. I rationalized it in my own mind as being simply a case in which there were so many things that worried her, that she could spare no additional anxiety. But this tendency far predated Prairie du Chien or even my father's illness. I remembered once when my brother and I were in elementary school and my teacher had noticed that we had no coats to guard against the cold of January. She called my mother, who apparently had failed to notice this, but that afternoon it was not my mother but the teacher who took us down to a department store and purchased winter coats. This became part of family legend, but the story was always told with much laughter, as if my mother's failure to make sure her children were warm was merely an example of artistic eccentricity, instead of simple neglect. Certainly, there was never any suggestion that she had done anything wrong.

Surveying the gaggle of reservists grouped around the Red Cross tent in the morning, Al commented, "Must really be serious now. They brought in the weekend warriors." He seemed more interested in a nurse who was working the tent, but Joey and I concentrated on creasing our caps in the proper way and getting our new boots dirty.

By the end of the second day, the water had begun to recede and the rain, though promised, had still not come. At dinner, Al said, "I've had it. What do you say we get back to a place where they don't wrap the toilet seats in paper?"

Joey and I wanted to stay, but by morning the National Guardsmen had actually begun to dismantle the dikes and the cleanup of the town was beginning as the receding water revealed dirty stripes of debris on the houses and buildings. We packed our new clothes in the car and by early afternoon Al was pulling up in front of our apartment house, which stood as gray and unappealing as ever.

Charles was at school and I supposed my mother was at work, but I was surprised that my father wasn't home when I came in. I walked through the hall and found Anna sitting at the kitchen table. She had been crying and I immediately assumed something had happened to Jesús, though why that should have brought her to our apartment I didn't know. She took me in her arms and mashed my face into her bosom and then she started crying again. It was some time before I could disentangle myself and ask what was going on, why she was sitting alone in our kitchen in the middle of the day. I hope she wasn't going to start cleaning again.

"It's your father," she said at last.

"What happened?" I felt a sudden pressure in my chest, as if my breastbone were about to collapse.

"He fell in the shower and broke the glass door and cut open his face. Jesús happened to hear him and came in. Otherwise, he might have bled to death."

I felt a terrible foreboding come over me. It was only a few weeks before that we had been playing catch on the front walk and now my father couldn't safely take a shower by himself.

"Where is he?"

"Your mother went with him in the ambulance to Columbia. I was just waiting here because we had no way to contact you."

This was probably more a statement of fact than an accusation, but I felt guilty. If I hadn't been out turning back the floodwaters of the Mississippi, I would have been here and it wouldn't have happened. Or so I thought. But my guilt or responsibility wasn't really the point. Our adventure on the river was over just as my father's remission was. I kissed Anna on the cheek and thanked her for letting me know. "I'm going over to see him now," I said and left.

My father had a private room at the hospital and when I arrived a nurse was just finishing changing his dressing and they didn't see me immediately. He was wearing terrycloth shorts and his gown had fallen away, revealing his long arms, bony shoulders, and hairy chest. In that moment of vulnerability, as the nurse cradled his head in her arm and swathed my father's broken face in gauze, I saw, or felt I did, our whole life move past, his, mine, ours together. I knew now there would be no more remissions, no piano recitals, no baseball, ever again. I would be his steward, cleaning up for him, making arrangements, softening his fall, finally becoming his guardian, and though I didn't really understand all this then, I felt it, felt the change that had occurred while I was away concentrating on other things.

Now my father noticed me and jerked violently, knocking the nurse's hands away. "What are you doing here?" he yelled. "I told them not to tell you."

This was ridiculous and we both knew it, but he was embarrassed at my having found him this way, so I decided not to argue the point. "Anna told me," I said. "I came right over."

The nurse smiled and brushed herself off. "You must be Mr. Meyer's son," she said. "You look just alike." Then she cleared some papers off the only chair in the room and excused herself.

Having reacted violently, my father as quickly calmed down. "Take a load off your feet," he said. "Your mother should be back before long."

I sat down, unsure what to say. Despite my father's disability, he had always been the ultimate authority on anything in our family. He was sick but he was still unquestionably the boss. It had been confusing and difficult for me growing up, but he was now clearly in a subordinate position because he was the patient and I was visiting him. The bandage covered half his face, including his right eye and nose. "That's a big bandage," I said. "Are you going to be all right?" What I really wanted to know was whether or not he could see, but that was a big question and I thought I'd lead up to it gradually.

"It was stupid," he said, ignoring my question. "I leaned against the shower door and the damned thing broke, that's all. It could have happened to anyone."

We both knew this wasn't true, but it was typical of him. It was as if his disease were something incidental, and not worth paying attention to. Things like this were normal, or so he wanted to pretend. Still, there was no point in arguing about it. "How long will you be here?" I asked.

"Your mother's talking to the doctor now. How was the flood?"

He asked this in the same tone of voice he might have used to inquire about a movie and for a moment I didn't understand. Everything seemed inconsequential compared to his injury. Then I remembered where I had been for the past two days. I was surprised he had even noticed I was gone. "It was pretty bad. The whole town was underwater; people were going up and down the streets in rowboats."

"Like Venice," my father said, and we both smiled at the odd conjunction of the Wisconsin river town and the Grand Canals in Italy.

"Sort of," I said. "No gondolas, though."

Without either of us acknowledging it, we were having a quiet moment together, talking as any father and son might do, which might have been normal, but not for us. For the first time that I could remember, my father acted as if my life might have some interest independent of him. "I used to play songs from musicals like *Showboat*," he said. "Not often, but sometimes for an encore, you know. Something everyone would recognize, something they'd like." And then sensing I didn't see the connection, he added, "That's a musical, Daniel. It's by Jerome Kern and Oscar Hammerstein and there's a famous song in it called "Old Man River." Paul Robeson used to sing and I used to play it. The whole thing takes place on the Mississippi River. That's what made me think of it."

This seemed amazing to me. *Huckleberry Finn* was the only thing I knew to have been written about a river. "Do you have it?"

"I've got a recording of it somewhere," my father said. "Not the music. I can't play it anymore. I can't play anything anymore." Then he smiled. "Maybe you could, though. Maybe we could get Professor Braun to teach you to play "Old Man River." Wouldn't that be something, Danny?"

I had no idea who Kern and Hammerstein were, nor who Paul Robeson was for that matter. I didn't know what Professor Braun would think of this kind of music or if he would teach me to play the song, but in that dismal hospital room I felt as if somehow the torch had been passed and I knew that if I never played another piece of music in my life, if I gave up the piano and music entirely, that before I did I would learn "Old Man River," and that I would play it well for my father.

Eighteen

Summer

Summer came suddenly one day in June. Throughout the prolonged spring, there had been exacerbations of winter during which we would put aside the light jackets and pastel clothes we had bought to cheer ourselves, and put on once again heavy coats and hats, gloves and mufflers. Then, abruptly, it was over and it was ninety degrees and humid. Because we lived relatively close to the lake, there was some slight breeze every afternoon, which my mother optimistically referred to as "the pneumonia front," but since there were barely five feet between our windows and the house next door, my brother and I realized scant relief from this and spent most of our time outdoors on the stone stairs. It seemed like years since I had spoken to Charles, but he appeared to be better somehow, though he still spent much of his time alone playing chess against the grandmasters of the past. At eleven, he hadn't lost his baby fat entirely, but he had striking coloring, thick black hair and blue-gray eyes, and I found myself oddly drawn to him now. One evening after dinner I asked if the men from Mars were still paying nightly visits.

Charles might have construed this as mockery, and in a way it was, but he seemed to take my question in and think about it before answering. "They had another assignment," he said simply, as if he hoped to see them again someday.

This was reassuring to me. I wasn't close to Charles, but I didn't want him to be living another life while the rest of us were trying to figure this one out. This might seem selfish, but selfishness has been given a bad name over the years. It's hard to care sincerely about the lot of others if you feel shortchanged yourself. I wanted to make things as easy as possible for myself, but the truth was that life had not been easy for any of us for a long time. A crazy brother just made things more complicated, and I suspected Charles didn't like it very much either. Beyond this, I found his madness frightening, as if the existence of a psychosis in the bedroom next to mine made me more vulnerable. As awful as my father's illness was, I found mental disease to be more terrifying than physical disability, the loss of emotional tethers to be the most profound loss of all.

"Mom's going to fire Daisy," Charles said now, surprising me.

"Bullshit," I said. I was my mother's confidant, the apple of her eye; if she were going to do anything like this, she would have told me first.

He shrugged, not caring if I believed him or not. "It's true," he said.

Something about Charles' calm demeanor made me think he might know what he was talking about. "How do you know?" I asked.

He was playing jacks with a beat-up golf ball and spoke only intermittently, intent on his game. I looked away in embarrassment, though there was no one around to see us. My brother seemed to have no idea what was appropriate for a boy. He played no sports, unless chess could be called a sport, and he collected butterflies, which he then mounted in frames on his walls. Once I had caught him playing dolls with a little girl across the street but even my mother drew the line at buying Charles a dollhouse. "I heard Mom and Daddy talking," he said. "Daddy's getting sicker."

The matter-of-fact way he said this irritated me. There had been more emotion in his description of the Martians leaving town. "I know he's sicker," I said. "What's that got to do with anything?"

Charles hardly seemed to be listening. He had a tough pick-up of two jacks triangulated by a third. He bounced the golf ball once, twice, then knocked them all on the grass, ending the game. The kid couldn't even play jacks worth shit, but this didn't seem to bother him. Nothing did. "They think Daddy needs a real nurse," he said.

I felt physically affronted by this and while there is no question that part of my irritation had to do with learning all this from my little brother, I also felt responsible for Daisy. How could my mother just fire her? What was Daisy going to do without us? Where would she go? In my fevered mind, I imagined she'd have to go to work full-time as a prostitute and imagined her in provocative dress leaning against a brick wall in the Inner City trolling for business. Previously, I had imagined sex for pay to be a voluntary activity, something she would do occasionally, on the side, as a man might moonlight at a second job to pay off some holiday bills. But when I thought of her walking the streets of the ghetto or approaching idling cars full of white men on Twenty-seventh Street, I felt oddly complicit, as if my interlude with her had somehow tipped the balance and sent her irremediably into a life she would never escape. Not that I had great plans for Daisy; I had never seen her going to college or even finishing high school. But having known her, as they say, in the biblical sense, I was interested in her future happiness, even if I was having trouble with my own. In an obscure way, I cared about her.

When my mother came home, I asked about Daisy and she said they had already spoken and Daisy wouldn't be coming back to work. They had given her a month's severance pay, which seemed generous. "She asked me to give you this," my mother said, handing me a small blue envelope. She was smiling, as if she expected me to say something, but I just put the envelope in my pocket. I didn't want to discuss Daisy with my mother. "What's going to happen now?" I asked.

My mother sat down and smoothed her tweed skirt across her knees. There was something reassuring in that gesture, that is, I think it reassured her, as if she was reliving some ancient instruction from a parent about how young ladies should sit. "I've been talking to Mr. Goodstein," she said.

I didn't see the connection. I hadn't even known Abe was back in town. He had spent most of the spring in Vegas. Now I imagined my days as a runner for him were over. First Daisy, and now Abe. I was not having a good day. "About what?"

"He came by the studio. He wanted to buy some art for his office. You remember? He spoke to us about it that day."

I did, but I was surprised anyway. I hadn't thought Abe was really interested in art. Representative studies of kids and dogs lined the walls of their apartment and I couldn't really see my mother's expressionist bursts of color hanging there. But it was a mistake to judge people too quickly in these areas; I was always wrong, or so it seemed. The steelworker would have a fondness for grand opera; the notions salesman would be reading Wallace Stevens on the bus. Who ever really knew about people? Besides, Mrs. G. would have chosen the art for their apartment. Nevertheless, I didn't see what Abe had to do with our conversation about Daisy.

"I was asking Mr. Goodstein about getting help for Daddy," she continued. Now her eyes glistened and she took a handkerchief from her purse and dabbed at them.

I didn't think the job would appeal to Al or Pete, though I knew the gambling business had been slow lately and they'd been spending a lot of time hanging around Andy's barber shop looking menacing. "Does he know any nurses?"

She shook her head. "No, I don't think so." She hesitated now, her lips pulled over her slightly bucked teeth, as if she were trying to hold back what she knew she had to say. "Your daddy might have to go to a home," she said.

At first the words made no sense to me. Insofar as my father had a home, this was it, but slowly I began to understand her meaning. "You mean somewhere else?" I suddenly felt shaky, as if my balance had been affected; it seemed disloyal to be talking this way and I was irrationally angry with my mother. "Why don't you do something?" I said. This was a cruel thing to say and I knew it, but I couldn't help myself; I couldn't help feeling that there *was* something to be done, that there must be.

My mother dropped her head for a moment. Then she said softly, "I'm doing the best I can, Daniel. I work very hard and I don't make much money. You know that. I didn't make Daddy sick and it's killing me that he is sick, but that doesn't change anything. It's not my fault, but I'm the one that has to deal with it."

I wanted to say that it wasn't something for anyone to deal with, that my father wasn't a problem to be handled, but I knew that in part he was that, whether I liked it or not, and I knew that given the kind of person he was, he would never be an easy problem, for my mother or anyone else. "He can stay here," I insisted, knowing it was futile. "We can take care of him. I don't want him anywhere else."

She took my hand and kneaded my knuckles so hard it hurt. "I know," she said. "But the trouble is we can't take care of him anymore. I can't and you can't either. You need to go to school and see your friends and play ball and do whatever you want to do with your life. Daisy just wasn't enough and I can't afford a full-time nurse."

"How can you afford a home then?" It made no sense.

"That's the worst part," my mother said quietly. "If he's here, no one will help us. Believe me, I've asked. But if he's in a home, there are special programs that will pay for it."

I knew that if my mother said this, it was true, but there was something she wasn't saying that I only sensed. Some slight sibilance in her tone told me there was another element here that she didn't really want to talk about, the reason beneath the completely reasonable explanation she was giving me. She was forty-two years old. Always thin, she was now drawn and exhausted, not only with the actual demands of her life but with what she thought of as her responsibilities, both to us and to him. My father's illness was draining her. In order for her to do well at her job and perhaps someday even be promoted, she had to spend less time catering to him. She had to be able to stay late at the studio working without wondering if he was lying on the floor bleeding to death. But the conundrum was that while she knew this was necessary, it was also impossible for her to do what she needed to do while she was my father's only support. She needed for him to be taken care of in order to take care of herself. For her, that was the only way, and I knew that she felt guilty about it. It was tragic: a choice had to be made and my father was the unlucky one. Still, neither of us could really say this. Instead, I said weakly, "He's too young for a nursing home."

My mother nodded. "You're right. Most of the people there would be thirty years older, his parents' age, if they were still alive. Nursing homes are bad enough, but at least most of the people there have already lived their lives. Your daddy hasn't. It's awful, Danny, but there's nothing we can do about it."

"Why did you talk to Mr. Goodstein?" I asked. I had the random, wild thought that Abe could teach my father to gamble and he could make millions from his wheelchair and then we'd be out of trouble. But my mother's explanation was considerably less dramatic.

She brushed her knees again. "He's a lawyer," she said. "He might be able to help get your father into the new Jewish Home down on the lake, next to the Jewish Community Center. Don't you think he'd be happiest there?"

It seemed somewhat disingenuous for my mother to be talking about this move in terms of my father's happiness. He wouldn't be happy anywhere, much less in a home populated by *yentas* and old guys who would be more at home in the *shvitz* than a concert hall. He had once told me that he was so anti-Semitic that he had seriously considered suicide. I thought he was kidding, but I was never sure. The fact was that he had not associated with Jews at all since coming to Wisconsin, had few Jewish friends, and had never belonged to a synagogue. As far as I knew, the only time he had been to the Jewish Community Center was to play a concert and that had been years ago. Why should the Jewish Home be any different than anywhere else? All nursing homes were the same to me and I suspected they would be to my father as well. "What do you mean get in?" I had only heard of people avoiding nursing homes, not clamoring for admittance. She made it sound like applying to college.

My mother smiled. "It's more complicated than you think," she said. "They usually expect a donation, and I just don't have anything to give them. We're barely getting along as it is."

Now the picture began to come clear. What my mother was telling me with great difficulty was that not only were we going to consign my father to a nursing home, but that in order to make this possible my friend Abe Goodstein was going to make a donation in our behalf. It was the kind of thing Abe would do, like buying me a suit, and I knew that he would do it with the best of intentions, out of sincerely wanting to help, but I felt embarrassed just the same. Embarrassed not only by our poverty, our need to ask for help from anyone, but by the long, laborious way my mother had found to tell me that she had taken a lover.

～

I did not open Daisy's note until later in the day and so it was only then that I realized with some surprise that I hadn't known she was literate. It was one of the peculiarities of our life that due to my father's condition we shared intimacies with a variety of people who really had little in common with my family. I would come home from school and find the delivery boy from the drugstore doing errands for my father or perhaps playing chess with him. Or if not the delivery boy, then perhaps someone from the grocery or even on some occasions a rather somber Presbyterian minister who enjoyed hearing my father tell dirty jokes. In each case, I would feel a sense of invasion along with the wish not to share personal details of my life with strangers, something which led me in later years to what amounted to a mania for concealment in which I hid almost every detail of my life from other people, even things which didn't matter and would have been of little interest to anyone. Privacy became my greatest luxury.

Yet I hadn't minded sharing with Daisy, and despite the vast disparities of our lives and expectations, for nine months, four days a week, we had brushed against one another in the hall, eaten at the

203

same table, talked of this and that, and even made love. It was all of a piece and I did not feel more intimate with her when she was sitting in my lap in the basement than I had when we were both working to lift my recumbent father from the floor to his bed, trying to ignore the acrid smell of urine and the fact that he was crying out of humiliation. Had I been raised with servants, I might have felt differently about it, might have had clearer ideas of boundaries and distinctions between us. I might have known more about class differences, not to mention racial ones. Due to the liberal color blindness of my parents and the necessary self-involvement of childhood, I assumed without thinking about it that my experiences were more or less universal and that Daisy and I were much the same in our outlook. I thought of Daisy as a family friend, as my friend, and I was concerned about her.

Her note, which was written in pencil, was short and to the point: "I going to miss you, Dan. Cum an see me sometime."

I was touched that she had bothered to write, particularly because she had to use my mother as an intermediary, but her meaning was not entirely clear; that is, I didn't know if she was inviting me to visit her in a professional way or simply being polite, or neither. Whichever was the case, I had saved thirty dollars from my work with Abe and now I decided that Daisy should have it. I knew little of her life away from us, but I knew that she rented a room above a bar on Third Street because my mother and I had dropped her there once, so the following Saturday, without telling anyone, I took the Locust Street bus into the ghetto hoping to find her. Looking back, I am impressed with my temerity in doing this, since the divisions between black and white in Milwaukee were probably as great as anywhere in the country, the city having earned the somewhat dubious distinction of being the most segregated in America. But I don't recall thinking much of this at the time, perhaps because my visits to my mother's studio had made me nearly as comfortable around black people as she was.

A strange metamorphosis took place as the bus moved west on Locust: at first, most of the people riding were working-class whites, but as we crossed the river and moved beyond Holton Street, the clientele changed subtly until finally I was the only white person aboard. And while I was aware of this, no one else seemed to notice except for a small girl across the aisle who studied me with unwavering brown eyes as if I were the most remarkable thing she had ever seen or hoped to see. Otherwise, there was only a palpable air of exhaustion as the bus made its leisurely way through the Inner City, as if the people were as broken as the tattered vinyl seats upon which they sat.

I got off at Center and Third and began walking south, as the bar was three blocks down. Third Street had previously been the Jewish main street of Milwaukee and many of the old brick buildings remained, some with the names of the original owners engraved above the door: Schuster's, Oberdorfer's, Steinhafel's. Yet, while the street remained lively, now the tenants of the buildings were quite different. There were small barbershops, soul food restaurants, funeral parlors, dime stores, newsstands, and in the odd vacant lot a few cars with prices written in soap on their windshields along with promises of a fair deal for the lucky buyer. The sidewalks were crowded with an amazing assortment of people, young, old, and in the middle, but all claiming a piece of the scene. Old men sat in front of checker games in the window of the barbershop, while women extended themselves out of windows calling out in high-pitched voices. There were sullen young men moving silkily along in pastel tuxedo shirts with collar pins dangling, their high-waisted trousers and conked hair speaking of a higher life than was displayed here this morning. I was aware of music, funk, jazz, rhythm and blues, and somewhere in the background gospel, all working together in a kind of contrapuntal stew that merged nicely with the cars and buses in the busy street.

It was hot and I began to sweat, though part of this was due to anxiety and a growing sense that perhaps I had not acted wisely in coming down here without telling anyone. I was uncomfortable in my tan chinos and polo shirt, especially with the wad of bills in my jacket, which I now imagined was visible to everyone. In my mind, I was completely transparent: a white boy with money looking for a woman in the ghetto. And yet, though this was probably very much the way I actually did appear, I walked the three blocks in peace.

Curly's Bar occupied two storefronts and even now there were men inside drinking and playing pinball. I hesitated at the entrance and when I looked up, a large brown man was examining me with amusement. "What we got here?" he said. "Ain't no pale boys downtown, you hear me?"

There seemed to be no direct answer to this if in fact it was a question. But I wanted to go inside and my desire made me cocky. The man was wearing a white shirt and soft camel trousers. A part had been cut in the middle of his scalp and I could smell muscatel in the air. "I like your shoes," I said.

He looked down at the gleaming black Stacies on his feet, lifted his cuffs, and moved his feet from side to side in an exaggerated soft shoe. "Eighty-five dollar," he said. "Got five pair just like them at home." Now that we were discussing clothes, his manner seemed to soften. He looked me up and down and shook his head. "I got to tell you," he said. "Those clothes are terrible." He shivered and backed away as if contact with me would somehow infect him with bad taste.

I liked my clothes, but this didn't seem the time to argue. "Excuse me," I said, and moved past the man into the cool interior of the bar. I had never been in a tavern without an adult and realized that, among other things, it was illegal for me to be in Curly's alone, but I couldn't imagine I was the first underage patron to set foot in the place. The first thing I noticed was the sweet smell of malt, though I couldn't be sure it wasn't from the Schlitz brewery, just down the street. As my eyes adjusted to the light, I noticed three or four men sitting at a long bar and a man with blue-black skin and a magenta T-shirt standing behind it. Now he motioned me over. "Something I can hep you with, Youngblood?" he asked casually, wiping the bar down with a rag.

I was aware that all talk around us had stopped, though no one had moved toward me. I didn't really want to be drawn into conversation with the bartender, but there seemed to be no other way. "I'm looking for Daisy," I said, suddenly aware that I didn't know her last name. "I think she lives here."

The bartender slapped his rag against the bar and ducked his head. "No shit," he said, winking at the others. "And what would a nice young white man like you want with Daisy, even if she does live here, which I'm not saying she does yet."

"I just want to talk to her," I said. "We're friends."

The other men seemed to find this hilarious, slapping hands and saying "Oh, yeah," and "That's right," over and over until finally the din subsided and the bartender took over again. "Man wants to talk," he said meditatively, and then he laughed a low, bitter laugh.

There seemed to be nothing to add to this so I just stood there for what seemed like an hour but was probably less than two minutes. Finally, I said, "Could you tell me where she is then?"

The man nodded again. "Oh, yeah, I can do that. Matter of fact, I'm sort of her manager, know what I mean? So I always know where Miss Daisy is."

I waited but he added nothing to this. It was my first experience of this kind of sarcasm and while fear caused me to sweat beneath my shirt, it also made me mad. I had been ignored before, but once noticed people had not treated me as an object of ridicule. Still, I knew that anger wouldn't help me in this situation; patience might.

"Do you know where she is *now*?" I asked, surprised by my tone of voice, but emboldened by the fact that I had survived thus far.

The man looked at me with new respect. "Why, yes, yes, I do. But you know you can't just come in here and talk to Miss Daisy without I know what this talking is all about, we understanding each other? That's disrespecting me, see? I don't know nothing about you and you say you want to talk, but how do I know that? How do I know if you're even talking straight to me, young man?"

This impasse might never have been resolved had Daisy herself not appeared at this point. "Leave him alone," she said. "He's my friend, just like he said." She had apparently entered by a rear door and now she emerged from the gloom and smiled at me. "Hi, Danny."

The bartender seemed to find this interruption disconcerting, but his pride wouldn't allow him to back off. "Since when you got young white boyfriends, girl?"

Daisy ignored him. "Come on," she said and led me to the back where a door opened on a flight of stairs. Stains that could have been left by piss or blood or both discolored the staircase; the stench was overpowering and I felt sorry for Daisy having to live in such a place. But once we got to her room, it was as if the outside world fell away. There was a single bed with a tattersall bedspread covered with pillows and stuffed animals. Flanking the bed was a club chair and a writing desk with a leather cover. A portable television set rested on a highboy in the corner and on the TV set was a framed picture of our family. When Daisy saw me notice, she said, "Your mama gave me that. I never had a picture before, not one with a frame."

Otherwise, the walls were bare and this was the strangest thing of all to me, for while our home wasn't lavishly furnished, there had always been art everywhere, paintings my mother had done or had traded for with friends. The idea of life without visual distraction struck me as being true poverty. "That man said he was your manager," I said, not wanting to embarrass Daisy but curious about her life.

Daisy snickered at this, holding her hand up to her face. "He wishes he was. That man's my daddy. At least that's what he says."

The idea that one's parentage might be in doubt was exotic to me, though no more so than Jesús' uncertainty about the circumstances of his birth. But I chose not to pursue this. It wasn't why I had come, though the homey room was reassuring and far different from what I had imagined. I took the money out of my pocket and handed it to Daisy. "I brought this for you," I said.

Daisy smiled and giggled again, which made her seem even younger than she was. Then she counted the bills, "Man," she said. "This is a lot of money. For this, you can stay all night. We'll have some fun."

She was wearing a red halter-top and blue jean shorts and looked like any teenaged girl. It made me sad that she should have to make her living sleeping with strange men, or even with me. I wanted to tell her that she didn't have to fake enthusiasm, that we actually were friends as she had told the man she thought was her father. "It's okay," I said. "I just had a little saved and I felt bad that Mom had to fire you, that you aren't going to work for us anymore. I'll miss seeing you."

"Yeah," she said, but Daisy wasn't the sentimental type. She didn't worry about sleeping with men for money and she didn't seem overly affected by having to leave our employ. It was just life to her and life would go on. "You know Miss Marie paid me a month ahead," she said now. "That was pretty nice and ain't no one can hep what happened to Mr. Sam. That's a fact." She seemed lost in reverie for a moment, her lips slightly parted, her eyes set on something in the distance. "That man was always good to me and, you know, he could play that piano like no one else."

"He played for you?" I found this surprising, though one's parents are always surprising, especially in their vulnerabilities.

Daisy laughed. "Oh, yeah! He played all the time, whenever I wanted, whatever I wanted. I'd just hum something and then he could play it right out, just like that. I never seen nothing like it, even in a club or on the TV. That man was something. And he was *nice*." Now her voice dropped. "All of you were real good to me, I can say that. That's why I wrote you the letter. I felt bad that I had to go, but you know, I understand why Miss Marie had to do it. I do." She fingered the money I had given her, as if the bills were playing cards. There was an incongruity here and we were both aware of it. Though a sexual relationship would have been out of the question unless it was on a cash basis, my giving her money as a gift made her feel obligated. We might say that we were friends, but the nature of Daisy's relationship with my family was financial. I could tell she felt awkward taking money from me without giving value in return. She seemed to be working this over in her mind as we sat in her hot little room. "I think I got to do you," she said at last.

My desire for her was constant, but this didn't seem right. "Just take the money, Daisy," I said. "Don't worry about it. I'll be fine."

The idea that I could be refusing a sexual offer of any kind was incredible, but standing there above the barroom full of men who might be enjoying her services later in the evening made me magnanimous. I knew what their presumptions were and I wanted to go against them.

She shook her head, and now I saw that despite whatever principles I might have felt I was respecting, she had values of her own. "I can't just take money off you," she said. "I always work for what I get. I ain't on welfare or nothing."

Prostitution as an antidote to welfare was not something I had considered before, but I still felt compelled to object. "You're taking my mother's money," I said, referring to the severance pay.

"That's different," Daisy said, and of course she was right. I had come down to see her not only out of friendship but also because I felt a responsibility for what I imagined was her sordid life and now she was denying me this patronizing view of her world. In effect, Daisy was asserting a kind of self-respect I would not have thought was there, and now I saw her in a new way. It might be fashionable on the East Side to think of blacks as being wholly passive victims, helpless before the economic imperatives of society, but Daisy wasn't buying it.

Now she crossed to me and began to massage my groin. My response was, of course, immediate, but this time she didn't laugh and I didn't feel self-conscious. We were past all that. Instead, we undressed slowly, as if we were real lovers and not acting on a contractual basis. Then, in the most tender way possible, Daisy took me into her with a sigh that spoke of destiny, acceptance, even love, for in our way, in that time, to the extent that we were allowed, we did love each other, and I thought we could continue to even if we never met again.

Nineteen

Uncomplicated Bereavement

The school year was drawing to a close and already the other kids were making plans for high school, as I had, or rather as Miss Harmon had for me. In a way, we were separating before the fact, finding it easier to move on than to say our good-byes. Miss Harmon had planned an eighth-grade skit for the graduation ceremony. It featured Madeline declaiming something by Blake that seemed to have little to do with Milwaukee, Campus, or our class, but you couldn't blame Miss Harmon for being ambitious for us. In the event, Madeline went over well with the parents, most of whom had no idea who Blake was and thought perhaps he was a neglected Wisconsin author who deserved a wider readership. Then Dr. Patterson handed out diplomas and the deed was done. We were graduates, though even we knew enough not to make much over graduating from the eighth grade.

At the reception afterwards, parents and friends milled about the enclosed playground set with long tables of meat and cheese while the graduates did their best to avoid them. Al came over and congratulated me, though I knew he was there as Miss Harmon's escort, the ride home from my Country Day interview having ignited a torrid affair between the two of them that I found both unexpected and piquant. Abe patted my cheek and gave me a hug. "Nice going, kid," he said. "You'll have plenty more graduations to celebrate, take my word." Then he slipped an envelope in my pocket and moved away. Though I had nothing against him for befriending my mother, their relationship had inevitably created a distance between us that neither of us knew how to dissolve.

I gravitated toward the chain-link fence where Maddy and some of the girls were standing. They were all in tears and now Maddy threw her arms around me and said, "Oh, Danny, I wish you every best."

It was an awkward moment, because I knew neither of us was going anywhere. Still, I hugged her back out of a sense of duty. She was wearing a pink organdy dress, her makeup was smeared, and her matted hair had fallen out of the chignon and descended down her back. Yet, she had a kind of hopeless charm that I found appealing. "We'll still see each other," I said.

"Really?" she said doubtfully, blowing her nose into a sodden handkerchief.

"Sure," I said with more assurance than I felt. "We've got all summer."

She was going to Holy Angels Academy in the fall and I knew that the different schools would provide a convenient way for us to drift apart if that was what was going to happen. Campus was lax in its moral counseling, but the nuns would no doubt be more demanding. The rumor was that Catholic girls were wild because of their oppressive upbringing, but seeing the Holy Angels students pristine in their blue and white uniforms, it was hard to imagine them acting out. I patted Maddy on the shoulder and said, "We'll be fine. Don't worry."

Then I excused myself and walked back to the food table where Anna had taken up residence. One thing I liked about her was that she was unapologetic about her weight. "I like to eat," she said simply, "and I hate to exercise. So I'm going to be fat. There are worse things to be in life."

Jesús stood loyally by, in case she needed help, but Anna seemed to be doing fine on her own. She had two plates working, one filled with cold cuts, potato salad, bread, and cheese and the other devoted to cake, cookies, and brownies. Now she looked up at me and smiled. "It's the graduate," she said. "Congratulations, Danny. Very nice."

I had done nothing during the ceremony, but I accepted anyway. Jesús smiled and patted me on the shoulder. A man of few words, as always. "Have you heard from Dr. Kissinger?" I asked. I was being a wise guy, but I felt entitled. It was my graduation, after all, and considering the fact that she had dragged me to Guatemala and back for her convenience, I thought Anna should be tolerant. Besides, I was curious and wanted to maintain my slight contact with the great world outside of Milwaukee.

Anna wasn't in the least put off. "I don't bother him unless it's important," she said. "When we got back, I sent him a thank you note and a picture of all of us standing in the square in the village."

"You sent Kissinger a picture of me?" I was unaccountably pleased, though I couldn't have said why.

Anna smiled. "He's probably got it on his bulletin board. Now you're Henry's friend too, Danny."

For some idea the idea of Henry Kissinger having a bulletin board in his office with pictures and cartoons posted seemed funny and we all laughed there in the bright sunshine, even Jesús, who had no idea what we were talking about. Then Anna said, "Alfred is coming back, at least for part of the summer. That Joe doesn't treat him very well."

I knew she didn't approve of "that Joe" and while I had never met the man, I didn't either. Yet the more interesting question to me was why people arranged their lives as they did, since so often it was the structure of relationships that led to disillusionment and heartbreak, not any particular incident or crisis. It was certainly true of Alfred and Joe and of Anna and Paul. Irrespective of the changes any of them might have undergone, the relationships seemed doomed from the start. I had even begun to wonder about my parents. Flushed with significance, I wanted to say something about this, but it didn't seem the right time to discuss the meandering path of love and Anna wouldn't have been interested anyway. She wasn't a romantic. She took what life gave her and made what she had to from it. No unreasonable hopes, no regrets. "I'm glad," I said. "He'll be here for the baseball season."

Jesús perked up. *"Béisbol,"* he said and dropped into a crouch. Then he rose quickly and helped Anna to a picnic table with her two plates.

My father hadn't come to graduation, in part because he objected to ceremony, but I suspected the real reason was that he didn't want to be seen in a wheelchair. Having been a public figure for so long, he still assumed that his slightest gesture would be reported in the papers, and if this had been an exaggeration when he was healthy, it was pathetic now. But I was glad he wasn't there, glad I didn't have to feel the tug between my friends and ministering to his needs. I had been doing that all year and had not forgotten the incident with Greta Garbo and the chocolate nut sundae. The only sense in which I felt otherwise was that my father's absence seemed to confer approval upon my mother's new friendship with Abe Goodstein.

The conundrum was that I couldn't bring myself to resent any of them. No one could have been kinder to me than Abe, and it might have been nothing more than an overactive imagination that constructed an intrigue out of Abe's assiduous attention to my mother's every need at the reception. He might simply have been acting gallant. Certainly it didn't bother Mrs. G., who was wearing a broad-brimmed yellow hat and carried on an earnest conversation with Dr. Patterson about the merits of Shorewood High School, where she planned to enroll Joey in the fall.

As I surveyed the scene, it was impossible not to remember the unspeakable dreariness of the fall, that time when I felt as hopeless as I ever had in my life. Things at home were not measurably improved, in fact in some ways they were worse, but my mother's contract with the university had been renewed for another year and I had the Country Day scholarship. These modest successes could not, of course, cancel out the significant tragedy of my father's continued decline, but for this day, I decided to push it far enough away to enjoy myself.

Miss Harmon approached, rather drunk, I thought, wobbling on satin high heels, a wine glass in her bejeweled fingers. "Daniel Meyer," she announced, as if I was about to receive an award. "Our Sidney and our perfect man." Then, she stopped, apparently thinking better of herself since the poem she quoted was, after all, about a dead pilot. Still, I appreciated the sentiment even if I had no intention of dying at an early age.

Now Al took her arm and steadied her. Though he had taken care to dress appropriately, choosing a navy blazer in preference to his usual leather coat and wore only one gold chain around his neck, they made an odd couple. "Take it easy, Irene," he said. "You're going to spill that on Danny." Then he winked at me and steered her to a nearby chair.

Miss Harmon looked outraged at first but then she began to laugh uproariously, her red gash of a mouth pulled back to reveal long yellow teeth. "I have no intention of doing anything of the sort, Al," she said. "I merely meant to congratulate the young man." Then she rose unsteadily and enfolded me in her arms, burying my face deep in her décolletage, until I nearly fainted from the smell of violets and sex. When she released me, she held my head tightly in her hands and whispered in her hoarse voice, "I have great hopes for you, Daniel. Great hopes. I expect to hear of you in the future. Don't let me down." Then as quickly as she had come, she was wobbling off in pursuit of some other student, with Al walking gingerly in her wake.

⌿

Which should have ended things. The Goodsteins moved to Shorewood so Joey could attend the village high school; Madeline went off to join her parents in Geneva instead of attending Holy Angels;

215

Anna and Alfred and Jesús resumed their odd ménage, managing an uneasy accommodation to the intellectual, emotional, and physical needs of all concerned; my brother, having forsaken the Martians and sleepwalking, was admitted to Campus for the following fall, beginning a life-long compromise with madness and instability which would result in his being a dull, fat, unfulfilled man in middle age. Yet as this is a story at least in part about the vicissitudes of brilliance, it would not be complete unless I returned to my father's attempt to make peace with the wreckage of his life.

If my parents argued about the next step, or blamed one another, they never did so in front of me. I assumed that whatever decisions were made or would be made were joint ones, and yet during our year in Milwaukee the balance in the family had shifted unalterably in favor of my mother. She would never have pressed her advantage, but the sad fact was that she didn't need to. In a short time, my father had gone from being a person who was dominant in every area of life to an invalid incapable of going to the bathroom by himself. It was a chilling lesson, one that I have never recovered from. It has given me, though given seems the wrong word, a particular bleakness so gray and all-encompassing that when it descends it is virtually impenetrable and my only hope is to lie low until it passes. And it has made me distrust genius and achievement, or at least to regard these things with the transient interest one might reserve for a parade. At the age of fourteen, I learned the crucial, unsentimental lesson of life: nothing lasts and nothing can redeem your fate.

But my feelings were not in question then; there were more urgent matters to worry about. My mother appeared in my room one morning dressed in a white blouse and black skirt and said simply, "I need you to come with me, Daniel. I have to interview the staff at the Jewish Home and I don't want to go down there alone."

It did not occur to me to refuse, though it did seem odd that my father wouldn't be attending the meeting. I think he had decided to absent himself from the whole thing, as if being there would confer upon the discussion a seriousness it did not merit. But my mother was serious. And that morning, she was continuing to do what she

216

had always done—casting me in roles normally reserved for adults. However inappropriate it might have seemed to others, it made perfect sense to her to bring her young son to a meeting whose purpose was to decide his father's eventual fate. But whom else could she have asked? She had told me not long before that she had seen a psychiatrist who suggested she rely upon her family for support, not him. Whether or not he knew that her family consisted of two adolescent boys and an invalid husband is lost to time, but he said she had no need for him, for therapy, because she wasn't mentally ill.

"You're sad a lot of the time, though," I said.

My mother nodded. "I know. It's very tiring, isn't it? But the doctor said that was natural under the circumstances." Now she gave me a wry smile. "They even have a name for it, Danny, this kind of sadness I seem to have developed. They call it uncomplicated bereavement." She waited a moment for my reaction, and then she said, "Can you imagine that? It takes modern science to decide that grief could ever be uncomplicated."

These weren't words I used very often, but I knew what she meant. Yet I would have taken it a step further since I found all experience to be endlessly complicated and confusing. "What does it mean?" I asked.

My mother puffed out her cheeks and shrugged. "I guess sometimes it's just natural to feel bad and cry and think everything's hopeless, the way I've been feeling."

I understood that part; it was the converse that was difficult. "So when is it complicated?"

"If it goes on too long, I guess." She held up her hand. "And don't ask what's too long because I don't know."

The idea of there being a time limitation on proper grieving, after which it became medically unacceptable, made me nervous. I imagined squads of white-coated psychologists with stopwatches keeping tabs on my mother and I worried that her depression would not lift during the prescribed period. Then I tried thinking of instances of complicated bereavement, perhaps mourning the misfortunes of people one didn't know or didn't like? Simone Weil starving herself to death? Maybe just feeling bad but not having a good reason. But who decided whether or not your reasons were justifiable? It was a difficult concept and I was getting nowhere thinking about it. Moreover it was no help at all in our present situation.

—z—

The Jewish Home had only opened recently and was the result of enlightened public health planning. Rather than putting the old and infirm of the community in some hard-to-reach suburb, the notion was to locate them next door to the Jewish Community Center, in a modern lakefront building, where the grandchildren could walk over easily after a swim or bowling to visit. Whether this ever actually happened was uncertain, but on the day we visited I saw no one in the home who was under seventy.

My mother and I were taken to a large, paneled conference room where shortly we were joined by an administrator, a nurse, and a woman named Ms. Robins, who introduced herself as the Supercare Social Worker for the home. Ms. Robins was an imposing figure, nearly six feet tall in a puce pants suit with rings on every finger and big teeth set in an uneasy smile. The administrator, whose name was Mr. Rose, was a small man in a brown suit and I noticed that he seemed to wince every time Ms. Robins spoke.

Being unfamiliar with the argot of social work or even with social workers, I had no idea what was meant by "supercare," yet instinctively I felt it had nothing to do with extra sensitivity toward patients, and I was on my guard. While one might have assumed that such a label would imply that the home intended to render my father care so exceptional that they had created a special category for it, one look at Ms. Robins gave the lie to such thoughts. There was nothing nurturing about her manner and it was clear from the outset that her primary concerns in the meeting were financial. I thought of referring her to Abe, but it seemed best to keep quiet since it had never occurred to me that caring for my father would present extraordinary problems for a place as large and apparently prosperous as the Milwaukee Jewish Home.

Yet, of course, there were problems. The home, like any other such place, had a payroll and fiduciary obligations, and according to rumor, the admission process was extremely competitive. Ms. Robins never said this exactly, but it cut no ice with her that my father had been a concert artist or, for that matter, a professor. As she talked, I studied her, and against my best intentions, I created a mythical biography for the woman that began at North High School in the Inner City, where I imagined she had sung in the choir and later graduated with honors. There would have been no money for college; in all likelihood no one in her family had ever graduated from high school. But a small scholarship had been found for her by an interested teacher and this took Ms. Robins to one of the less prestigious state universities, River Falls, say, or Stout. Following graduation she had come back to Milwaukee and worked in a nursing home while pursuing her studies in social work at the university extension. Finally, she had graduated after years of part-time study and, thanks to the War on Poverty, had moved up in the system until she found herself working at one of the best nursing homes in the city. To her, patients like my father, who would likely require more care than the senile sacks deposited in their wheelchairs in the commissary each morning, would represent an organizational problem. It was her responsibility to act as a gatekeeper. Given her background, there was little chance she'd feel overly sympathetic toward us. Things were tough all over. After a half hour, Ms. Robins said she had an appointment and left.

Alone with Mr. Rose and the nurse, whose name was Mrs. Stein, my mother began crying openly. "I'm sorry," she said. "It all just seems so tragic."

Inexplicably, this made things easier in the room. Grief was their turf, and everyone relaxed. Mr. Rose recognized calamity as an everyday occurrence and Mrs. Stein took my mother's hand in hers. "I understand, dear," she said. "But this is a wonderful home. You'll see." Then she brightened unaccountably. "I understand Mr. Meyer was a musician," she said. "Each Wednesday we have a sing-a-long. Do you think he'd be interested in joining us? We have a very nice piano."

The fact that my father's whole professional life would be understood in this way, as if he'd played the accordion in an oompah band, hit my mother hard. I heard her sharp intake of break and prepared for the worst. "I think he'd absolutely hate that," she said.

Mrs. Stein smiled and nodded, as if my mother had answered in the affirmative. Then Mr. Rose said, "We also have a group that gets together once a week for a Yiddish lunch. Perhaps that would be more to his taste?"

Realizing that it was in her interest to seem positive about something, my mother nodded, though we both knew that my father's primary use for Yiddish was telling dirty jokes to his musician friends. "He's really not very social," my mother said carefully, understating it nicely. "He likes to play chess."

This appeared to be the opening they'd been waiting for and talk followed of the vast supply of board games possessed by the home. There was an infinite variety of clubs and residents regularly went on field trips. I understood Mr. Rose's need to make the whole thing seem as attractive as possible and I appreciated his sensitivity toward my mother, but nothing could disguise the lachrymose reality of our joint task. People came to nursing homes when they were unable to care for themselves and there was no one else willing or able to do so. The halls were filled with people in wheelchairs who had lived vigorous, useful lives and now waited in various states of sentience for the end to come. A good nursing home was one that didn't stink. All the sing-a-longs and Yiddish lunches in the world could not change that, nor was there any way to sugarcoat the reality that my mother was considering signing papers that would consign my father to this place at the age of forty-six. It was this act of betrayal, for that is unquestionably how she saw it, that had caused the onset of her crying and I was powerless to affect it, because, essentially, I agreed and was her partner in crime. But no one at the table even looked at me.

My mother took the sheaf of papers in her hands and shuffled them. I remember her hands, her fingernails cracked and blue with old clay, the chipped diamond ring that had once been her mother's and before that her grandmother's. I knew that in her family one did not desert family members just because they were ill; I knew that her grandfather had employed a moronic uncle in his wholesale grocery business for twenty years before he died; I knew that this was killing her. Yet there was really no choice; this year had proven that. And hadn't we been deserted ourselves by these same aristocratic relatives because of my father's religion? For that matter, where was his family? My father had only my mother and me and Abe Goodstein. And despite Ms. Robins, the Jewish Home was the best we were going to do in Milwaukee.

I leaned over and put my arm around her. "It's all right," I said, wanting to reassure her. "You've done everything you could. You've done everything anyone could do."

My mother sobbed audibly at this because it was so obviously untrue. Then she squared her shoulders and stacked the papers on the table. "I'm sorry," she said. "I thought I was ready, but I'm going to have to think about this some more."

Mr. Rose sat back in his chair as if he had been hit, but Mrs. Stein was quick on the uptake. "That's right, dear," she said. "You just take all the time you need and call us when you're ready." Then the nurse gave my mother a hug.

We took the elevator and left the home in a state approaching shock. I was convinced that telling my mother she had done all she could was the thing that had paradoxically convinced her that she hadn't done enough. My accusing silence, on the other hand, would have made her pugnacious enough to sign. It is an irony of life that defining moments seldom announce themselves and it is only later that we can look back and say, yes, that was the time everything changed for good. But this was one such moment in my life. Standing there in the afternoon sun facing the crush of Prospect Avenue traffic, I knew that although our business that day had primarily concerned my mother and father, something had happened to me as well and it went beyond a new appreciation of human frailty.

I had lost one world and gained another, lost paradise, at least as I knew it, and gained the reality of Abe Goodstein and Alfred and Anna and Daisy. I had gone from long afternoons of baseball and swimming with my friends to hauling cinders and running numbers. I had traveled to Guatemala and knew the value of having friends in high places. And though my relationship with my father would deteriorate further and remain riddled with conflict until it was too late to do anything about it, the experience of caring for him would eventually prove to be as empowering as it was disturbing. What I had learned that year was that however limited life might seem, there would always be a way to survive and even live well. I had learned that from watching my beleaguered parents, but also from Abe and Anna, two wholly dissimilar people who would have been justified in sinking into pessimism but hadn't.

It was only seventy-five miles from Madison to Milwaukee, but the psychic distance was much further than that. Standing holding my mother's hand that day outside the nursing home, I felt stronger than before. I was no longer a boy, if not quite a man. In that moment, I had only a dim realization of all this; I did not know then that I would always be an exile from my past. The important thing was that I was on my way, even if I had no idea where I was going. And I knew with the vague unspoken gravity of real truth that whatever would come later would be affected in ways I neither knew nor saw by what had happened to me in this year, when I became aware for the first time of the limitations of security and the hard lessons of eternity.

Library of American Fiction

Melvin Jules Bukiet
Stories of an Imaginary Chidhood

Rebecca Goldstein
Mazel

Jesse Lee Kercheval
The Museum of Happiness: A Novel

Alan Lelchuk
Brooklyn Boy

Curt Leviant
Ladies and Gentlemen, The Original Music of the Hebrew Alphabet and
    Weekend in Mustara: Two Novellas

David Milofsky
A Friend of Kissinger: A Novel

Lewis Weinstein
The Heretic: A Novel